MW00884576

MULTIVERSE

M.A. ROTHMAN

Primordial Press

Cover Art by M. S. Corley
Interior Art by M. S. Corley

Paperback ISBN: 979-8-8479216-2-6
Hardcover ISBN: 979-8-8484532-6-3

ALSO BY M.A. ROTHMAN

Technothrillers: (Thrillers with science / Hard-Science Fiction)

• Primordial Threat

• Freedom's Last Gasp

• Darwin's Cipher

• Multiverse

Levi Yoder Thrillers:

• Perimeter

• The Inside Man

• Never Again

• The Swamp

Alicia Yoder Novels:

• New Arcadia

• Operation Thrall

• Vatican Files

LitRPG:

• The Plainswalker

• The Sage's Tower

Epic Fantasy / Dystopian:

• Agent of Prophecy

- Heirs of Prophecy
- Tools of Prophecy
- Lords of Prophecy

CONTENTS

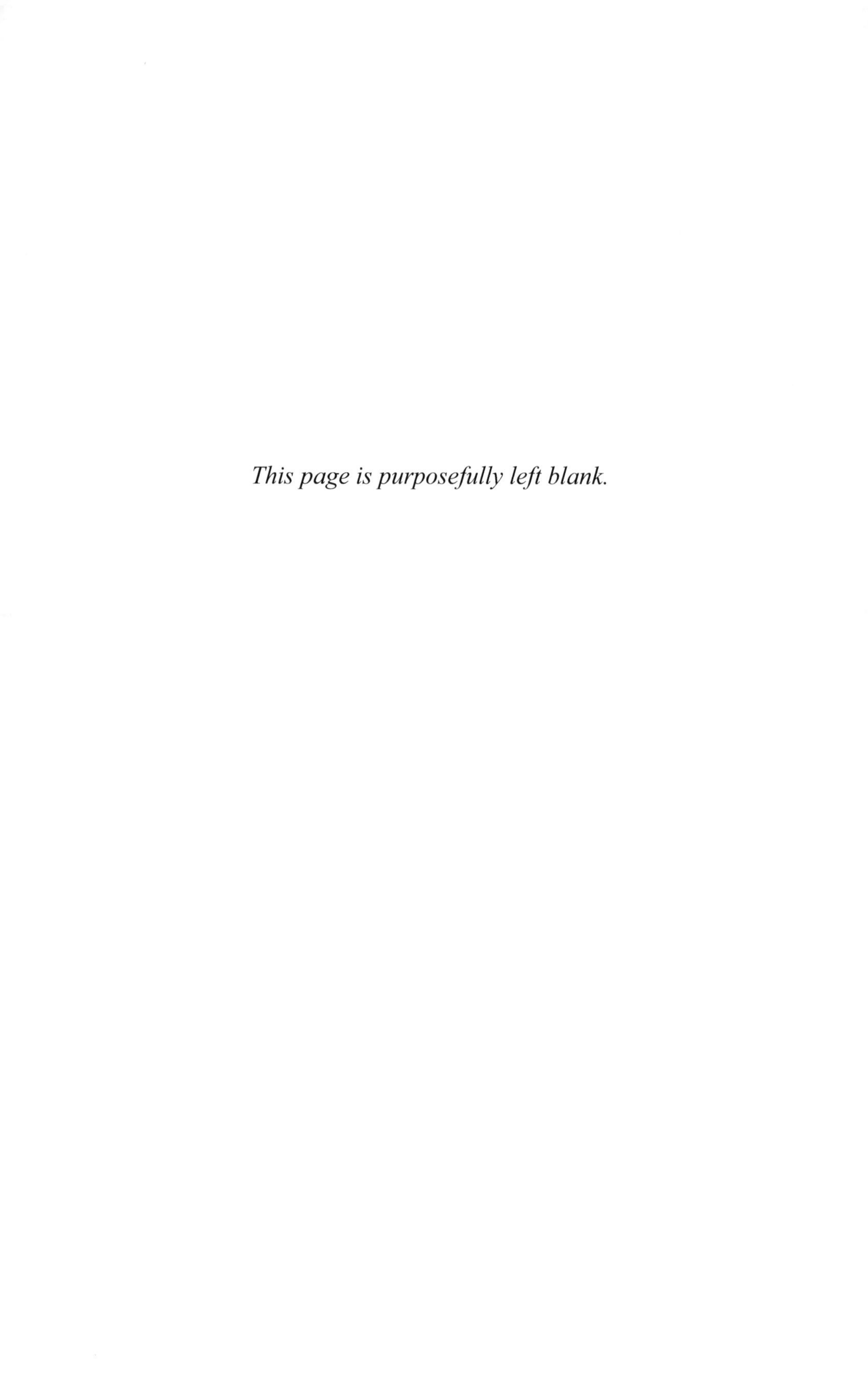

This page is purposefully left blank.

When Michael Crichton's novels first landed in the thriller section of bookstores, most discerning folks realized that his melding of science with thriller was really a form of science fiction. But it was only a fluke of marketing that Crichton's science fiction works were placed in the thriller section, giving birth to a new thing call a technothriller.

I recognize that in this book I am standing on the shoulders of the giants who came before me, and I would like to dedicate this novel to both Greg Benford and Larry Niven. Both who I consider friends, and wrote seminal material in the genre I now work in.

Professor Gregory Benford is a fantastic author and was one of the first to bring superluminal particles to the science fiction masses. It pleases me to no end that I've had the chance to discuss with him the finer details of the technology that I lay out in this book as well as the past and present research on the topic. We are both looking forward to future advancements in this domain.

Larry Niven, whose works were among the foundation of what many now call hard science fiction, was also a huge influence not only in my writing but has forced countless millions of readers to ask the classic question of "what if?" when reading about future-looking technology in the form of a story. And I hope to also carry that torch and force future readers to continue to ask that same question.

"Modern thinking is that time did not start with the big bang, and that there was a multiverse even before the big bang. In the inflation theory, and in string theory, there were universes before our big bang, and that big bangs are happening all the time. Universes are formed when bubbles collide or fission into smaller bubbles."

—Michio Kaku, Theoretical Physicist

CHAPTER ONE

Michael Salomon lurched into a sitting position and felt a wave of dizziness as he blinked the sleep out of his eyes. His heart raced, and he was having difficulty catching his breath as the gauzy memories of a dream fled from his now-conscious mind.

Something had just happened, and he wasn't exactly sure what it could be.

Definitely not a dream. Not with the growing anxiety he felt. Some kind of nightmare…

He glanced at the clock on his nightstand. It was just past seven. He'd gotten to bed only four hours earlier, but waking up at this time was habit. During the school year he'd be frantically climbing out of bed to go teach physics at Princeton. But it was the summer, and he dedicated all his attention to his research.

That was what had kept him up late last night. A discovery

that ended with him leaving the lab after two a.m. in a state of shock.

He had wanted to tell someone. Anyone. But it was late, and he couldn't trust himself to talk to his colleagues until he could verify everything with a clear mind. Triple-check the data. Then, and only then, would he risk his reputation.

He stood up from the bed, only to immediately sit back down with a sudden bout of vertigo. Maybe it was his body telling him he needed more rest.

And then he caught the scent of bacon.

He didn't remember making any bacon when he got home from the lab. He had been too exhausted to do anything but go directly to bed. But when he opened the bedroom door, the scent was unmistakable, wafting up the stairs from the kitchen.

And something more.

Someone was humming.

Standing at the top of the stairs, he was about to yell out an empty threat that he had a gun, but his words were choked away when he saw a woman approaching the base of the stairs, carrying a coffee mug. She had straight dark hair hanging to her mid-back, and naturally tanned skin. And she was very pregnant.

Maria.

Their German shepherd puppy, Percy, followed her every step, his nails clicking on the wooden floor.

Before Michael could say a word, Maria's face lit up. "You're awake!" She held up the steaming mug of coffee. "I was going to bring this up to you and tell you I made breakfast."

He merely stared, not believing that this could be real.

Maria waved for him to come down. "The baby is really moving," she said, putting a hand on her stomach. "Come down and feel her."

The puppy looked up at him and barked joyfully.

Michael's skin felt cold and clammy, like he was on the verge of passing out. But he managed to walk slowly down the stairs, unable to take his eyes off the woman he'd loved for nearly a quarter of his forty-two years on this Earth.

Maria grabbed his hand and put it on her stomach. "Do you feel that?"

He nodded. "What—" He cleared his throat. "What day is it?"

Percy whined for attention.

"You poor thing, you're barely even awake." Maria smiled, handed him his coffee, and scratched the top of Percy's head. "It's Thursday, and you practically passed out the moment your head hit the pillow. You didn't even get undressed."

That part was true. He was still wearing the same clothes from last night at the lab.

Still unbelieving, he pressed his hand to Maria's belly once more, feeling the movement as life stirred within her.

Their baby.

His throat tightened with emotion, and he felt like he was about to explode.

"Ay, *mi amor*. What's wrong?" Maria wiped away an unbidden tear that had rolled down his cheek. She wrapped her arms around him. "Whatever it is, it'll be fine. Did something bad happen at work?"

He kissed the top of her head, a storm of emotions raging through him. "I guess I just had a nightmare."

"What about?"

"I don't want to say it out loud."

"Come." Maria grabbed his free hand and gently pulled him toward the kitchen. "Have a seat, and I'll serve up breakfast. I'm sure everything will look better after you've gotten something in your belly."

Michael sat at the kitchen table and watched as his wife of eight years, pregnant with their child, busied herself in the kitchen.

He watched, knowing it was impossible. Because his memories told him of a cascading set of events that had led to Maria disappearing.

First was the late-term complication with the pregnancy. Their daughter was delivered early, and though she should have lived—the odds were with her—she didn't make it. That was the beginning of the end for their marriage. There were arguments. Bitter and nonsensical fights. And then, one day, Maria left and never came back.

He vividly remembered the pain of waking up and finding her gone. Her clothes still in the closet. Her car in the garage.

He filed a missing persons report with the police. They told him she was an adult and maybe she'd just needed time away.

But Maria had literally *vanished*. Gone from his life.

For years.

Until now.

And then there was Percy. The puppy was now watching

his mom prepare scrambled eggs, his tail wagging furiously as she scooped some into his bowl on the counter.

Percy was alive… and still a puppy. He had whined for weeks after Maria disappeared. And then one day he escaped from the back yard and got killed by a car.

But apparently that never happened.

It was all a lie. A nightmare.

Percy hopped from side to side with anticipation as Maria mixed his puppy kibble with the eggs. When she set it on the floor, he dove in and devoured it.

Michael smiled at the sight. His wife was really here with him, and as his gaze trailed down to her bulging belly, it took all of his self-control to not break down and begin sobbing right then and there. Their daughter wasn't dead. She was having a little party inside Maria's belly.

Everything was good. Everything was as it should be.

Maria set down two steaming plates of scrambled eggs and bacon, poured herself a glass of orange juice, and sat down beside him.

He sipped the coffee. It was hot, strong, and black. Just like she'd always made it.

She looked longingly at his mug and sighed. "That's the one thing I do miss. My morning *tinto*."

Tinto was what Colombians called a black coffee.

He smiled, reached under the table, and patted her belly. "It won't be long. Would you prefer that I don't drink coffee while you're pregnant?"

Maria gave him a hard look. "Why, are *you* pregnant? Don't be silly. Besides, the orange juice is good for the baby."

She took a sip, then pointed at his plate with her fork. "Don't let your food get cold."

"Yes, ma'am." Michael smiled and shoveled a forkful of eggs into his mouth.

Yet even as he chewed, he felt a nagging sense of wrongness.

But then Maria smiled. He returned the smile as he took a bite of bacon.

Everything was perfect.

It was just past ten, and Michael was driving south on US-1 heading in to work when he saw a cluster of brake lights up ahead. Traffic slowed, and then stopped altogether. He sighed, not seeing any cause for the traffic jam. It was a simple two-lane highway, and never got backed up.

"Someone must have gotten into an accident," he muttered.

As he sat in the car, making no forward progress, his mind drifted back to last night's experiments. His area of research had to do with superluminal particles, otherwise known as tachyons—a niche field that occupied one of the darkest recesses of special relativity. And there was good reason for that: no one had ever detected a tachyon. They were the stuff of science fiction.

Tachyons were particles that could go faster than the speed of light. And if there was one thing that everyone understood—or misunderstood—about Einstein's groundbreaking theory, it was that *nothing* could go faster than the speed of light.

This wasn't exactly true.

To be more accurate, Einstein said that nothing that *initially* moved below the speed of light could be accelerated to move beyond the speed of light. And thus the question arose: could tachyons exist?

Up until last night, that question had gone unanswered.

Michael was roused from his thoughts at the sound of tires screeching behind him. He looked in the rearview mirror and saw a vintage Cadillac swerving, seemingly out of control. No cars had stopped behind Michael, and the barreling Cadillac was no more than fifty feet away from crashing right into him.

Everything seemed to slow. Michael saw the panicked look on the driver's face as he wrestled with his steering wheel. The driver had clearly lost control of the giant boat of a car. It fish-tailed, smoke billowing from the tires.

The professor braced himself for impact.

And… the Cadillac skidded to a stop beside him, facing backwards. The driver was literally within arm's reach.

Under normal circumstances, Michael would have thrown his entire inventory of curse words at the man who'd nearly hit him, and would likely have invented new ones for good measure. But he was shaking with the sudden dump of adrenaline into his bloodstream, and he found he couldn't form a coherent sentence. The world was spinning, and he thought he might throw up.

He needed to gather his wits.

So he turned off into the breakdown lane, moved ahead several car lengths, and pulled into the entrance to a parking lot. It was for some kind of medical complex—a sign read

"Rothman Orthopedics." But he barely noticed it. He just needed air.

He parked, got out, and took in a slow, deep breath. He felt as though the ground beneath him was tilting. He'd never passed out before, but he was sure he was about to.

Clinging to his car door to keep from collapsing, he closed his eyes and focused on his breathing.

In his mind's eye he saw a verdant field of grass.

It was more than an image; it was a crystal-clear vision, unfolding as though he were experiencing a dream through a camera lens.

He saw a man in the distance, kneeling. Michael involuntarily moved toward him, despite the fact that the closer he got to the figure, the more anxious he felt.

The man was in a graveyard, kneeling before a tombstone.

Michael's breath caught in his throat. He recognized the man before him.

It was *him.*

But not exactly him. An older version of him. He was thinner. Too thin. A noticeable amount of gray in his hair. A scraggly beard.

Then Michael looked at the tombstone, and his blood ran cold.

Felicia Batsheva Salomon.

We had you only one day, but know this: If love
could have saved you, you would have lived forever.

. . .

Below the inscription were two dates: birth and death. They were the same date.

And the date… was tomorrow.

Michael's tires screeched in the driveway as he parked, jumped out of the car, and rushed into the house.

"Maria!" he yelled.

He heard the dog's bark in response, coming from the back yard.

His heart pounding, Michael raced to the sliding glass door leading to the back yard and yanked it open. "Maria!"

"Honey? I thought you were going into work?"

Maria was sitting on a lounge chair in partial shade from their patio umbrella. She looked uncomfortable.

He rushed over and gingerly scooped up her hand. "Baby, are you feeling okay?"

She shrugged. "I'm feeling very pregnant right now. So, the usual. But also my lower back is really hurting today. I thought this chair would help but… no. What are you doing home?"

Michael couldn't explain. "I—I want to get you checked out by the doctor. You look… overly tired."

"Why today? I already have my appointment set for tomorrow."

He pasted on a smile. "Just do me this one favor. It's your

job to be pregnant, and my job to be worried, right? I just want to make sure everything is okay with you and Felicia."

Reluctantly, Maria allowed him to help as she slowly levered herself up from the lounge chair. "I haven't even showered yet."

"No one cares about that. Please, just humor me."

"Fine." She rolled her eyes. "But at least let me change my clothes."

He gave her a quick kiss on the forehead. "Deal."

The ultrasound technician placed warm jelly onto the business end of the wide transducer and then placed it on Maria's belly. "Okay, let's take a look at the little cutie and get some measurements."

Maria gripped Michael's hand as the sound of a rapid heartbeat played through the ultrasound machine's speaker. She looked over at the technician. "Is that Felicia's heartbeat?"

"It sure is. Felicia is a beautiful name. It means 'smile' in Spanish, doesn't it?"

"Close, but not exactly. It's more related to *feliz*, which means happy."

The technician continued moving the probe across Maria's belly with one hand while working the machine's keyboard and mouse with the other. "Do you have a middle name picked out?"

Maria smiled at Michael. "We're not sure yet, but I was

thinking about Batsheva. It's his grandmother's name; she passed not too long ago. What do you think, honey?"

Michael nodded, but a chill raced up his spine. That was the name on the tombstone.

Felicia Batsheva Salomon.

The technician stopped suddenly and lifted up the probe, making the screen go black. "Wait here a moment," she said. "I'll be right back with Dr. Sakata."

Though her voice was calm, Michael spotted the look of concern on the woman's face as she got up from the stool and left the room.

Maria squeezed his hand. "I should ask Sakata if there's anything I can take for my lower back. I'm not sure I can handle another eight weeks of this."

Michael gave her a warm smile, but inside, he was freaking out. What had the technician seen? There shouldn't be any big surprises in the beginning of the eighth month; it should be smooth sailing at this point. At least, that's what all those damned pregnancy books said that Maria had made him read.

The door opened, and Dr. Sakata walked in. "Hello, Mr. and Mrs. Salomon. I understand we're doing a wellness check. Did you have any spotting or other symptoms that made you come in today?"

"Spotting, as in bleeding? No." Maria hitched her thumb at her husband. "He's just worried, and wanted me to get checked. The only new symptom I have is back pain. But I guess that comes with the territory."

The doctor sat on the stool. "Well, let's have a look."

As the physician slid the probe across Maria's belly, the

ultrasound screen showed various structures that meant nothing to Michael. Still he watched closely, his eyes moving from the screen to the doctor's expression and back, looking for some kind of reaction.

Sakata stopped on one fuzzy image that looked like all the rest, clicked something on the keyboard, and zoomed in. He shifted the angle of the transducer slightly.

The sound of the baby's heartbeat thudded loudly in the room.

"Is there something in particular you're looking for?" Maria asked.

The doctor glanced at her. "You said you're having back pain?"

She nodded. "It's much worse today. I normally don't sleep on my back, but I fell asleep that way waiting for my husband to get back from work." Maria gave Michael an accusatory glare, then squeezed his hand and blew him a kiss.

Sakata zoomed in on different parts of the image and clicked more buttons, causing small printouts to roll out of a slot in the machine. After about a minute of that, he lifted the transducer, wiped it off, and then wiped down Maria's belly with a fluffy white towel.

"Well," he said, "let's start with the baby. She seems to be under no distress and is about where we'd hope she'd be for a gestational age of thirty-two weeks. That's all good. But it's also good that you came in today." Sakata held up one of the images and pointed at something that was hard to make out. "Maria, you have a minor placental abruption. That means that the placenta has partially torn from the wall of the uterus."

Maria gasped. “What does that mean for the baby?” Her eyes welled up with tears and she squeezed hard on Michael’s hand.

“Like I said, it’s minor. But I would like to keep you overnight for some tests. We need to check the blood chemistry of the baby and make sure she’s still getting everything she needs. It’s likely the tests will come back okay, but you two should prepare yourself for the possibility that we may have to deliver early.”

All Michael could see at that moment was the birthdate on the tombstone. His voice sounded far away as he said, “But she’s only thirty-two weeks…”

Sakata patted the air and tried to smile reassuringly, with minimal success. “A fetus that reaches thirty-two weeks’ gestation has a ninety-five percent chance of survival. The important thing is that you’re here and we know about this issue. I’m going to prescribe antenatal betamethasone, which is a corticostcroid to help with the baby’s lungs. It’ll help them mature in anticipation of a possible early delivery.”

Maria asked with a quavering voice, “You think we’ll deliver early?”

Sakata smiled, and this time it seemed genuine. “We’ll do everything we can to keep your little one inside you for as long as possible. We’re just preparing for other eventualities.” He leaned forward and patted Maria’s foot, then shifted his gaze to Michael. “I’ll have the nurse give you a list of things to get from the house. I’m going to call admitting and get your wife checked in for tonight.”

“How long do I have to stay?” Maria asked.

"At least through tomorrow morning. By then we'll know more. If this is a developing issue that needs immediate treatment, we'll address it then. But it may well be that we can treat this with careful monitoring and bed rest."

"Bed rest, as in *at home* bed rest?" Michael asked.

Sakata nodded. "*If* things are stable, then yes." He gave them both a sympathetic look. "I know this isn't what you wanted to hear. But at least we know about it now, and you're where you need to be. In the meantime, let's try our best not to worry about things that may well not happen."

As the doctor left, Michael could think only of the tombstone.

He leaned down and gave Maria a kiss. "It'll be okay."

"Th-thank you," Maria stammered as she let out a shuddering breath.

"For what?"

Maria began practicing the breathing techniques she'd learned in one of their many pregnancy classes. "For feeling paranoid today. You probably saved the baby."

Michael leaned down and held his wife close so she couldn't see the worry on his face. He wanted to believe her, believe the doctor, and assume everything would be all right.

But he couldn't. His mind's eye couldn't look away from the haunting image of tomorrow's date carved in stone.

Birth… and death.

His fear wouldn't lift until tomorrow had passed safely.

It's only a vision, not a prophecy.

He held his wife tightly and tried to believe it.

CHAPTER TWO

Michael stood over Felicia's incubator, staring down at the newborn delivered only eight hours earlier. The last thirty-six hours had been the most harrowing experience of his life. Maria had spent the night in the hospital, but after some observation this morning everything seemed to be perfectly fine. There was even talk of being able to go home on bed rest. And then suddenly Maria was being wheeled into the operating room for an emergency C-section. Throughout it all, the memory of that tombstone weighed heavily on his soul.

"Mr. Salomon?"

One of the neonatal intensive care unit's nurses approached with a growing frown. He knew that he'd breached the hospital's protocol by entering the NICU without having checked in with one of the nurses, but once Maria was out of recovery and had fallen asleep in the hospital room, he'd needed to see his little girl.

"I'm sorry," he said quickly. "There was nobody at the desk, and I just wanted to make sure she's okay."

The nurse paused at the foot of the incubator, shook her head, then checked the digital readout on the monitor. "Heart rate is one thirty-five, respiration is at fifty, and her blood oxygen is ninety-eight. All within a very healthy range."

"She's so small," he said.

The woman picked up the clipboard attached to the lower frame of the incubator. "Three pounds, fifteen ounces, sixteen inches long, with a head circumference of eleven and a half inches. All good sizes for someone her gestational age." The nurse's voice took on a more upbeat tone. "Felicia's had quite a birthday, maybe you should—"

"Honey, how is she?"

Michael turned and his eyes widened. His wife was walking toward him, dragging along an IV pole on wheels. He rushed over to her.

"Maria, what are you doing on your feet? You just had surgery, are you crazy?"

She smiled and patted his cheek. "I'm okay. The doctor said I'm supposed to get on my feet and walk around." She looked to the nurse. "Is she okay?"

The nurse smiled. "She's doing fine. I'll leave you two alone to visit for a little bit." She glanced up at the clock on the wall. "We change shifts in just a few minutes, at midnight. I'll let the new shift nurse know you're here, but you should check in with her as well."

Michael gave Maria his arm to hold on to, then led her over to the incubator, where she gazed down at the sleeping baby.

"She's beautiful," Maria said.

Michael agreed. "Are you sure you're okay to stand? I can bring a chair."

"I'm fine." She squeezed his arm and put her hand on the clear plastic of the incubator, unable to take her eyes from Felicia. "She's a miracle."

They both stared down at the baby, and Maria began softly reciting a prayer.

"God bless Felicia behind the plastic wall.

"She has been taken from my womb without warning and I long to hold her in my arms.

"Lord, I ask in your name that Felicia be healed.

"God give her the strength to make it through another second, minute, hour, and day, as each moment is a blessing and a triumph from heaven.

"Lord, we are at your mercy for the life of our child. Please leave her here on Earth and know that we will provide all the love and understanding that Felicia needs. We accept the challenge and will be your humble servants, dear Lord."

They both said, "Amen," and Michael kissed the top of Maria's head.

"It all happened so fast." Maria looked up at him with a serious expression. "It's a miracle we were even in the hospital already when everything went wrong." Her voice quavered with emotion. "How did you know?"

"Know what?"

"You know, about getting me to see the doctor."

He looked up at the wall clock and watched it tick over to midnight. Somehow, seeing that big hand point to twelve lessened the fear that had been gnawing at his guts ever since he'd had that vision. That tombstone would never be real. It was now the next day.

He met Maria's gaze and smiled. "You'd think I was nuts if I told you."

Maria arched an eyebrow.

"Okay, fine," he said. "I saw it in a nightmare."

"Saw what?"

"Felicia's tombstone."

Maria's eyes widened.

Michael pointed at the clock. "It's past midnight, thank God. But that damned tombstone had yesterday's date on it."

"That's awful." She pressed her lips together and held a troubled expression. "Why didn't you tell me about your nightmare before heading off to work?"

Michael winced as he recalled the screeching of tires that had led to his vision. "Because… I hadn't had it yet?"

Maria looked confused.

"I guess it wasn't exactly a nightmare," he explained. "Is there such a thing as a daymare? On the way to work, someone almost rear-ended me on US-1, and I was so freaked out I pulled off the highway and parked. That's when the nightmare hit me. It was the strangest thing, but it was so vivid. Just like —" He cut himself off. That morning's memories—of not having Maria by his side and all the rest—it was still a raw emotion that he couldn't stand to even verbalize. "It was just like watching a movie."

“It was just a dream,” she said, taking his hand. “I’d say I’m sorry you had to see it, but I can’t. Because it gave you the warning that saved Felicia’s life.” She looked down at their daughter once more. “It truly is a miracle.”

As Michael rinsed his mouth and put the toothbrush away, he heard the dog whine. He turned from the bathroom sink and saw Percy gently reaching up with one paw to touch the top of Maria’s leg. It was almost as if the dog was finally noticing that something was missing—namely the baby.

Maria was struggling with a wide elastic band wrapped partially around her midsection. “Come here and help me with this abdominal binder,” she said. “I need you to pull it tight across my belly while I pull the other side.”

“Isn’t that going to hurt your incision?”

“They told me I have to use this thing every day,” Maria huffed. “Just help me get it on.”

As she gripped one end of the band, Michael pulled on the other.

“Harder!” she groused, more impatient than usual this morning.

Reluctantly, he pulled the elastic band taut around her midsection and pressed it flat on the Velcro portion so it would stay.

“Ah, that’s better,” she said with a sigh of relief.

He was doubtful as she walked out of the bedroom. It had been only a week since the surgery, and she was supposed to be taking it easy. Maria didn't seem to understand what "taking it easy" meant.

Michael followed her down the stairs. "Are you sure you don't need any help today?"

She shook her head. "Stop asking me that. I'm fine. I just need to get everything ready for the baby." From the moment the doctors had said Felicia would likely be able to come home tomorrow, Maria had thought about nothing else. "I love you, but you drive me crazy asking me if I'm okay every five seconds of the day. Go to work. Show the world how smart I know you are."

"What about food and—"

"Are you kidding me? Our neighbors and your colleagues have filled our refrigerator with more food than we can possibly eat in the next month." Maria pulled him down for a kiss, aimed him at the front door, and gave him a light push. "Go, before I have to kick you out." She pointed with authority in the direction of the door.

Michael got the message. It was time to get back to work.

Michael slowed as he approached the bridge spanning across Washington Road and turned right onto the private road. Despite Princeton's prestigious name and reputation, it always amused him that there were utterly no signs here indicating that he was now on the campus. After a quick left, and then another, he approached Jadwin Hall, where most of the physics labs were located. As it was the beginning of summer session, there wasn't much competition for parking spots, at least compared to other times of the year, and he actually managed to park close to the building.

As he climbed the six steps to the side entrance of the hall, a voice shouted, "Michael!"

The chair of the department was standing by the entrance, with a tall, slim, blonde woman standing next to him.

"How goes it, Herman?" Michael said, walking up to the entrance. "Why are you standing outside in the humidity?"

The man held up his ID and shrugged. "My badge isn't working." Something about the professor's deadpan delivery and native Dutch accent always made it sound like he was making a dry joke.

Michael unclipped his own badge and swiped it on the badge reader. The door buzzed and he pulled it open, letting the two into the air-conditioned building.

As they walked in, Herman made introductions. "Michael, this is Doctor Carmel Harrington, a research fellow at the Children's Hospital of Westmead out of Australia. Carmel, this is Professor Michael Salomon. His work on high-energy particle detection in empty space may lead us into places we never imagined possible. More importantly, his wife just had a baby girl." He looked at Michael. "Congratulations, by the way. How is Maria holding up?"

Michael beamed. "She's doing great. We think we'll be able to bring the baby home tomorrow."

"Excellent. You'll have to bring the little one by so we can all coo over her. Only when mother and daughter are up to it, of course."

"Of course. I'll be excited to show her off."

Herman checked his watch. "Actually, Michael, since you're here, would you mind guiding Carmel to the lounge? I'll be escorting her to give a talk at the Lewis-Sigler Institute in a few minutes, but I need to make a quick call first. You can ask her about her research. It's fascinating."

"Not a problem."

As Herman hurried off, Michael led Carmel down the familiar route, past the first-floor laboratories and into the open-air lounge, which was equipped with several well-stocked refrigerators and even an industrial-strength cappuccino maker, which he'd never actually used before.

Michael grabbed a Diet Mountain Dew and Carmel selected a V-8, and then they took seats at a table. "So," Michael began, "what kind of research do you do at the children's hospital?"

Carmel, who looked to be in her mid-to-late fifties, sipped at her drink. "Professor Salomon—"

"Please, Michael is fine."

"Michael," she said. She had a very slight Australian accent. "Are you familiar with SIDS?"

"Sudden Infant Death Syndrome? I know what it is, but not much more." He shuddered at the idea of having a child stop breathing for no apparent reason.

"Well, I've been studying the subject for thirty years. Ever since my son, Damien, died of it."

Michael set down his drink. "I'm so sorry to hear that."

She waved dismissively. "Ever since then, many people have thought I'm mental for being so single-minded in my pursuit of answers. Or really, just one answer. *Why?* Why did my otherwise healthy son die? At the time it happened, I was actually a lawyer, though I had a biochemistry background. I quit my job, went back to school, got my PhD in sleep medicine, and dove into research. And it's been worth it. My studies have identified a biochemical marker that can help detect which babies are more at risk of SIDS."

"That's amazing." Michael leaned forward, elbows on the table. "What's the marker?"

She warmed to her subject. "It's an enzyme called butyrylcholinesterase, also known as BChE. Babies with a low amount of it are more susceptible to SIDS. We believe that the low level of the enzyme represents a dysfunction of the nervous system, and poses an inherent vulnerability to SIDS for those infants. We're currently working on a treatment protocol."

"Wow. You represent quite the inspirational story," Michael said. He couldn't help but think of Felicia. "As Herman said, I've just had a child. She was born last week, eight weeks premature, and she's coming home tomorrow, the doctors think. I don't suppose this enzyme test is already rolled out to hospitals yet?"

She smiled. "No, that's still a long way off. We haven't even published quite yet. But I'm hopeful that in the next eighteen months we can be rolling out recommendations to government agencies around the world. Your FDA, the UK's NHS, and others."

Just then Herman appeared in the doorway. He nodded at the drinks on the table. "I'm glad to see you don't share

Michael's affection for Diet Mountain Dew. I don't know how he can drink that stuff."

Carmel laughed. "Most people say that about me drinking V-8." She smiled at Michael. "To each their own."

"Well, I'm ready when you are," Herman said.

Michael and Carmel stood. "It was very nice meeting you," Michael said. "I look forward to seeing your work put an end to SIDS around the world."

"I was telling her the same thing!" Herman put in. "For physicists, the victories in our research never feel quite so tangible as that."

As Herman and Carmel hurried off, Michael considered what Herman had said. Physics research often didn't provide the same level of tangible results, and yet…

He thought back to the work he'd been doing the last time he was in the lab, a week ago, on that fateful night before his vision. Would he be able to reproduce those results?

Only one way to find out.

Michael frowned, as he always did, at the name on the sign above the lab's entrance. Although he'd worked in the basement-level lab for nearly a decade now, it had been labeled the "Salomon lab" last year when he attained tenure. That was a thing at Princeton—naming labs after the professors that headed the research within—but to Michael it felt pretentious.

He swiped his badge on the reader and pushed his way inside. He found Ken, one of his post-doc researchers, already at work, showing a lab notebook to a summer institute grad student whose name Michael couldn't recall.

"Hey Ken, were you able to get any of those higher-speed CCDs from that MIT contact I gave you?"

The post-doc nodded vigorously. Ken Lee was a brilliant researcher, and his almost savant-like talent with numbers manifested itself in his ability to solve complex math equations in seconds. Michael loved working with the guy; he was practically a human calculator. But Ken also had severe speech apraxia, making it very difficult for him to communicate in a verbal manner. Instead, he often relied on a notebook-sized dry-erase board that he always kept handy.

As Ken started to scribble a response, the grad student hopped up from his stool and gave Michael an uneasy look. Michael understood; he had a reputation for being a hardass with the students. "He's hella smart, but will tear you a new one if you ask him a stupid question" was a common comment in his student-based reviews on RateMyProfessor. Everyone who made it to Princeton was smart, but Michael felt strongly that smart wasn't good enough. All too often, these kids were lazy and didn't want to put the work in. He wasn't at all forgiving when students asked questions about things that were clearly explained in the textbook.

Michael finally remembered the kid's name. "Josh. This isn't going to be like one of my regular classes. You take your cues from Ken. He knows what he's doing, and you'll learn a lot. If you have any questions, ask. I'd rather you ask a question than stare dumbly at us and not learn anything from this summer's experience. Got it?"

Josh nodded. "I totally get it. Thank you for letting me join for the summer, Professor."

"Don't thank me yet." Michael grinned. "You'll probably work harder than you've ever worked. You'll need to keep up."

Ken turned the whiteboard toward Michael, with his response to Michael's question about the CCDs.

"Yesterday we received a dozen high-speed CCDs direct from Professor Johnson's photonics lab. I've incorporated them into the rig, and combined with the new synchronizer, I think we can get frame grabs in the vacuum chamber with a timing resolution as low as 250 picoseconds."

"That's fantastic. At 250 picoseconds, how far will a photon travel?"

Ken wiped the board with his sleeve and wrote, *"Approximately 7.5cm."*

Josh raised his hand.

Michael grinned. "We're not in the classroom; there's no need to raise your hand. Just ask your question."

"Um." The grad student hesitated for a second. "Professor, if I understand correctly, you're trying to capture proof of certain high-speed particles in the lab's vacuum chamber, right? So, I was curious about why you need a faster cycle time for the cameras. The vacuum chamber has a diameter of one hundred twenty-two centimeters—a full four feet—and the CCDs we had before had a timing resolution of around one nanosecond, so that would mean we could get an image of, let's say a photon traveling about thirty centimeters across the chamber. Meaning we'd get anywhere from three to four images. So… why is that not enough?"

"Very good question," Michael said. "You're just thinking of the wrong kind of particles. You're thinking of luxons—massless particles that always travel at the speed of light, such as a photon. But what if I told you that we're trying to measure something traveling faster than that."

Josh's eyes widened as he looked back and forth between Ken and the professor. "I didn't think—"

"That there were such things?" Michael said. "That's what we're here to prove."

"Or disprove."

"If you have a proposal on how to prove a negative, I'd like to hear it, but no. Our goal is to positively prove the existence of what I think has been buzzing around us since the dawn of time." Michael turned to Ken. "Are the capacitors charged? We ready to run an experiment with the new setup?"

Ken nodded and made a quick scribble on the whiteboard. *"Ready when you are."*

Michael grinned. "Okay, let's do it."

Michael sat in front of a computer, looking at a live image of the vacuum chamber, as Ken walked over to the wall and flipped a red lever. In the upper right-hand corner of the monitor was another video feed coming from the building's roof.

He looked over at the grad student. "Josh, do you understand what we're doing?"

"Ken's opening up the reflector dish to gather whatever it can. It's the same principle as a satellite dish, right?"

"Yes and no. The dish is certainly receiving whatever signals it's being bombarded with, but we aren't reflecting any of the particles nor are we using an LNB to convert any of the signals received into another form. This dish isn't about to receive HBO or anything." Michael watched as the mirror-like petals of the dish unfolded, resulting in something that looked very much like an oversized—and extremely expensive—funnel. "It's a clear day, so we should get a pretty reasonable stream of signals coming in. When we launch the experiment, the funnel will briefly activate a high-gauss magnetic field that will feed the signals into the routing pipe at the base of the funnel. Do you know why we need the magnetic field?"

The grad student furrowed his brow. "Is it sort of like the same problem a particle accelerator has to deal with—you don't want those particles touching the sides of whatever you're piping them through?"

"Exactly right. It's the same consideration they have at the Large Hadron Collider, at Brookhaven National Labs in New York, at Fermilab, and at the smaller accelerators throughout the world. We may not be as famous as them, but I've got a special flavor of the same concept built in this very building. Right now, you and I are sitting in a heavily shielded compartment for an experiment that will last all of about one millisecond.

"That funnel out there is receiving radio waves, visible light, background cosmic radiation, et cetera. Most of which will, of course, be traveling at roughly the speed of light.

That's *not* what we want. So we've set up the magnetic fields with a very unusual configuration. The incoming stream of particles will curve, as they do in any accelerator, but we're also forcing the beam to pass through an aperture, such that those particles going at or below the speed of light will bend too far and not make it through the aperture. It's like a race where you have cars going around a track. The slower cars will make the turns as they're supposed to, but a car going too fast will fly right off the track. Those are the particles we're looking for."

Josh grinned. "This is *so* cool. And I was thinking more about the faster cycle time on the cameras. With your setup, even if a particle came screaming into the building at three times the speed of light, meaning it would travel about 22.5 centimeters in 250 picoseconds, we could still catch multiple images of it as it passes through the chamber."

Just then Ken motioned for Josh, who hopped off his stool and joined the researcher at an L-shaped table with a single monitor and keyboard. Michael took the opportunity to look over the equipment. At the heart of it all was a high-density compute cluster, connected by a thick black cable to the synchronizer with the banks of CCDs—in effect tiny cameras capturing whatever light was visible in a 64-by-64 square of pixels. The CCDs were arranged in a grid pattern, and the captured data was fed to the synchronizer, which mapped all the data into an image in the compute cluster's memory.

Michael turned to Ken. "Hey, now that we're pumping CCD frames across to the compute cluster at four times the previous speed, can the computer's memory handle a full millisecond of that data? These are better resolution CCDs than we used before, right?"

Ken began scribbling, and Josh looked over his shoulder and read the words aloud.

"Sorry, Professor, I forgot to mention that. Yes, the CCDs are higher resolution. We have plenty of total memory on the cluster to spool to, but the expected four million frames we'd receive in the span of a millisecond would overwhelm our bandwidth, and the caches can only hold so much. Across all the data channels we have interconnects for, and given that each DIMM has a peak transfer rate of about 35 gigabytes per second, *and* we have no more than 128 data channels we can feed, that gives us a peak spool of roughly 4.5 terabytes per second, or 4.5 gigabytes per millisecond. With these CCDs all pumping a portion of what ends up being a 768K image, the L1 caches will get filled faster than we can flush it across—"

"Okay, I get it. We need a bigger rig. How much wall clock time can we get spooled to memory?"

Using the heavily stained sleeve of his lab coat, Ken wiped the board and wrote a number down, which Josh again read aloud. "Roughly 1.4 microseconds."

Michael let out a groan. He hadn't taken into consideration how close the upgrades would take them toward their current data transfer rate limit.

"Okay, how long does the captured data take to spool to storage and start again?"

More scribbling, and Josh said, "Flushing the caches to memory and then to non-volatile storage will take almost a minute. We also have a limit on how many 1.4 microsecond bursts of data we can store on the storage array currently installed."

"That's fine. I figure if we don't find anything in a particular 1.4-microsecond image run, we can go ahead and delete it. Are we ready on your end?"

Ken gave a thumbs-up.

Michael went back to his console, pulled up the control application, and hovered the mouse arrow over the "go" button.

"Here goes nothing."

He clicked.

A loud thunk reverberated through the lab as several activities all happened seemingly at once.

"Ken," Michael said, "start saving the data and get us ready for another." He kept his focus on his screen, waiting for the first image as he replayed in his mind the steps that had just occurred.

The stream of particles, mostly photons, were captured from the rooftop and routed into the funnel. The conduit through which the particles entered had a very strong magnetic field applied to it, keeping the stream from contacting the walls of the pipe. As the particles entered the building, they raced around the circumference of the basement lab at unimaginable speeds, and on the last loop of their path, those particles traveling at or less than the speed of light were winnowed out. If anything remained in the pipe, it would have flown straight into the vacuum chamber.

The monitor flickered as the first of roughly 5,800 frames of visual data was received. Michael advanced it manually, adding 250 picoseconds with each click—a time period about two billion times shorter than the time it takes for someone to blink. The images all showed nothing—just the darkness of the vacuum chamber.

With his mouse, he highlighted the main portion of the vacuum chamber image, avoiding the time code. Michael clicked the "auto-scan" button, allowing the computer to start flying through the images, looking for any differences in the area he highlighted. In only a second it stopped at the end of the series with a popup message.

"No changes."

Michael nodded. Not unexpected. He glanced at the wall clock. It was ten a.m.

Josh called out, "We're ready."

The professor moved the mouse over the "go" button and repeated the process.

It was going to be a long day.

Michael grimaced. It was seven in the evening, an hour past when he'd told Maria he'd be home. She was used to his shenanigans, especially during the summer, but with the baby coming home tomorrow, he couldn't keep doing this.

"We're ready, Professor." Josh sounded tired.

Michael's obsession wasn't fair to these two any more than it was fair to Maria. "Okay, guys," he said. "This will be the last one for the day."

He clicked "go" again, and the familiar thunk blasted

through the room while Michael stared bleary-eyed at the monitor.

The first image came up looking like it always did, with the edges of the dark vacuum chamber only barely visible as varying shades of black and dark gray. Michael had long ago quit searching the images manually; he clicked right away on the auto-scan and waited for the computer to pop up the same message it always—

Wait.

Michael's eyes widened in disbelief.

There was a change.

In the 4,438th image of the series, on the left-hand side, was a tiny bluish smear.

As he zoomed in, he heard footsteps behind him. "Professor?" said Josh. "Is that what I think it is?"

There was a squeak of a dry-erase marker on the whiteboard, then Josh added, "Ken says it's the same color as what he saw in the core of the Advanced Test Reactor at Idaho National Labs."

Michael couldn't wipe the grin off his face. "One second, guys." He zoomed back out, then advanced to the next frame.

A chill raced up his spine.

The blue smear had elongated slightly and had advanced halfway across the screen. He pointed at the tail end of what now looked almost like a minuscule blue comet. "Look at how short that tail is. Evidently the Cherenkov radiation dissipates very quickly. No wonder nobody has ever seen such a thing."

He went back to the previous frame, grabbed a ruler from the table, and placed it against the monitor where the faint blue light had first appeared. He then moved forward one frame and shook his head in amazement.

"The particle has traveled roughly one third of the way across the chamber in 250 picoseconds." He looked over at Ken, who'd already started scribbling while smiling ear to ear. He turned his whiteboard around.

"5.333c!"

Michael advanced the frame once more, and the blue smear was still just visible near the right-hand edge.

They had done it.

"Save this data!" Michael almost yelled. Ken raced back to the compute cluster and tapped quickly on his keyboard.

Michael's heart thudded in his chest as he kept advancing and rewinding through the three frames of evidence.

"Professor, it's saved," Josh announced as Ken got up from his chair with an excited expression.

Michael rose to his feet and fist-bumped them both. "Gentlemen, we just captured a particle going over five times the speed of light."

CHAPTER THREE

Michael lifted the bassinet from the kitchen table and put it on his lap. As Felicia's big blue eyes stared up at him, he couldn't help but think she looked a bit like a stern and wrinkled Yoda. She'd been home for only a couple of hours, and it all felt so weird and new, having a baby at home. Maria had just come back from walking Percy around the neighborhood, trying to get him to calm down. He'd been overwhelmed by the new smells of the baby.

They were now gathered in the kitchen, and Maria patted the seat of the chair next to her. "Up, Percy, up. I can't pick you up right now. Mommy's still healing."

As if understanding completely, the puppy hopped up onto the chair. He turned around and let out a yip.

"Percy," Maria chided. She put her arm against his chest. "This is Felicia, your baby sister."

Percy's sniffer was working overtime as he leaned closer to

the bassinet. His butt wiggled and his tail swished back and forth. But Felicia seemed unfazed, and Michael brought the bassinet a little closer so the two of them could see eye to eye.

"Percy, be gentle," Maria said. She held Percy around the chest, and the oversized puppy leaned forward and licked at the edge of the basket. "She's still very tiny. But soon enough you two will be able to play together."

Felicia's arms and legs stiffened, and she made a small sound that sent Percy scurrying back against the chair.

Michael laughed. "Just like her mom, she's a tooter."

"As if!" Maria gave him a dramatic look of outrage, which was quickly replaced with a grin as she shifted her attention back to Felicia. "Look at her, she just yawned."

"They do that, you know." He grinned and watched as their little girl closed her eyes. "Can you believe it? We're parents."

Percy climbed down from the kitchen chair and wandered away, likely looking for his chew toy.

Maria motioned toward the stairs. "It looks like she's falling asleep. Take her upstairs to our bedroom, turn on the baby monitor, and close the door so Percy doesn't get in. I'll prepare dinner and we can both stare at her while we eat."

Lifting the bassinet off his lap, Michael got up carefully, trying not to wake the baby. As he climbed the stairs, his phone vibrated, and he was glad he'd thought to turn off the ringer.

"Whoever it is, call back later. I literally have my hands full."

Maria hummed a tune as she zipped around the kitchen, messing around on the stove at one moment, then moving to the counter to chop ingredients. How she knew what to put in the pot and in what measures was beyond Michael's ken. She finished off by tossing a large sprinkle of seasoning into the steaming pot, then she stirred its contents and tasted a spoonful of the broth.

Michael just watched all this with a smile on his face. His wife always seemed happiest when she was doing something in the kitchen. And he knew he was lucky she loved to cook. If it were up to him, it would be blue box mac and cheese every night.

"How's your incision doing?" he asked.

Maria filled two bowls with the chunky soup. "It's still a little sore, I guess, but fine. With the abdominal binder on, I can barely feel a thing."

"Just don't overdo it, okay?"

She placed the bowls on the table. "You worry too much. Have a seat and eat your *sancocho*."

Michael took a sniff, and his mouth watered from the savory scent that wafted up from the bowl. In the broth were chunks of corn still on the cob, stewed chicken thighs, tomatoes, and other bits and pieces he couldn't identify.

"It smells spicy," he said.

Maria blew on a spoonful and sipped it with a contented expression. "I put a little *aji amarillo* in there. Not too spicy. My mom used to make this when one of us was sick. It reminds me of home."

Before meeting Maria, Michael had hated spicy food.

She'd slowly converted him into at least tolerating it. But he knew that "not too spicy" for her probably meant "extremely spicy" to him. Still, her mention of her mom meant that Michael was going to have to tough it out. Her father had been a police officer, and because of his work, he, along with all of Maria's family apart from herself, had been killed by enforcers from one of the Colombian drug cartels. That all happened not long before Michael met Maria. It was also why she got permission from the US government to stay here, even before they were married, given the danger she'd face if she went back.

He gulped down a spoonful, and at first he was surprised at how much it reminded him of his own mother's chicken soup. But then he was hit with a sledgehammer of spice.

"Do you like it?" Maria asked.

"Mmm. It reminds me a little of the soup my mother used to make." With his thumb and forefinger, he picked up one of the chunks of corn and nibbled the kernels off the cob, hoping it would calm the heat.

It only made it worse.

"How are you handling the spice?"

"It's..." He cleared his throat and took another spoonful. "It's fine. I can feel it in the back of my throat. But it all tastes amazing."

"I'm impressed. You're doing much better with spice. I should probably add a little more—"

"No. No more spice," he said quickly. "This is about as much as I can handle."

Maria reached her bare foot under the table and ran it

against the back of his calf. "Your face is all blotchy. It was too much spice?"

Michael laughed and chewed on a succulent piece of chicken thigh. "Any more and I think I'll melt, but this is good."

His phone vibrated once again, and this time he retrieved it from his pocket. "Yes?"

"Michael? Did I catch you at a bad time?"

"Herman? No, I can talk." Michael glanced at his watch. It was just past eight. The department chair never called him this late. "What's up?"

"Remember how we were talking about the possibility of getting some government funding to expand the research on your project? Well, the DARPA guys called from DC. They want to come and meet with you. I think your funding problems are about to vanish."

Michael sat up straight. "You're kidding?"

Maria looked across the table at him with a quizzical look.

"I'm not in the least, considering the importance of your recent findings. I'm just surprised that you reached out to them without consulting me first. As you know, these requests are tricky, and we don't want to burn any funding bridges."

"Wait a minute. This isn't *your* doing? I haven't talked to anyone about the project. I mean, no one outside of you and my team."

"Really?" There was a moment of silence on the line. *"Maybe one of your team members then... Either way, they're going to be here at nine a.m."*

"Well, yeah. Okay, sure. I'll be there."

"But that said... I do *want to know how they came to be aware of your research. If one of your people has talked out of turn, that's a serious breach of confidence. You understand that, right?"*

Michael understood it well. The thought that Ken or Josh might have broken their NDA—and Michael's trust—made him sick with anger.

"I understand, and I'll take care of it."

"Good, then we're clear. I have a conflict tomorrow morning, but I'll come by the lab later in the day and you can fill me in on what happened. Have a good evening."

"You too."

As he put the phone back in his pocket, Maria raised an eyebrow. "Good news?"

Michael nodded. "Yeah. Mostly good."

She smiled and took another spoonful of her soup. "That's better than mostly bad."

Michael sipped at his coffee as he watched the examination through the one-way glass. It was seven a.m., and he'd set up two appointments, one for Ken and another for Josh.

Josh now sat in the chair on the other side of the glass, with a blood pressure cuff on his right arm, and two pneumography tubes wrapped around his chest and stomach to measure his breathing. The tubes and cuff were attached to a box on a table in the corner, which was in turn attached to a laptop.

In the room with him, fiddling with the box, was a licensed

polygraph examiner who also happened to be a professor of forensic science that Michael had befriended a few years back.

The examiner hit a few keys on the laptop. *"You are Mr. Joshua Whitley, am I correct?"*

The examiner's voice carried to Michael's observation room through a small speaker in the ceiling.

Josh nodded. "Yes."

"We'll be going over the answers to your questions you filled out earlier. I need to let you know that..."

Michael walked out of the room and into the adjoining observation room. Through this wall of one-way glass, he should have seen Ken filling out the same questionnaires as Josh, in preparation for his own turn with the examiner. But Ken wasn't here yet.

It was very unlike Ken to be late.

Michael breathed in deeply and let the air out slowly as he walked back to the other observation room.

"Mr. Whitley, I'm going to ask you a series of control questions that are intended to create your baseline physiological responses. These will help me calibrate the equipment. After I ask each question, please say 'no' as your response. Do you understand?"

Josh nodded.

The examiner shifted in his chair. *"Mr. Whitley, you are twenty-four years old, is that correct?"*

"No."

Michael knew that particular answer was a lie. Josh was twenty-four.

"Are you the current president of the United States?"

"No." Josh grinned.

"Please try not to move during this examination. Even facial reactions can throw readings off. Let's try that again. Are you the current president of the United States?"

"No."

"Have you ever told a lie?"

"No."

Was there a person who had never told a lie? Probably not.

After finishing with the control questions, the examiner quizzed Josh on recent events. These were questions that Michael had set up with the other professor ahead of time.

"Are you happy working in the Salomon lab?"

"Yes."

Josh's gaze was focused on his own lap.

"Do you find the research topics being covered in the Salomon lab interesting?"

"Yes."

"Do you think others might find them interesting?"

"Yes."

"Have you communicated with anyone outside of the laboratory environment, in any way, about the Salomon lab research topics?"

Josh hesitated. *"No."*

"Are you nervous?"

Josh looked up at the examiner. *"Yes."*

"Do you know if anyone has communicated anyone outside of the laboratory environment about the experiments being conducted within the Salomon lab?"

"No."

"Have you in any way violated your non-disclosure agreement that you signed as a condition of joining the Salomon lab?"

"No."

"Are you excited to continue working in the Salomon lab?"

"Yes." Josh failed to keep a grin from peeking through his otherwise somber expression.

The examiner tapped again on the laptop's keyboard. *"Okay, Mr. Whitley. I'm finished with the questions. I'll be right back to disconnect you from all of this stuff."* He closed the lid of the laptop, detached it from the box that was still connected to Josh, and walked with it out of the room.

A minute later, the door to the observation room opened and Professor Itzhak Mizrahi walked in. He had a troubled expression as he took a seat next to Michael.

"Your other student isn't in the lobby or the examination room. That's not very promising."

"I don't understand it. He's never late."

Itzhak shrugged and held up the closed laptop. "Let's talk about Mr. Whitley."

"What's the verdict?"

"I found his physiological responses to be fairly unpredictable and there were signs of what I like to call response normalization."

"What's that?"

"That's when people learn to maintain some control over their physiological response. The intelligence community trains some of their operation officers in this technique, so that they can pass one of these tests even while lying. It can be effective, but it's also detectable. Basically all it achieves is masking truth from falsehood, making both look the same in both the control and actual tests.

"In this case, your student had minimal dynamic physiological responses, which implies that there were some attempts at masking his reactions. Given his age and background, I wouldn't presume he'd been trained to fool polygraph analysis, but when some people are nervous and trying to control their nervousness, it can naturally resemble conscious response normalization. I believe your student might fall into the small percentage of people for which polygraph analysis doesn't yield a definitive yes or no result. However, even though these results were rather inconclusive, given his age and background, I'd say Mr. Whitley likely committed no conscious violations of his agreements with you and your lab."

"That sucks. I mean, it's good, but it kind of sucks as well."

"You were hoping it was him."

"I mean no, but… yes."

"You mean to say, you don't want it to be the other guy."

"Exactly. I've known Ken a long time."

"And now he's not even showing up. I assume he'd have called you if something came up?"

Michael nodded. "Like I said, he's never late. But if he were… he'd have texted."

"I'm sorry. And even though I can't really form an opinion about the other person without examining his responses, the idea that he didn't show up for a polygraph test… doesn't bode well." He stood and shook Michael's hand. "I'd better go disentangle your student from the rig. If the other guy shows, just give me a call and we can set up another time."

Michael's stomach gurgled with anxiety. Ken was a raw talent and a real workhorse. And a good guy. As far as Michael was concerned, Ken was worth five Joshua Whitleys.

He texted Ken yet again: *Where are you?*

Ken was never without his phone. And Michael couldn't think of any occasion where Ken hadn't immediately returned his text. But now, nothing.

He dialed Ken's number. This was something he'd never done before. There was no point in talking to Ken on the phone, since Ken didn't talk back. The phone rang four times and then a woman's voice began speaking.

"Hi, you've reached Ken Lee's voice mail. He's unavailable to talk for obvious reasons. Please text him whatever message you have, and he will return your text as soon as possible. Thank you."

Michael shook his head. He hoped desperately that there was another explanation for Ken's absence than the one Itzhak had quite clearly implied. But there was nothing he could do about it right now. He had a meeting to keep with the folks from DC.

Standing in front of Jadwin Hall, Professor Salomon watched as four men climbed out of a dark sedan and headed in his direction. The entire group looked like factory-cloned examples of each other. They seemed to be roughly his age, in their early forties, but they were all wearing suits and ties, which he most definitely was not. Dressed in khakis, a navy-blue polo, and a white lab coat, he suddenly felt underdressed for the meeting.

The lead suit nodded and gave him a toothy smile as they shook hands. "Professor Salomon, I'm John Hawkins with the Defense Sciences Office out of DC. It's good to meet you."

"It's good to meet you as well. Come in, let's get you guys out of the humidity." The professor swiped his badge on the reader and opened the door. "I'll show you to the conference room."

"Actually, Professor, I think we'd rather take a look at the lab, if you don't mind," Hawkins said. "We're interested in seeing what you're currently working with."

"Of course."

Michael led them down the stairs to his basement lab. There was no one else there; he'd told Josh that other than this morning's polygraph there wouldn't be any work for him today. Though in truth, that was mostly because Michael had anticipated that Josh had betrayed him. Still, his absence was just as well.

"Professor," Hawkins said, trailing his gaze along the shielded piping that came through the wall and led to the vacuum chamber, "who else is on your team at the moment?"

"It's a very small crew. Just me, a post-doc researcher, and a graduate student." Michael walked over to the main terminal, patted the keyboard, and pointed at the monitor hanging from the ceiling. "This is the control panel, and—"

"Where are they?" Hawkins asked. The other three men

had yet to say a word, but were now busily taking notes on their iPads.

Annoyed at the question, Michael shrugged. "Knowing that you folks were coming, I gave the others the day off." Then, without thinking about how the question might be taken, he blurted out, "I know you spoke with the chair of the physics department, but I'm curious as to how you even know about our work here. For that matter... what is it you think we've discovered?"

Hawkins seemed unfazed by both the question and Michael's challenging tone. "Sorry," he said with a friendly smile, "I suppose we didn't start this conversation in the right place." He pointed at himself and the others. "We're all physicists, with varying focus areas. We *are* talking about first proof of the existence of tachyons, right? Faster than speed of light transmission?" He pointed at the heavily shielded mass at the center of the lab. "I'm guessing you've gotten proof by detecting them in that vacuum chamber."

"Through Cherenkov radiation trails?" said one of the others.

So the others can speak, Michael thought.

"Again," he pressed, "can you tell me how you guys know that we did this? It literally *just* happened. I haven't even written up any of the reports yet."

The physicists all turned to a man who'd been hanging at the back of the group. The man had very light blue eyes, almost like an Alaskan husky's. And in one eye, instead of white surrounding the iris, his was all a dark red.

Michael had had the same thing happen to him once a few

years ago, though not nearly to the same degree. One morning he just looked in the mirror and noticed a large red splotch in the white of his right eye. It didn't affect his vision, and he didn't even feel it when it happened. The docs said it had probably happened when he'd coughed or exerted himself in some way.

The man looked up as if only now noticing that everyone was staring at him. "Sorry, I was taking notes about the lab. What's the question?"

Michael tried to keep his voice light and friendly. "I'm sorry, you are…?"

"Apologies for not introducing myself. My name is Carl Sundenbach."

"Carl. How did you guys find out about what we've been doing in our humble little part of New Jersey?"

"Oh, that. I got a call from someone named Ken? He told us you have visual evidence of superluminal particle trails in a vacuum. He wasn't very specific, but he didn't need to be. News like that… well, you can understand how excited we were. As I'm sure you must be."

"Wait." Michael felt his heart thudding loudly in his chest. He had feared Ken had broken his NDA, but this… this was impossible. "You say Ken *called* you about this? And you spoke to him?"

Carl nodded. "Yesterday, in the morning. After a discussion with our higher-ups, it was decided that the four of us would come up and talk to you directly."

Michael tried to put together in his mind what had happened yesterday. He had taken the day off from work to pick up Felicia from the hospital and get her settled in at home. He'd left instructions for Ken and Josh to archive the video images and research solutions for capturing the still frames in real-time. And while he was gone… Ken made a phone call?

"I'm curious," he said to Carl. "Did Ken sound odd at all?"

The man looked at him quizzically. "What do you mean?"

"I mean, did he sound at all unusual?" Michael smiled, trying to hide from his voice how troubled he was. "It's just that I've rarely ever heard him speak, so I was wondering what made him call you. It's sort of an unusual breach of norms around here."

Carl shrugged. "He didn't sound particularly stressed, if that's what you're asking. He certainly didn't say he was breaching a confidence. In fact, the conversation was pretty casual and matter-of-fact. It made me wonder if he was pulling my leg."

"He didn't sound particularly stressed…"

"The conversation was pretty casual…"

Michael recalled the first time he'd met Ken. The man had tried desperately to speak, to not let his impediment get in the way, but he was practically unintelligible. Michael quickly agreed to relying solely on the whiteboard as a workaround. Still, over the time they'd worked together, he'd heard Ken answer the phone a few times… and every time was a struggle. The man was utterly incapable of a casual verbal conversation in any way, shape, or form. And, at least as far as Michael knew, there was no voice synthesizer good enough to mimic *natural* human speech, complete with "casual" pauses, pacing, and intonations.

Which meant either someone else had called Carl, pretending to be Ken, or…

Carl was lying.

Hawkins seized control of the conversation once more. “Perhaps you could show us what you’ve found, Professor? There *are* images, right?”

“Yes, I’d be happy to show you what I have.”

Michael went to the computer and pulled up one of the images with the blue ghost of a tachyon. “Gentlemen,” he said, “this is the first of a three-frame sequence capturing a particle exceeding the speed of light in a vacuum.”

“Is this color-adjusted?” Hawkins asked.

“No, this is exactly what was seen in the chamber without any color processing whatsoever.”

The men all began to speak at once.

“That’s the same shade of blue we saw over in…”

“…you can almost imagine the cavitation…”

“Can you determine the speed of the particle?”

Michael answered the one question he heard in the hubbub. “I can tell you the exact speed. We aren’t using the standard Ring imaging Cherenkov detectors due to the nature of how we’re collecting the source particles. We’re literally taking 250-picosecond sequence images with a line of high-speed CCDs.” He clicked with the mouse and advanced to the next frame. “This is one-quarter nanosecond later, and you’ll see the particle has advanced nearly forty centimeters. Which computes to 5.3 times the speed of light.”

“Whoa…” Hawkins looked back and forth between the monitor and his fellow physicists. Everyone was wide-eyed, even the liar with the red eye. "You're confident in these results?"

Michael shrugged. "I have three frames showing a particle that seems to be progressing at an unheard-of speed. I personally believe this is exactly what it seems to be, but I also won't be shouting about this on the rooftops until I've done this experiment several times."

"So you've only managed to capture this the one time?"

"Actually… no. This is the second time I've produced these results. Once with slightly less sensitive equipment. With the new setup, I have little doubt I'll be able to make more observations."

One of the men nudged Hawkins. "John, we should get some of our equipment down here and see if we can calculate the four-momentum of the particles. We have no idea what kind of particle this is. This could be huge."

Michael pulled a sheet of paper out of the desk and handed it to Hawkins. "You'll see on there some of the next steps I'm working on. Gathering an identity of the particle is just one of the things on the list." He pointed at the pipe running from the wall and into the vacuum chamber. "For instance, I have a sorting mechanism already established here to separate luminal and superluminal particles, and if it's as easy as it seems, I've got all the equipment I need to hypothetically collect them, normalize their speeds, and create a stream of such particles. Of course, some of the more interesting items on my list would require significant funding; I would need equipment that the school doesn't have access to. I've already talked with the chair of the department, and we're willing to discuss an arrangement where we'd work with the government on the advancement of this research."

The men began talking to each other as if Michael wasn't even there. Talking about the things on his checklist, equipment, authorizations, and much more. But Michael could already tell that the poorly funded project he'd been working on for a decade might suddenly be injected with all the financial support he could have hoped for—and more. He maintained a neutral expression, but on the inside he was popping the cork on the champagne.

The door to the lab buzzed, and Michael looked up to see Herman walking in with a grim expression. The men from DARPA had left hours ago.

"Herman? You're not looking very happy. What's up?"

Michael stood as the man approached, but Herman motioned for him to sit back down.

"Trust me, you'll want to be sitting when I tell you this."

"Is this about the DARPA guys? Because when they left, I felt pretty—"

"No, it's not that. It's about Ken Lee." Herman pulled in a deep breath and shook his head. "There's no good way to say this. He's dead."

Michael's mind went blank. He'd prepared himself to hear almost anything but that.

"He's... How?" The word came in a barely audible whisper.

"I only know what I was told by HR. Looks like a car accident. Evidently the police found his vehicle at the bottom of the Delaware Raritan Canal off Old Lincoln Highway."

Michael felt a wave of emotions wash over him. He didn't know what to think, how to act, what to feel. "You said the police… was there foul play, do they think?"

Herman's eyes widened. "I wouldn't think so. Is there a reason why—"

"No," Michael said quickly. "I guess I just don't know how to react."

Herman put his hand on Michael's shoulder. "Here's how you react. Finish up whatever you've got going on and let me drive you home."

"You don't need—"

"Nonsense. I know you were close with him. You need a little time to absorb the news. I'll go to my office and get my things. I'll be right back."

As Herman left, Michael looked around in a daze. Ken… gone. It didn't seem possible.

He tried to follow Herman's advice and close out his work. But his mind kept drifting back to what Carl had said.

"He didn't sound particularly stressed if that's what you're asking… The conversation was pretty casual."

Michael was now more certain than ever that the man with the red eye had been lying through his teeth. Everything about this felt wrong.

He looked over at the chair that Ken always sat in. The chair he would never sit in again.

"I'm sorry, buddy," he whispered. "I'm going to miss you."

CHAPTER FOUR

The moment Michael walked in the front door, he froze. A wide-eyed Maria stood not more than five feet away, a cast iron pan held above her head, ready to swing.

She then muttered a string of obscenities in Spanish as she lowered her impromptu weapon. "Why the hell did you scare me like that?"

"What do you mean, scare you? I just opened the door."

She pushed the front door closed and gestured at it as if the answer was obvious. "You always come in through the garage." She looked out the window, and her frown deepened.

Michael turned to see what she was looking at. Herman's Cadillac was backing out of the driveway.

"Is that… where's your car?" Maria demanded, all the while keeping her voice low.

He was surprised she wasn't yelling at him. Maria was a sweetheart of a girl, but when surprised or angry, she was most definitely a yeller. Then he realized, the baby must be asleep.

"Well..." He wasn't sure how to begin.

Maria cupped his chin with her free hand and stared into his eyes. "*Ay, mi amor*. I can see it in your face, something's wrong." She gently grabbed his arm and pulled him toward the kitchen. "Come, dinner's not ready yet, but the supermarket had some really nice watermelon I just cut up. We can snack on that and you can tell me why your boss just dropped you off at home."

Michael let himself get led to the table, then watched as Maria gathered silverware, dishes, watermelon, and a pitcher of freshly squeezed limeade, which was a favorite in their house. The baby monitor was on the kitchen counter, and he could see Felicia lying in her crib, sleeping. Percy's rear end and tail were just visible in the picture.

"You're good with Percy in the room by himself with her?"

She nodded as she sat down across from him. "It's interesting—he somehow knows not to bark when he's near her. So I figure he's less likely to wake her when he's with her than when he's down here barking at me. He hasn't quite figured out that sound travels." Maria smiled. "But you should see it. If Felicia even twitches, he comes running down to get me and starts barking up a storm. It's adorable."

She stabbed a fork into one of the big cubes of watermelon, took a bite, and looked him in the eye. "Now tell me. Why did your boss drop you off at home?"

Michael started by telling her about Ken's death. She was as horrified as he was; she'd never met Ken, but he'd talked about the man frequently. Then he went on to tell her about the leak to DARPA, and the government's claim that Ken was the one who called them.

Maria frowned. "But you said Ken can barely speak aloud."

"That's right."

"So how could he have talked to that government man?"

Michael pointed at her with a speared fork of watermelon. "That's exactly it. He couldn't—like, he literally couldn't. Besides which, I would never have taken Ken as someone to violate his NDA like that. Not even accidentally. He knows how this stuff works. He knows he's not supposed to talk to anyone about what he does at work."

"But you talk to me about your work. *I* didn't sign one of those papers. Maybe he mentioned it to a friend and it was a friend who called? I mean, you said that you guys had a big discovery. I can tell you're excited about it, and I'm excited for you. Maybe Ken trusted someone like you trust me, and that trust wasn't well targeted. And then that someone called the government people, pretending to be him. Maybe they even thought they were doing him a favor, when they really were getting him in trouble."

Michael stared at his wife for a full five seconds as he processed what she'd said. Then he smiled. "Maria, sometimes you're just brilliant."

"Sometimes?" She arched her eyebrow and harrumphed. "Finish the watermelon and get yourself changed while I go ahead and get supper ready. And if you check on the baby, *please* don't wake her. She's been up all day and she just went down a few minutes before you got home."

As he headed upstairs, he thought through Maria's explanation. It was simple, and he wanted it to be the truth. He wanted for Ken to not have betrayed his trust.

But then again, for Ken to get killed the very day that these DARPA men showed up…

No. He shook his head. It was just a coincidence.

When Michael walked downstairs after his shower, he was hit with the scent of cumin, and he smiled. Fajitas were one of his favorite dishes that Maria made. She always reminded him that fajitas were an American dish and not from south of the border, but he didn't care where they originally came from. Maria added her own spices, and whatever they were always made his mouth water.

Maria's eyes lit up as he walked into the kitchen. "It's about time, you slowpoke. I was going to call 911 in fear that you might have drowned up there."

"Nope, just enjoying a hot shower."

Felicia's bassinet was on the kitchen table with Percy lying underneath, his tail wagging. The dog looked as if he wanted to bark at Michael's arrival, but then settled for a whine, as if trying his best not to bark around the baby. That dog was amazingly smart.

As Maria set a platter of seared meat on the table, she gave Michael a suggestive look. "I hope you left some hot water for us later."

"Us?" Michael blinked as his wife turned to get some plates

from the kitchen. His eyes followed her sashaying hips, and he grinned. "Wait a minute—you had a C-section just a little over a week ago. We can't have sex yet. Can we?"

Maria laughed as she put out a plate of grilled vegetables and a container of steaming-hot corn tortillas. "Not everything is about sex, my dear husband."

Michael stared at her, perplexed, which made her howl with laughter.

"I'll explain later, you silly man."

Percy poked his head up from under the table, looking for a head scratch, and Michael obliged. As he roughed the puppy's fur, he heard a jingling noise. The dog had on a new collar.

"Percy! Where'd you get that snazzy collar?"

The dog lolled his tongue out in a big smile.

"It looks amazing, doesn't it?" said Maria.

Actually, Michael thought, *it looks expensive.* It was a heavy silver metal with a designer look to it—more like a thick necklace than a collar. If it were made of gold, it would look quite at home on a rapper. Not the kind of thing Maria usually bought.

"How much did you pay?" he asked.

"Nothing. We got it for free."

"Huh?"

Maria pointed at his plate. "Make your burrito. Your food will get cold."

He obediently grabbed a tortilla and smeared refried beans on it, then added medium-rare grilled and marinated steak, shredded cabbage, rice, sauteed onions, and mushrooms.

Maria nodded in satisfaction, then explained. "Felicia and I were out taking Percy for a walk when this old car stopped just down the street from us. It was one of those fancy ones with the flying person's statue on the front? I forget what they call them."

"A Rolls Royce?" Michael asked with his mouth full of food.

"Yes! That's it. Anyway, there was this elderly couple inside, and when we walked past them, the old man rolled down his window and said Percy looked just like a German shepherd they used to have years ago. They still had the dog's collar in the glove box, had never felt right getting rid of it. But when they saw Percy, they knew it had a home. The man said their dog wore it for almost seventeen years, so it should bring good luck."

"Seventeen years? That's a good long time for a German shepherd. And that was very nice of them. Did you get their names?"

Maria shook her head. "They said they were just passing by and wanted to say hi to Percy. Do you think it's expensive?"

Michael shrugged. "I have no idea. Looks like stainless steel. But if it was owned by someone who drives a Rolls Royce? Who knows, could be made of platinum."

Her eyes widened in a look of concern. "Do you really think so? Or it could be silver."

"I wouldn't think it's silver. Silver tarnishes pretty easily. After seventeen years on a dog's neck, it wouldn't still have this shine."

"Well, maybe we should have it checked."

"No, I was kidding about it being platinum. I'm sure it's

just stainless steel. It might be some designer thing, which means it was expensive when they bought it but wouldn't have any resale value. We should just let Percy enjoy it."

Maria looked down at the dog. "Percy, you like your new collar?"

Percy gave a cautious yip and wagged his tail.

She patted the top of his head. "Then it's settled. Daddy and I say it's okay for you to keep it."

Michael took a swig of the limeade and grimaced.

"Too sour?"

"No, just not as sweet as you normally make it."

"Sorry, *mi amor*, I ran out of sugar. I have to go to the grocery store tomorrow, I'll pick some up." She pointed at his plate. "Now eat up. You're going to need your energy for what I have planned."

Michael quickly grabbed another tortilla. He was suddenly very curious about what Maria had in store for tonight.

It was almost pitch black in the bedroom when Michael awoke, his senses tingling with an awareness of something being not quite right. Percy, on his doggie bed on the other side of the bedroom, raised his head and looked over at him, then went back to sleep.

Michael looked at the clock on the nightstand. It was three a.m. The house was entirely quiet. Maria was beside him, sound asleep. The baby was in her crib making soft breathing noises.

So what had woken him?

He closed his eyes, and immediately he sensed lingering images of a farm. He could even smell the manure.

Had he just had a dream of being a farmer?

There was a building pressure in his head… the beginnings of a headache. But he was too tired to get up and get some Tylenol. He wondered if it was the result of the massage Maria had given him earlier. The massage had been her surprise for that night, and when she told him that, he was excited. But it turned out the kind of massage she had in mind involved smooth rocks being pounded into his muscles. Maria had read about the technique in some book—a book he planned on finding and lighting on fire. She loved the experience when he did it to her, but when she did it to him… well, he tried not to let on, but all he felt was pain.

He needed to get some rest. Hopefully he wouldn't wake up in the morning feeling like his muscles were made of chewing gum.

He let his mind drift, trying to find sleep once more. But instead, he once again saw images of a farm. It was no place he'd ever been before, that much he was sure of; he'd grown up in suburbia and had only ever seen a farm on TV. But the feeling of his shoes sinking into the soft earth, and the smell of the dew in the morning was so strong, he could have sworn he was actually there right now.

"Where are the sheep?" he muttered to himself. "If I must dream of a farm, the least they could do is let me count sheep…"

He tried to think of nothing but darkness. But he had the

strangest sensation. It was as if he was seeing snatches of images that came and went before his conscious mind could even process what he'd seen.

It was a long time before he finally drifted off to sleep once more.

CHAPTER FIVE

The four months after Michael's first meeting with the men from DARPA—and the subsequent influx of funding—saw a great deal of change in the lab. For one, Michael was now supervising not just one graduate student, but an entire team. Four computer engineers, two mathematicians, an astrophysicist, and four additional lab assistants whose backgrounds ran the gamut from mechanical engineering to physics. Despite all the people, however, he finally stopped worrying about additional leaks. His government partners had insisted that every member of the team undergo a security screening and register with a government database to be allowed to even know about this work, much less participate in it.

Michael was thrilled with the resulting pace of progress in his research. If anything, he sometimes worried DARPA wanted him to rush things too much—although he'd never actually been given a deadline, and they hadn't interfered with his research. Which was lucky for them, because if they had, he'd have ignored their demands and given them all the middle finger. No, thus far, the folks out of DARPA had been the perfect partner: very generous with the funding and yet hands-off when it came to management of the project.

And the project was amazing. The latest images from the vacuum chamber showed not just three blue smears, but an unwavering blue line that grew across the screen as a beam of tachyonic material shot across the vacuum chamber. The engineers had been working long hours to get the lab infrastructure updates configured just right, enhancing what he liked to call a "particle sorter" into a viable tachyonic accelerator. The result was a mechanism that could not only collect tachyons into the accelerator tubes circling the building, but to normalize the disparate particles into a stream of tachyons, all of which were traveling at the same speed—and all of which he could control.

In truth, his experiments had progressed further in the last three months than they had in the previous three years. And now they were about to try something that would have seemed like a pipe dream only months earlier.

One of the engineers crawled out of the vacuum chamber, resealed it, and unzipped himself from his sterile garb. "Professor, the mirror is good to go."

Michael gave him a thumbs-up, and the man slapped his hand on a flashing red button. The sound of the air pumps filled the lab as they evacuated all the air from within the chamber.

Michael looked over his shoulder and called out across the lab. "Charlie, what's the story on the calculations?"

A reedy man in his fifties walked over with a legal pad that had longhand equations scrawled all over it. "Professor, I had Sarah double-check my work." Sarah was the project's astrophysicist. "We think we're good on the CMB movement calculations."

"Let's pretend I'm not an astrophysicist. CMB?"

"Sorry, Professor—"

"Don't sorry me, just explain what you mean."

"Yes, well..." The man looked flustered, which made Michael feel less than confident about the data he was about to receive. "Well, we're moving at roughly 368 kilometers per second through the IGM, the intergalactic medium, but after talking with Josh and going over to the experts on such things, we determined that the most accurate means of determining our actual speed as we're moving through the universe is to calculate it using the rest frame of the CMB, which is the cosmic microwave background. To make a long story short, it's how Hubble and other space telescopes keep their orientation and it's the best method we know of how to predict where we are from one moment to the next as we float through the universe. Or in our case, predict where we will be or where we were at different intervals."

Michael nodded. "Okay. With all that, can we can get the bounce to occur within the chamber?"

Charlie nodded. "We should. But it's going to strain our power resources. The mechanical engineers are sweating bullets over the capacitors. We're probably good for a very short tachyonic burst at such a low speed."

Michael glanced at his watch. It was two minutes before

the experiment would begin. "Fine. Make sure somebody from the computer lab calls into the bridge. I want the entire team on this conference call."

Charlie hurried away and Michael put the desk phone on speaker as he dialed into the meeting. A beep sounded, and then a voice said:

"Who joined?"

"It's me."

"Hi Professor, it's Josh. Looks like it's just you and me at the moment."

Another beep, and then: *"Carl from the Defense Sciences Office."*

The DARPA guy with the red eye. He was a regular lurker in these calls. Never said a word, but was always in attendance. Typical of a lot of the DC types. He'd been appointed by the higher-ups in DC to "oversee" the project for the government and report back to his management.

"Hi Carl," said Josh. *"We're going to start at five after the hour, just to give everyone enough time to get on the call."*

Josh had gained a lot of confidence in the last several months. He was a far cry from the timid grad student Michael had first known. These days he was acting less in a technical capacity and more in an administrative one, helping Michael coordinate and keep tabs on the different tasks involved across the various departments that were now involved in the project. In effect, he'd become the group's project manager.

More people joined, and Michael waited until the clock ticked over to five after.

"Professor," said Josh, *"everyone is on the line."*

"Thank you, Josh. Okay folks, as a reminder, today's experiment will be to initiate a test bounce of a tachyonic stream. First, the hope is that we *can* bounce the stream from one surface to another via a tachyonic mirror. This is by no means a guaranteed thing. We already know that these tachyons that we've captured have a charge, so unlike neutrinos we can manipulate them to an extent. If we do get a bounce off a mirror, then we move on to our second goal, which is to try and measure some of the physical characteristics of whatever this beam is composed of. Most of the latter part we'll do as a post-processing exercise by analyzing things frame by frame. So: let's get rolling. How are we doing with the chamber atmospherics?"

"Professor, we're just now reaching ninety-five nanopascals of pressure in the vacuum chamber, and based on our prior tests I predict that we should be able to hold steady at about ninety-three."

A perfect vacuum was relatively impossible to achieve on Earth due to innumerable factors—outgassing of the materials the chamber was made of, virtual particles, etc. But at below one hundred nanopascals, the vacuum was so complete as to statistically claim that there would be no stray molecules within the chamber that could interfere with the tachyon beam.

"Great. Engineering? How are we on power?"

"Professor, this is Jan Halvorsen. I've voiced my concern before, and I'll do it again. The power needed for this experiment is stretching our resources to the point where I'm becoming uncomfortable with our ability to keep the power running to the lab. We're already cooling the capacitor banks

to maintain a clean power spigot at the lab's current power demands. The power spike required for this experiment is going to be very hard to support for any length of time."

Michael sighed. "I understand your concern."

Over the last four months, he and the crew had learned a lot about these faster-than-light particles. Among their characteristics, they seemed to have an elastic property associated with their speed. Unlike photons, a tachyon's speed seemed to be all over the map, which made them hard to control and observe. But their natural speed could be influenced by adding or taking away energy. And strangely, adding energy slowed them down, and draining energy sped them up. Ultimately, the key point from the engineer's point of view was that creating a stream of same-speed particles was an energy-intensive process.

Michael explained the situation to those who weren't familiar with this aspect of the experiment. "For the rest of you, Jan is talking about an issue with how the tachyonic particles behave. We already have to pull a lot of energy from our grid in order to maintain the stream at a somewhat average tachyon speed, which for these particles seems to be around 4.3 times the speed of light. Today's experiment involves slowing that down to as close to the speed of light as we can achieve. That puts a massive drain on the grid." He addressed Jan once more. "Jan, what's the longest period of time that we can cause a spike on the grid before something fails?"

"Professor, you don't want me to answer that, because I'd argue the answer is zero. But if I'm forced to give you a non-zero answer, I..." He paused. *"How long do you need?"*

"How about two nanoseconds as measured from launch of the beam to the beam's cessation?"

"I suppose I can... yes, I'll make it work. But we still need to online more capacitors for the grid. We're already past anything sensible."

"Good, then that's settled. We'll work out the capacitor issues after this experiment. Visual, how are we doing with our CCDs?"

"Hi, Professor, this is Tony. The CCD arrays are active, and we have a good signal from both the side and top views."

"Compute? How are we doing on the streaming interface? Can we handle both visual orientations?"

"Yes, Professor. I worked with Tony and we should have a real-time stitching of both optical streams into a single synchronized video stream."

"Good. I want the CCDs capturing at least two microseconds before we launch the beam of particles."

"Two microseconds before *the beam is released?"*

"Yes."

"Roger that, but realize that we can only do up to four microseconds of spooled data right now, in total."

"That's fine. Part of that will just have to be two microseconds before the stream is released. That's a hard requirement."

"Got it, I've made the adjustment on the synchronizer. We're good."

Michael was always excited in the moments before they launched another experiment. They could only do one per week, partly because of setup time, but also because they needed that much time to collect enough tachyons for the stream. The more particles they had, the more data they could gather.

He clapped his hands together. "Okay folks, this is what we've been working toward. Peeling back one more layer of the onion to discover something new. If anyone has any issues or concerns with initiating this experiment, speak now."

There was silence.

"In that case, Josh, start the ten-second countdown. On zero, I'll initiate the sequence."

"Okay, Professor. Starting the countdown now."

A computerized voice on the line began a countdown. *"Ten, nine, eight..."*

On his computer, Michael adjusted his real-time view of the chamber. He had his screen set up with a bird's-eye view of the chamber on the top, a side view on the bottom. When the beam launched, he wouldn't actually see anything, of course; it would be far too quick, and the stream of particles too gossamer-thin for the human eye to see. The real data would come from the high-speed footage the computers captured. But he always watched anyway.

"Three, two, one, launch."

A loud *thwack* sounded in the lab, and Michael stared impatiently at the monitor, waiting for the first frames of data to show up.

"We've got the spooled data, Professor. The computers are processing and you should have a searchable video in... now."

The screen refreshed, and the search buttons activated in the viewing window. Michael advanced a couple of frames manually, verifying that both the upper and lower images had the same timecode, with each frame separated by 250 picoseconds. Then he highlighted the main portion of the video, excluding the timecode, and clicked on the "auto-scan" button.

The timecodes became a blur as the video fast-forwarded and stopped at the first "difference" it encountered in the highlighted area.

"Okay, folks. My screen is shared, right?"

"I shared it with the bridge," Josh said. *"Everyone should be able to see it."*

There were a couple of affirmations from the others on the call, and Michael began.

"Then you can see it too," he said. "We have our beam." Michael smiled at the blue line that appeared on the left-hand side of both the top and bottom video streams.

Someone on the call asked, *"Why does the timecode say only forty-three nanoseconds have elapsed? Didn't Professor Salomon ask for a two-microsecond lead-in before the beam launched? There shouldn't be any changes until after that lead-in period is over: a full two* thousand *nanoseconds."*

The computer engineer responded, sounding a bit panicked. *"There must be a mistake. I programmed it in."*

Michael kept his voice steady. "Let's move on and see if we get a bounce."

He advanced the video stream by a frame, and the beam progressed slowly across the screen. "Everyone notice that the beam is only advancing about eight centimeters per captured frame. That's just a little bit above the speed of light. That verifies yet again that we're able to collect wild tachyons of various speeds, normalize their velocity, and shift them down to very close to their minimum speed."

As he advanced through another fourteen frames, the beam slowly progressed across the screen. The very last frame showed the beam reflecting back, but at a very slight angle.

"Interesting," Michael said. "First, we've just learned that we can in fact deflect a tachyonic stream with a mirror. That's a major new piece in the puzzle to understand these particles. But also, notice the angle of deflection. Unlike a normal particle that's affected by gravity and momentum, this stream… well, at first glance I'd say its angle is unaffected by our own movements. I refer of course to our high-speed movements through the universe: the Earth rotating, the solar system moving within the galaxy, the galaxy itself moving across the universe. We'll need to run the numbers, but this *could* be an indication that tachyons aren't affected by some of the common forces we'd expect them to be affected by."

"Professor?" someone said. *"Why is the top view off-center? I thought the CCDs were lined up along the path of the beam, but the top shows the beam near the edge of the screen."*

"It should be centered," Tony replied, sounding defensive. *"Maybe there a processing issue?"*

"I don't think so. We're taking whatever—"

"Guys," Michael interrupted. "Work out the kinks later. Let's keep our minds focused."

He continued to advance the frames until the screen turned black. Then he clicked yet again on the "auto-scan" button. The stream fast-forwarded through more of the images and then stopped at the next change it found.

The hairs on the back of Michael's neck stood on end.

"Wait a minute, what just happened?" someone asked. *"Are we replaying the video?"*

"No, the timecode says we're 2.046 microseconds in, unless... did the video get processed incorrectly?"

"Hold on," Tony said, his voice taking on a triumphant tone. *"Look at the top image: it has the beam dead-center. I told you, there must be a problem in the video stream stitching algorithm on the compute side—"*

"Guys, guys... this isn't a problem in stitching." Michael smiled as he gazed at the monitor. "Remember, the timecode is inseparably part of the visual frame capture. If it was an inadvertent duplication, the timecode would also be duplicated, and it's not." He started advancing through the images. "Look: the beam progresses and is reflected just like we saw in the earlier capture. It's exactly like the first beam we saw, with one major exception. Anyone else notice what that difference is?"

"The top view of the beam isn't off-center," someone said drily.

Michael suppressed a chuckle. "Well, that's definitely one thing. No, folks, the reason I asked for a two-microsecond lead-in video capture is because we wanted to be able to capture evidence of something happening that has up until now only been theorized.

"What does this world do as time elapses? I'll tell you: the world moves through space at roughly 368 kilometers per second. That means in two microseconds, we move roughly 73 centimeters. And just for a moment, imagine if we had taken the beam of tachyons that we released and sent it back in time two microseconds. The entire world, including this laboratory, would be offset by about 73 centimeters."

"Wait a second," said Josh. *"Are you saying the beam actually went* back in time*? And the movement of the Earth is why we're seeing the beam in a different location?"* Josh asked.

"I'm sure as we analyze the details of the footage, we'll learn more. But this wasn't an error in stitching. The timecodes incrementing throughout the stream is proof enough of that. And yes, it *is* my belief that these two streams of tachyons we captured on video are actually the same stream. If I'm correct, folks, we have just captured the first evidence of a stream of particles passing backward in time by almost exactly two microseconds."

There was the sound of a sharp intake of breath on the line, and someone began coughing.

"Of course," Michael said, suppressing his excitement, "this is not yet definitive. We've seen it once, and we'll need to reproduce this multiple times, with various parameter shifts, and so on. But I believe history will declare that this is a foundational moment in science. We have, for the first time, witnessed something controlled by man traveling to the past—and we have visual proof of it.

"This is as big a step as the first step Neil Armstrong took on the moon. Maybe even bigger."

CHAPTER SIX

Michael hit save on the report he was only about halfway through writing, leaned back in his chair, and looked up at the ceiling tiles in the lab. He didn't have to look at the clock to know it was way past the time he should have gone home.

The door buzzed and Josh walked in.

"Josh? What are you doing here so late?"

The grad student held up a three-ring binder. "I just got Jan's report from the power substation. The last one I need is yours. Dr. Sundenbach said he needs a full report by this Friday."

"The DARPA guy? Well, he's just going to have to wait until I'm done. I don't take orders from him, nor does he dictate my schedule. Anyway, it's only Wednesday." He looked up at Josh. "What did you think of what we saw today?"

Josh sat on a stool. "You mean the history-making moment

when you proved that something can go back in time? What did I think of *that*?" He gave the professor a lopsided grin.

"Well, I admit I may have gotten a bit grandiose in the moment. We didn't exactly *prove* anything yet. We don't call anything known unless we can reproduce it and study it further from all different angles. But yes, what are your thoughts?"

Josh's wide-eyed expression made him look much younger than he was. "Honestly, I'm wondering what in the world we can do next that will build on that? I mean, it's kind of hard to top. And I've been thinking of practical uses for this… you know, if we do prove it. What could we accomplish with this? I mean, without diving into science fantasy, though some might argue that what you did today was straight out of a science fiction novel."

Michael nodded. "That's always a good question: what next? But in this case, we've got a lengthy agenda already. As you know, there's a lot we still have to learn about these particles. We don't even know what they're made of yet. This is as new a field of research as there is.

"But I can tell, you're thinking of a slightly different question: what else can we make them *do*. One thing I'd like to tackle in the next year or so is to see if we can accumulate a large enough stream of tachyons to have an effect on baryonic sub-light-speed material like the stuff we're made of. Are these microscopic specks that just flit by and rarely ever interact with normal matter, like a neutrino, or can we actually get 'touched' by a tachyon? We've already proven they're charged, so perhaps the computer engineers could set up an unshielded wire in the path of a tachyon beam and see if we can have an effect on the data going through the wire."

Josh grinned. "That would be awesome. You could have live network traffic flooding through that wire, and if you have someone monitoring the data packets on one end of the cable and another capturing what comes across the other end, you could compare the two data sets and probably tell very easily if some zeroes had been flipped to ones or vice versa."

Michael nodded appreciatively. "That's not a bad idea. I might suggest we take an approach like that."

Josh's grin widened further. Michael could tell that the wheels in his head were turning at a rapid pace.

"I was curious about something else," Josh said. He motioned to the monitor, which still had the professor's report on the display. "I know you're writing up your report on particle velocity normalization. And, well..." Josh held an embarrassed expression. "I'm sure I'm just missing something basic, so don't yell at me for it. I totally get that when you add energy to a superluminal particle it slows down, and it speeds up when you bleed the energy away."

"I hear a *but* coming."

"Well, yes. I've seen how you're doing rather complicated flip-flops of electric fields to control the particles' speed, like what CERN does and most of the other accelerators, but I was wondering whether or not temperature, making things hotter or colder, could serve the same effect? Isn't that in essence adding or taking away energy?" He winced. "Even as I say it out loud, it sounds stupid to my ears, but I don't have any idea *why* it's stupid."

Michael shook his head. "It's not a stupid notion, but you have to realize that temperature is an indirect measure of average kinetic energy, and it is necessarily collisional. While non-Maxwellian, non-equilibrium kinetic energy distributions technically don't have a 'temperature' but, they kind of do, as long as the collisions among the particles aren't destructive.

"In the same way the temperature of the moderator reduces the eventual free speed of particles to a distribution that is in equilibrium with the moderator temperature, the opposite is also true: particles diffusing from cold to warm physical moderators increase in average speed. But the effect is diffusional, by definition it's random direction, and the collisions need to be dominated by lossless ones.

"I know it may sound like I'm speaking in cursive, so how about this: Temperature is like a demolition derby for microscopic particles. The colder things are, the slower the crashes; the warmer they are, the faster the crashes. But because it's a demolition derby, there isn't much in the way of organization. The directional velocities are going to be all over the map based on how these collisions occur. If a particle gets smashed by something heading in the opposite direction, that's going to slow it down, even though you're trying to speed things up. Or, to switch analogies, temperature is like herding cats; it's just not an effective way of dealing with individual particles. With the electric fields, we're taking a much more direct approach to organizing the particles and moving them along a path."

Michael smiled. "I know that was a long-winded explanation, and probably overly detailed, but to answer your question about whether temperature could be used to manipulate the energy associated with the tachyons, the answer is no, but also yes, but *probably* no for weird stuff like the tachyons we're dealing with."

Josh grinned. "I think I got that. The demolition derby example is a good analogy. Thanks… that helped." He glanced at the clock. "Yikes, it's almost ten."

Michael locked the computer screen and got up from his chair. "Yes. And I don't know about you, but I've got an early day tomorrow. Are you taking off?"

Josh shook his head. "Not yet. I still have to write my daily status report to Dr. Sundenbach."

"Don't stay too late, okay? I'll see you tomorrow."

The house was quiet as Michael walked up the stairs and entered the bedroom. The only light was coming from the night light, which cast the various hues of the rainbow as it slowly cycled through its visual recitation of ROY-G-BIV. Maria was asleep on his side of the bed, with his fidget spinner in her hand —the same toy she made fun of him for using whenever he was thinking about something, usually something about work.

Percy lay on his doggie bed, and though he didn't bother to open his eyes as Michael walked past, his tail twitched, a sleepy wag as greeting.

Michael of course went straight to Felicia. As he peered into the crib, he couldn't help but smile at the sleeping face of his little angel.

He quietly changed out of his work clothes and got into

bed. With a long day behind him, a wave of exhaustion washed over him as he felt himself meld into the mattress. But he felt like he'd barely closed his eyes when he heard Maria gasp.

"*Mija!*" Maria whispered as she scrambled out of bed, picked up the sleeping baby, and bounced around with Felicia's head against her shoulder.

"Maria? What's wrong?"

His wife's eyes were opened wide in the dimly lit room. She looked panicked. "I don't know. A dream… I think. Something scary."

Michael flipped the covers off of him and got up to help. "I can hold her. You get some sleep."

"*No.*" Maria said it abruptly, and suddenly she looked embarrassed. "Sorry, I'm just processing the nightmare. I didn't mean to bark at you."

Percy yawned, walked to the bedroom door, turned back to face them, and let out a soft yip.

Maria looked at Michael. "That's how you can help. You can take Percy to go potty. And since we're all awake now, maybe I'll make some coffee and a snack." She gave him a quick kiss on the lips and a smack on the rear.

Michael glanced at the clock on the nightstand. To his surprise, he'd gotten about an hour's worth of sleep before being awoken. But that was definitely not enough.

Percy yipped again, this time from down the hall.

"I'm coming, I'm coming…"

Michael waited in the darkness as Percy peed in his favorite spot: the trunk of an old magnolia tree. Given it was the middle of the fall, it was quite cool, but then again, Michael was rarely out and about at two a.m.

In the darkness on the far side of the yard, Percy let out a guttural growl and barked a warning.

"Percy!" Michael called out, snapping his fingers several times to get the dog's attention. The last thing he needed was the neighbors complaining about barking in the middle of the night. But the dog only growled even louder. Michael stomped his foot on the grass and gave a loud clap, and finally Percy ripped his attention from whatever had distracted him. He came loping back to Michael, his collar jangling.

As they went back into the house, the smell of freshly brewed coffee had already permeated the air. Maria was sitting at the table with two mugs, and Felicia rested on top of the table in her carrier. Michael couldn't believe how big she already was at just four months old. Various colorful objects hung above her from the carrier's handle, and she was preoccupied with batting at them. Maria said it was an exercise in hand-eye coordination, but Michael was just happy to see her having fun.

"What was Percy barking at?"

Michael sat down, sipped at his coffee, and shrugged. "I didn't see anything. His sniffer probably caught the scent of something new and interesting somewhere out there." He studied Maria's face; she still had that same haunted expression that she'd woken with. "Is the dream still bothering you?"

She shook her head. "I don't know… sort of. It's like when

you're searching for a word and you know you know the word, but can't remember it? It's sort of like that. Whatever it was that I dreamed, it just freaked me out, I guess." She sipped at her coffee. "Something really had your attention today for you to not even call to say you'd be late." She said it in a matter-of-fact way, but Michael knew she was angry, as she should be. He'd messed up. "I'm guessing it was that big experiment you were setting up? How'd it go?"

"I'm sorry I didn't call. I—"

She put a hand on his arm. "It's okay. But next time…"

"I promise." Michael smiled. "The experiment went exactly like I'd imagined it would, which is crazy, because I was imagining some really radical stuff. I still can hardly believe it actually happened."

Maria looked genuinely happy for him. "Tell me about it. Obviously not the science of it, but in general? Give me a taste of the 'radical' work my husband has done, so I can brag to all the bitches at the supermarket."

He laughed. "You know you can't talk about this with anyone but me. I explained to you what tachyons are, right?"

"Those things that go faster than light?"

"Right. Anyway, there's this thing called relativity, and without getting too detailed, science has known about how as you get closer to the speed of light, time slows down a bit. You're still moving forward in time, but as you approach the speed of light, time seems to slow and ultimately stops when you hit the speed of light. We've actually demonstrated this by experimentation. If you measure the time elapsed for someone on the ground and someone who goes on a very fast jet, when that jet comes back, the clock that went on the jet will be slightly behind the one that stood still.

"So, now imagine if you're *past* the speed of light. This is something that has never been experimented with, because we never had access to anything that went faster than light."

"Until you came along." Maria smiled.

"True. Anyway, the math says that if something can go faster than the speed of light, you'd be able to have something seemingly go backward in time."

Maria made a 'T' with her hands. "Time out. You're saying if a magical plane went faster than the speed of light, it could land before it took off?"

Michael shrugged. "It's a really good question. There's all sorts of paradoxes with traveling backwards in time. It's why many respected scientists truly thought it couldn't be done. It's the whole, what if I murder my own grandfather before my father was born, do I just go 'poof' or is that even possible? Unfortunately, we just don't know. We're trying to get at some of that with my work. And, well, the thing that was big yesterday was that… I'm pretty sure we witnessed something actually go back in time." He showed a sliver of space between his thumb and forefinger and said, "It went back in time just a tiny little bit."

Maria's eyebrows went up. "Wow."

"Yeah. That was my reaction too."

"So now you know it's possible. What's next?"

"My grad student, Josh, asked me the same thing. Sometimes with these deep physics theories, we never come around to how can we practically use it, or take advantage of it. It's always about the science, and too rarely do we get a chance to *do* something with it. And then Josh actually suggested an experiment that I'm seriously thinking I'll try. Have an unshielded wire carrying network traffic and see if we can affect any of that traffic with the tachyons. That's step one: can these tachyons reach out and touch things in our world? 'Our world' meaning the world of things *not* going faster than the speed of light."

Now Maria was definitely interested. Before she became a full-time mom, she'd gotten her degree in computer science and was very familiar with computer networking. "If you could affect the data flowing through the wire, what stops you from creating fake e-mails that literally came from the past?"

Michael started to answer. "I suppose you could—"

But Maria was on a roll. "Or if a virus snatched a password to someone's bank account, even if they changed the password, the virus could go back in time, *before* they changed it, and drain the account. That would be an entirely new class of viruses that would make quantum cryptography pointless." Maria's eyes widened, and she grasped Michael's hand. "*Mi amor*, this is a terrible thing. Do you have computer experts involved? How can software prevent an attack before it even knows it's being attacked?"

Percy whined under the table.

Michael felt a knot in his stomach. He had never intended to upset her. He tried to calm her fears.

"We aren't anywhere remotely close to that kind of thing yet. This is all theoretical for now. And yes, we've got comp-sci folks on the team, and eventually we'll want to experiment with things that are more practical, but I promise before we start applying any of this stuff, we'll put mitigations in place for these concerns you're talking about—and probably a lot more concerns that nobody has even thought of. Right now though, we're still very early. Just learning some fundamentals."

"But you said you are funded by the government. What if they want you to succeed so they can do things like this?" Her voice was filled with emotion. "They may already have plans for it. To use this thing you've discovered against an enemy we don't even know about."

"Maria, we're only talking about minuscule particles traveling across unfathomably small gaps in time. I doubt anyone can actually change the past."

"How can you *know* that?" Maria said, her tone challenging.

Michael really wished he hadn't gone down this rabbit hole with her. He had to admit, there could be scary implications to what he was working on, but he had faith in being able to ensure all these bad outcomes didn't happen.

"I suppose I don't *know* we can't change the past," he said. "But even if we could, it would be years, maybe decades, before we could even *begin* to think about such things."

"*Mi amor*." She squeezed his hand. "Are you sure this is the thing you should be doing? Why not just teach like you have been? Why take leave from the classes to do full-time research? Does this problem really need to be solved? I mean… you will laugh at me for saying this, but I'm serious: the scientist who built the Terminator was just trying to create a better CPU. It's the law of unintended consequences: you don't know what happens when you open Pandora's box. This could turn out very badly."

Felicia jolted awake in her carrier and began crying.

Michael pulled Maria's hand to his lips and kissed her knuckles. "Honey, it's late. Let's get back to bed. We can talk about this when we're not both so tired."

Maria stood, picked up the crying baby, made a silly face at her, and then cuddled her to her chest. "Just think about what I said. If it's money or something, we can make it work. I trust you, but I don't trust these people you're working with. They must have a good reason to be investing so much in your success. Just think about it, okay?"

Michael nodded. "I will."

And he meant it. What Maria had said—the last thing she'd said—had really struck home. The DC folks had been extraordinarily generous with their budget for this project. Even Herman had remarked on it. Would they do that if they didn't think there was an equally extraordinary payoff for them?

Questioning the funding was like looking a gift horse in the mouth. But Maria was right: the government never did anything without a purpose.

What was their purpose?

Maria smiled at her daughter as she kneaded some dough. "*Mija*, soon enough you'll be learning how to do this as well.

What do you think? You think your papa will like pizza for dinner?"

A spit bubble grew on Felicia's lips and popped suddenly, making the little girl's eyes grow wide with surprise.

"I agree. Your papa needs to eat more. He's getting too skinny for his own good."

The doorbell rang, and Percy began barking. He was the man of the house at the moment, and he took his job quite seriously. Maria grabbed a kitchen towel and wiped her hands as she called out, "Be right there!"

Growing up in Colombia with a father whose job it was to fight the drug cartels, she'd learned at an early age to never assume the best of people. That was a sure path to destruction. So she grabbed the sheathed filet knife she always had handy in the kitchen and tucked it into the back of her waistband before walking to the front door. Through the peephole she saw a man in a suit with a badge on his lapel.

Percy was still going crazy, so she led him into the guest room and closed the door. Of course he continued to bark anyway, but the sound was muffled. Anyone outside on his property was a threat as far as Percy was concerned, whether it was the newspaper boy or some official-looking man in a suit.

As Maria finally opened the front door, she saw two sedans in the driveway, both with heavily tinted windows. Two cars? For one visitor?

She faced the man, who stood two paces back from the door. He wore dark glasses and looked the part of a federal agent—or at least, that was how they looked on TV.

"Yes?" she said.

"Mrs. Salomon?" The man held up a billfold with official-looking credentials. "I'm Agent Conway with the Defense Intelligence Agency." He pulled out a sheaf of papers and handed them to her. "Ma'am, as that document will state, I'm here on official business. We've received credible threats against your husband regarding the research he's doing on behalf of our government."

"Threats?" Maria said as she skimmed the embossed paperwork. It had been signed by the director of some agency she didn't recognize. "What kind of threats?"

"I can't go into details, ma'am." Agent Conway motioned toward another man who had appeared next to one of the vehicles. "My partner and I are here to take you and your daughter into a safehouse while the proper authorities trace and eliminate the threat."

Maria took a step back into the house, feeling a bout of nausea. "What about my husband?"

"Officers are en route to his office as we speak. He's going to be collected as well. Your safety is our primary concern."

"I'm calling my husband." Maria pulled her phone out of her pocket and started to call Michael—but the phone flashed the words "*no signal*" at her. That was impossible. Her phone always had full signal strength at their house. Yet now she had zero bars.

She faced the agent and shook her head firmly. "I'm not going anywhere until I can reach my husband." She held up her phone. "Which means you'll have to wait, because I'm not getting any signal at the moment—"

Suddenly a strong arm grabbed her from behind and a cloth

was pressed down over her nose and mouth. She screamed and threw her head backward, but as she pulled in a breath, she was overcome by a sweet-smelling scent. Percy's barking faded into the sound of a mosquito buzzing, and she felt herself falling as the world turned black.

CHAPTER SEVEN

Michael held back a yawn as Josh handed him a thick report. It detailed the project's activities for the week, issues encountered, and capital requests. He was bleary-eyed from lack of sleep, but he forced himself to open the binder and flip through the pages. To his surprise, this week's report was marked with "TOP SECRET" classification markings on each and every page. He was quite used to seeing those by now, but this was the first time the entire report was so marked, including what he considered the "boring stuff."

He looked up at Josh. "Even time sheets are top secret now. The government is really getting buttoned up, aren't they?"

"Seriously. Did you notice the SAR markings everywhere?"

"Yeah, I see those too. And now, instead of SAR, they say SAR-PM. What's that? I know SAR is Special Access Required, but I've never seen the PM before."

"Actually it's kind of cool. PM means Project Morpheus. That's the codename the government has now assigned to our experiments. It's got a Mission Impossible feel to it, don't you think?"

Maria's warnings replayed in Michael's mind.

"The government may already have plans for what you're doing."

"It's the law of unintended consequences: you don't know what happens when you open Pandora's box. This could turn out really badly."

He wasn't nearly as enthused about the government's involvement as he was just a few weeks ago.

"Not only that," said Josh, "but they're converting us over to a secure network. As of next week, no e-mails or discussion about Morpheus happens on anything but the new accounts that are being set up for us on something called Jay Wicks."

"Jay Wicks?"

"It's an acronym. J-W-I-C-S. I actually don't even know what it stands for, but it's evidently what the intelligence community uses to communicate Top Secret content. There's going to be training and special access ports for using it. We'll be on an isolated private network."

Michael frowned. "I thought the dot-gov e-mails we were using were all we would need. This is getting to be a pain in the butt."

"Sorry. Don't shoot the messenger."

"No, I'm not blaming you."

"Good, because there's one more thing." Josh pointed at the document. "That copy of the report is registered specifically to you, meaning you're accountable for that particular copy. Officially, that copy can't leave this lab. Any movement of an official copy would require paperwork. Lots of paperwork, and maybe even a secure courier, but I don't yet know the details yet for transporting this stuff. Let's just assume you're supposed to file it in the security bin before leaving the lab."

Michael was about to balk, but instead he just sighed and said, "Fine." The truth was, he should have expected this earlier. He was probably lucky they hadn't locked things down a long time ago.

Before Josh could hit him with any more annoying news, Michael's phone buzzed, and he put it to his ear. "Hello?"

"Professor Salomon?"

"Yes, who is this?"

"Sir, it's the front desk at Jadwin Hall. We have an Officer Cross here. He says he needs to see you."

Michael wondered why security would want to see him. "Um, okay. I'll be right there." He hung up and turned back to Josh. "I have to go."

"But the report, it needs to be—"

Michael gave Josh a glare.

"I'll file it away for you, Professor."

Michael took the stairs two at a time to the main floor, all the while wondering what in the world the campus police could want with him. Did someone steal something from one of the labs? But as he entered the lobby, he realized this was no campus matter. The man at the front desk wasn't campus police but city police, complete with sidearm and the whole police officer regalia.

"Professor Salomon?" the officer said.

"Yes? Can I help you?"

"Sir, I'm Officer Cross with the city of Princeton police. I'm sorry for the inconvenience, but my sergeant sent me here to collect you. Evidently there's been some sort of incident at your place of residence, and you're needed there."

"At my home?" Michael's heart started to race. "Did something happen to my wife? My baby?"

"I'm told that your wife and child aren't at the residence. The sergeant merely asked that you be brought in to help sort some things out. I'm sorry, but I don't have any other information than that."

"I need to call my wife," Michael said, pulling out his phone.

"Of course. But can you do it as we go? I was asked to get you there as soon as possible. My squad car is just outside."

Michael was barely listening. "Sure, sure." He followed the officer as he called Maria. The line rang and rang, and voice mail eventually answered.

He felt nauseated. The only time Maria didn't answer her phone was when she was asleep. He tried again, and again got voice mail.

As he climbed into the front seat of what smelled like a relatively new police car, he dialed for a third time, and cursed himself for never having gotten the phone number of any neighbors. What on earth could be going on? Where was Maria?

The officer put the car into gear and weaved his way out of the school campus.

"Do you need the address?" Michael asked.

The officer tapped on a computer screen that was angled in his direction. "I have it all right here. Just relax. I'm sure the sergeant will be able to answer your questions when we get there."

Michael leaned his head back in the seat and tried to control his breathing. There was only one question he needed an answer to right now.

Is my family okay?

Alicia sat in her usual seat in the lecture hall, farthest back on the far left. The class was Neuro 516, a graduate-level neuroscience course; its full title was "The Neural Basis of Goal-Directed Behavior." That should have made it one of her favorite classes, but it was all so damned remedial. For three weeks now she'd been listening to the professor drone on, and she wasn't learning a damn thing.

"The brain doesn't store a lot of glucose, which is its primary source of energy. The means by which neurons become active requires pumping ions across a neuronal cell membrane in both directions. The energy needed for those pumps to work comes from glucose, and as it's depleted from the blood, more blood has to come in and thus transport additional glucose. All of this blood flow is localized to within three millimeters of the neural activity. The burning of glucose and use of oxygen changes properties of the blood, and helps us identify regions of activity through the use of a functional MRI."

The man spoke without slowing his stride. *"If I told you, then the bad guys would learn how to avoid the long arm of the law. My branch of government has been commissioned to eliminate crime as we know it, and working with the finest minds in our country, we are well on our way. Now if you'll excuse me..."*

The man climbed into the back seat of a sedan, and the car pulled away from the scene.

Alicia gazed up at the monitor with the rest of the people in the library, confused. An older woman standing next to her whispered to nobody in particular, "My nephew got put in jail for something he'd only been *thinking* about doing. He hadn't even done anything yet."

A few others nodded, as if they'd heard similar stories.

"It's unnatural," someone said.

The reporter was now facing the camera. *"That was the elusive Dr. Sundenbach with the Defense Intelligence Agency. The man in charge of what's become known as Project Morpheus. There's been a lot of debate about the methods being employed, but the results speak for themselves. We'd like to hear your thoughts—"*

Alicia gasped as she startled awake. Students had already begun to walk out of the lecture hall; class was over. She scrambled to shove her stuff into her backpack. But as she stood, she was struck by a sudden bout of vertigo. She had to grab on to her seat, worrying she was about to pass out or throw up.

What had just happened?

She had memories of things that...

Her heart raced as she looked around. She was in school. How was that possible? She'd graduated fourteen years ago…

She dug into her backpack, pulled out her makeup kit, and looked in the mirror.

At the sight of the face staring back at her, she was *definitely* worried she would pass out. The world was spinning. She pulled in a deep breath and let it out slowly.

The girl in the reflection was her younger self. When she was a college student.

What was real? What wasn't real?

Was she the college student working toward her PhD, or was she the post-doc researcher who'd been involved in what might have been the worst mistake in human history?

Either way… she needed to go talk to Michael.

He wouldn't have moved to DC yet. He was probably still a professor at the school.

She closed her eyes, and the world stopped tilting for a moment. She recalled the layout of the campus. She was only a ten-minute walk from Jadwin Hall.

But how could she approach him without him thinking she was insane?

"Hi, Professor Salomon. You don't know me right now, but in about ten years, you and I hook up, join forces, and ruin the world. We need to talk."

Yeah. That probably wouldn't go over well.

"Are you okay?"

Alicia looked up as a male student crouched by her side with a worried expression. "I'm just fine. Just peachy keen. You can leave now."

The student frowned and walked away.

She took another deep breath and slowly straightened up. "This is going to be an interesting conversation," she muttered to herself as she walked out of the lecture hall.

Michael stared wide-eyed as the police car he was in was waved through a barrier blocking off the street to his home. He saw the flashing lights of a fire engine and two more police vehicles, plus one sedan parked alongside his house that he didn't recognize.

The moment the officer stopped the car, Michael hopped out. There was shattered glass everywhere.

A man wearing a suit and an official-looking shield on his waistband walked over to him. "Are you Michael Salomon?"

"Yes."

"I'm Detective Connor from the Princeton Police Department. As you can see, we've had a bit of an incident here."

The garage door was up, revealing that his wife's car was still in the garage, but all the boxes and papers that had been neatly set on shelves were now strewn across the garage floor. A fireman was walking through the chaotic interior, examining the area where the furnace and water heater were located. It looked like something had exploded.

"Where's my wife?" Michael started heading for the front door.

"Sir." The officer grabbed his arm and held him back. "The area hasn't been cleared yet. The fire department is currently evaluating the situation. But we know there's nobody in the house, and the dog is in the back yard."

Michael realized he could hear Percy's yips over the noise of the fire engine's motor running.

"What happened?"

"We'll get the official read from the fire department, but it looks to me like some kind of gas leak."

Michael sniffed the air. Other than the diesel fumes coming from the idling fire engine, he couldn't detect anything. "It doesn't look like there was any fire—was there? I should check with the neighbors. Maybe Maria was visiting—"

"We've already checked, and we've evacuated the entire block. Your wife and child weren't within the evacuation radius. You were expecting your wife and child to be at home, is that right?"

"Yes!" Michael's heart raced. Where could she have gone without the car? "Is the stroller in the living room? Maybe she went on a walk with the baby."

One of the firemen exited the house and headed their way. The detective introduced them. "Harry, this is Mr. Salomon, the owner of the house. Mr. Salomon, this is Lieutenant Kinzinger with the Princeton Fire Department."

Kinzinger removed his helmet and wiped his sweat-streaked face. He nodded to Michael, then turned to the detective. "There's no doubt about it. This was no accident."

"What?" Michael blurted out. Despite the heat and humidity, he felt a chill run through him. "Someone did this on purpose?"

"I'm afraid so, sir. And they weren't even trying to hide the fact. There was a propane tank in the middle of your kitchen, and someone had lit a few candles in another room. But you're lucky—other than blowing out nearly every window, and of course making a mess of the inside of the house, there were no lasting fires inside the home. There's damage, but the home should be recoverable."

As they spoke, an unmarked sedan parked about twenty feet away, a blue light flashing on its dashboard.

"Is it safe for Mr. Salomon to go inside?" the detective asked. "The whereabouts of his wife and child are unclear, and he wanted to look for a stroller."

"Sure." The fireman motioned for Michael to follow. "Just don't touch anything. We've cleared the home from a safety perspective, but there's a forensics team coming to see what kind of prints and other evidence they can find."

Michael buried his hands in his pockets as he entered the house. The place was a disaster, with singe marks everywhere, as if a fireball had raced through the house—which perhaps it had. It really was a miracle the place hadn't burnt to the ground.

He walked past the foyer and looked into the living room. The stroller wasn't there, which gave Michael a surge of hope. Maybe Maria was simply on a long walk. And as he went through the rest of the house, he didn't see the stroller there either.

The upstairs was in better shape. Things had been knocked off shelves, and the flatscreen TV that had been mounted to the wall was now lying face-down on the floor, and of course the windows were blown out, but there was no actual damage to the structure. Still, every room reeked of smoke, and it would take a lot to get this place back to a livable condition.

"Why would someone do this to us?" he asked as he walked back down the stairs with the fireman. His mind suddenly drifted to the possibility that the people who killed Maria's family might have done this.

"That's a good question, Mr. Salomon. The city's forensics team is the best in the business; hopefully they'll find something."

Percy's barking traveled in through the shattered windows in back, and Michael asked, "Is Percy okay? The dog, I mean."

"He's fine. It looks like he was out back when it happened. But he's not letting any of my men near him. I can't blame him for being spooked." They had reached the kitchen, and the fireman pointed to a barrier that had been set up just outside the shattered sliding glass door to the yard. "We put that up to keep the dog from coming in. But you can just push it aside."

Michael moved the barrier enough to get out, then called to Percy. The dog let out a crying bark as he came around the corner, kicking up clods of grass and dirt. The overgrown puppy threw himself on Michael with all of his seventy-pound bulk, frantically licking and nuzzling while crying and yipping as if trying to tell him the story of what had happened.

"I know, big boy. We have to find your mom and sister."

Michael pointed at Percy's leash, still hanging on the wall. "Is it okay if I grab that leash and take him out of here?"

The lieutenant grabbed the leash and handed it over. "Let's walk him around the back. I don't want him getting hurt."

Michael clipped the leash to Percy's collar, and they exited through the back yard gate and around to the front, where a van had just arrived. Percy wagged his tail uncertainly at all the unusual activity.

The detective—Michael had already forgotten his name—was talking with a newcomer in a suit and dark glasses, but he turned when he saw Michael approaching.

"Did you find the stroller?"

Michael shook his head. "No, so maybe they're out for a walk. But she's not answering her phone, which is *very* unlike her."

The man in the dark glasses spoke up. "What about family? Could they have come by and picked her up?"

"Her family was killed years ago, back in Colombia."

The detective motioned to the man in the suit. "This is Agent Glen Bernstein with the—well, I suppose you should introduce yourself."

Bernstein handed Michael a business card and flashed a government badge. "Professor Salomon, I'm a member of the FBI, dispatched from our field office in Newark. Let's take a little walk, if you don't mind. There's a few things I need to make you aware of."

Percy let out a low growl as he looked up at the man.

"Percy, chill," Michael said as they started walking away from the house.

The dog reluctantly settled down.

"Professor Salomon—"

"Call me Michael. The professor thing is mostly for the students."

"Yes, sir. Michael. You may not be aware of this, but as

part of your security clearance process, various parts of our government were involved in clearing you. As a result, there's an existing FBI case file on you and every member of the team you're working with."

Michael hadn't known that, and would have objected if he *had* known. But at this moment, maybe it didn't seem like such a bad thing. Anything that would help find his wife and daughter.

The agent continued. "A little over an hour ago, I was read in on your team and the security concerns associated with each of its members, including yourself."

"Security concerns?"

"Yes, sir. I can't get into the specifics, but you, along with a handful of others on the team, are being assigned a security detail. I have an agent incoming who will shadow you going forward, just to make sure there aren't any more issues like what happened today."

Michael froze mid-step. Goose bumps rose on his skin and he felt like he was going to throw up. "Are you saying…"

"Professor… I'm saying we believe your wife has been kidnapped."

Michael's chest tightened. He felt like he couldn't breathe. "What makes you think this?"

The agent pointed up at the streetlight. "Do you see that gray tube up there? It's a camera. Strictly as a security measure, we've had your home monitored for some time now. And this camera recorded an incident this morning, a few hours after you left. I'll show you."

The man pulled out his phone, tapped on something, then

turned the screen toward Michael. He'd brought up camera footage of his house, before it had all the windows blown out. Two cars pulled into the driveway. Several well-dressed men piled out of them, and a few disappeared into his back yard, while one approached the front door.

His wife answered the door, and a conversation ensued. And then Michael watched as his wife was carried, seemingly unconscious, from the house and into one of the cars. Another man exited the house with Felicia in her baby carrier. In what seemed like no time at all, his family was gone.

Percy barked and his fur stood on end. The dog was sensing Michael's state of alarm. Fear was probably coming off of him in waves.

He looked frantically at the agent. "Is someone tracking down the vehicles? The license plates were clear on the video."

The agent nodded. "Trust me, we're doing everything we can to find your family." He put the phone back in his pocket. "Has anyone reached out to you about the project you're involved in? Asked any questions that seemed suspicious to you?"

Michael felt the world tilt, and fearing he might fall, he crouched down to sit on his heels. His stomach clenched, and he threw up on the sidewalk.

Percy whined and shoved his face into Michael's side.

Moments later he heard footsteps, and he was offered a plastic bottle of water. "Drink that, sir." The agent was crouched beside him.

Michael struggled to breathe. The world was swaying. His

throat was burning. He took a swig from the bottle, swished the water around in his mouth, and spit it out.

"Professor, I understand how upsetting this must be. Believe me when I say we have a lot of people working to find out who did this. But we're going to need your help. Has anyone tried to talk to you about the work you're doing?"

Michael shook his head. "No. No one." He looked at the agent with a panicked expression. "My wife's father was a police officer tasked with running down elements of a drug cartel in Colombia. The cartel ended up killing all of my wife's family. Do you think it might have been them?"

The agent frowned for a moment and it was obvious that the information Michael had just shared had been something the man wasn't aware of. "I'll make sure our people are apprised of that background data and follow up on it. However, pertaining to your work: if anyone contacts you with any kind of information, or asks questions that seem out of place, you need to let us know immediately. That might be the clue that helps us track down your wife and child."

Michael looked over at the agent. "You think someone will reach out?"

The man nodded. "We believe so."

Another unmarked sedan parked twenty feet away, and the driver got out and walked over. Agent Bernstein helped Michael to his feet, then introduced the new arrival.

"Professor Salomon, this is Agent Nick Cole. He'll take you back to your lab while I make arrangements for your temporary housing. Is there anything you need from me before you go back? Any questions?"

"Anything I need?" Michael wiped tears from his eyes and laughed bitterly. "I need to kill whoever did this to my family. That's what I need."

Bernstein patted Michael on the shoulder, then turned to Agent Cole. "He's all yours, Nick."

Michael wiped his face and collected Percy's leash, then followed Agent Cole to his car. Cole looked sympathetic as he opened both the front door for Michael and the back door for Percy. Michael focused on his breathing as he got in.

Turning back to look at the house, Michael couldn't get the image of his wife being dragged out of there from his mind.

Michael felt a red-hot rage building up within him and he took a deep breath and slowly let it out.

There was nothing he could do at the moment.

He needed to focus…

It had only been a couple hours.

The FBI was on the case.

Agent Cole piled into the driver's side of the car, put it into gear and slowly turned the car back toward the way he came.

Back to the lab…

Back to Project Morpheus.

CHAPTER EIGHT

A cool fall breeze blew across the campus. Michael and a handful of other scientists from the project were gathered at the hall's entrance, looking out at the eight police cars with flashing lights now parked in front of Jadwin Hall.

"I don't understand," Michael said to the FBI agents who had been waiting at the door when they came out. "Are we not even allowed to drive?"

Percy's ears swiveled as he looked around at all the different faces, his nose in the air catching all the new scents. The dog had been surprisingly good at the lab, especially considering the traumatic experience he'd just been through.

The agent in charge shook his head. "Sir, we're only following protocols. As part of your security detail—and this is for your own safety—you and your key scientists are all being escorted to a hotel that has been cleared for your stay. You all have rooms on the same hall, and agents will be stationed there around the clock."

"But what about our cars?" one of the scientists said. "Are we just supposed to leave them here?"

"You will move your cars to the hotel. Today only, you will drive them under police escort. It's a little over a mile away from this campus. But after that, you will be shuttled back and forth between the hotel and the lab."

"How long is this going to be for?" another scientist asked. "I've got a wife and kids. I'm all for security, given what happened to Professor Salomon's family, but this isn't tenable long-term, guys."

"We understand your concern. Your families all have uniformed officers watching over your homes, and we're doing everything we can to minimize interference with your lives. I assure you this is *all* temporary. As soon as the threat is identified and taken care of, things will go back to normal."

"But what about—"

"Enough," the agent said, raising an open palm. "This isn't a referendum on whether or not we're doing this. You are all under threat, and this is for your safety as well as the safety of your families. We'll make it as comfortable for you as we can, but this is the way it is." He motioned to the parking lot. "Now let's get you all situated. Hopefully this will be over before you know it."

Michael took it upon himself to lead by example. He turned to the others. "Well, I'll see you guys at the hotel. We can take out our frustrations on the dinner menu tonight. The dinner tab is on the FBI."

He walked to his car and situated Percy in the back, but by the time he'd gotten into the driver's seat, Percy had already hopped into the front. The dog was busy sniffing everything.

"New smells, eh, Percy? I guess you always take Mom's car."

The puppy whined and scratched at the glove compartment.

"Stop that. This car is still relatively new. I'd appreciate you not clawing it up more than necessary."

Percy lowered his ears, sniffed again at the dash, and again scratched at the glove compartment.

"Percy, there's nothing in there." Michael leaned over and opened the glove compartment. All it contained was the manuals to the car and the registration. "See?"

The puppy pawed at the contents, spilling it to the floor of the passenger's seat.

"Percy, geez. Get in the back, okay? You're making a mess." He grabbed up the manuals and papers and shoved them back into the glove compartment. As he did so, he spotted a business card.

Suddenly he was struck by an overwhelming sense of déjà vu. A memory that was powerfully etched in his mind. A memory of today. Except…

He could practically taste the smell of the neighbor's freshly cut grass as he stepped out of the house in the morning.

He could feel Maria's warm embrace as she kissed him on the front doorstep, the baby in one arm and Percy at her feet.

He felt all over again the overwhelming fear and then grief as he learned that his family had been kidnapped.

And now, at the end of the day—at the end of that *first* day—he saw the business card.

The business card that had changed everything.

As he saw himself retrieving the plain white card, he re-experienced the horror of seeing a fingernail taped to the back of it.

Maria's decorated fingernail.

There was no doubt about it being hers. He couldn't count how many times he'd seen her carefully place the three tiny rhinestones into the hardening gel of her manicure. Each represented a different member of her family that had been killed back in Colombia.

Scribbled on the card was a warning.

Trust them. For the sake of those you love.

Michael felt a surge of despair as he saw himself walking in an unfamiliar park, the Washington Monument visible in the distance. Someone in the crowd bumped into him and dropped another business card.

He picked it up.

On it were two fingernails. Maria's… and a smaller one. Very small. It had to be Felicia's.

They await the completion of your work.

More memories flooded his senses. Memories of things that had never happened, and yet they were so vivid, so detailed, he was certain he had lived them all.

Then, suddenly, it was over. He was back in his car, staring at a business card on the floor of his car.

He fully expected it to be the same card he'd seen in his "memory." But this one was different. The card he'd just seen, with the fingernail on the back, had been plain, unmarked. This one had a pyramid-shaped logo on it, with an eye at the center. It reminded him of the pyramid he'd seen before on the back of the one-dollar bill.

He remembered hearing it was called the Eye of Providence.

With a trembling hand, he reached down to grab the card. Taking a deep breath, and fearing the worst, he turned it over.

Taped to the other side was a lock of dark hair.

He put it to his nose. He clearly picked up the scent of Maria's lavender shampoo.

Beneath the lock of hair were four words:

You can't trust them.

They were in Maria's handwriting.

At that moment someone knocked on Michael's driver's-side window, startling him so badly that he dropped the card. An agent stood outside, and Michael rolled down the window.

"Professor? We're waiting on you."

"Oh, right. Sorry, I got distracted."

Michael rolled up the window, backed out of the parking space, and joined a line of cars on the way to their supposed safe house.

You can't trust them.

He could hear Maria saying those words aloud.

What did this mean?

Had Maria put that message in his car before she was kidnapped?

How? And if so, why the lock of hair?

Somehow, the lock of her hair was much less ominous than what he'd found taped to the card in the memory. Vision. Whatever it was.

As he turned right on Washington Road with half of the police escort trailing behind him, he tightened his grip on the steering wheel. It didn't make sense that Maria would have put that note in his car. She didn't know in advance she would be kidnapped. So who then? The kidnappers?

But why?

"Percy, what does it all mean?"

The puppy tilted his head, looking confused.

"Yeah, I don't know either. I feel like I'm being told something important… but I don't understand what it is I'm supposed to do with the information."

As he drove, Michael reached down between his legs and retrieved the business card. He sniffed Maria's hair once again, and detected no hint of smoke. For a moment he'd thought maybe someone had collected hair from her brush at the house after the explosion. But no smell of smoke ruled out that possibility.

He again imagined Maria writing on the back of the business card and taping a lock of her hair to it. It didn't make sense, but nothing else did either. Was she trying to warn him? And yet she knew that others might find the warning?

And what was the significance of the pyramid-shaped logo?

He had so many questions, and no answers. His wife and daughter needed him, and he was failing them miserably.

Alicia stood behind a group of trees just outside the Frick Chemistry building, watching as a convoy of cars with a police escort left campus. She used her phone to zoom in on the car at the back of the convoy. The quality of the image wasn't exactly stellar, but she recognized Michael's profile, and she felt a sudden pang of heartache.

This was all so strange. To all the world, she looked like a twenty-two-year-old grad student with all of her life ahead of her, but she felt so much older. She'd seen the future, and she knew that despite all the rules, she had allowed—would allow?—herself to fall in love with an older man. A senior member of a project she'd gotten involved in when her research team merged with his.

Michael had always feared what might be done with their research. She had been the fool who never saw it coming.

He was right. The government betrayed them all.

And now, this former version of herself along with his younger version, was tasked with undoing what had been done.

Yet there were huge gaps in her memory; not everything had transferred. She recalled that in the future, they'd be able to send someone's memories across time and space… but she couldn't remember how, or even what the mechanism was.

And as she watched Michael's car disappear, she realized just how much trouble she was in. How much trouble everyone was in. It wouldn't happen for another decade still, but it would happen. *Had* happened. She might not remember all the details of her research, but she did remember the basics of what had happened to her.

First came the government betrayal.

Then spent time in solitary confinement.

And then an escape. And with help, Alicia had constructed a plan to undo what she'd done.

What she and Michael had done.

But Michael… he had no idea about any of this. At least not yet.

Alicia gritted her teeth in frustration. It wasn't just that there were things she couldn't remember; it was worse than that, because she was aware that the gaps were there. It was like knowing you knew the alphabet, but not being able to recite it. Like the memories were there, but the pathways to those memories hadn't been formed yet. They hadn't transferred with the rest.

But Michael… she remembered him. Vividly. And that was

painful as well. They were supposed to have gotten married, but something happened.

Something…

She felt like she was losing her mind.

She needed to see him. Soon.

Percy pulled on his leash as Michael walked him. The campus presented a whole new host of smells to enjoy, and the dog was having a great time.

Michael was not. This was day four since his house had blown up, and the FBI had learned nothing. Not a word about Maria and Felicia. Nothing.

Making the experience somehow even worse was the somber shadow that was with him at all times. It wasn't always the same guy, but there was a member of the security detail with him twenty-four seven. The others on his team were even more annoyed, especially those with families. They were understandably outraged to be separated from spouses and children with no definitive end in sight. Truth was, this probably wouldn't last much longer before there was some sort of revolt.

Michael suddenly turned on the agent who was following behind him. "Is it normal for you to take this long to track someone down? You have video of these people, license plates. It's been four days."

The agent looked apologetic, even though it wasn't his fault. "I'm sure the SAC will contact you as soon as he learns something."

"Sack?"

"S-A-C, special agent in charge. Agent Bernstein. Do you want me to call in and see if there's anything new?"

"Yes. Please do that." Michael knew it was pointless, but he was losing his patience. His wife was out there somewhere, going through who knew what kind of hell.

"I understand how difficult this is for you, Professor. Everyone's doing what they can."

Which apparently isn't much, Michael thought.

A squirrel raced past, and Percy barked and pulled at his leash. Michael held him back. "Come on, Percy. Sir Chomps-a-Nut doesn't want to play with you right now."

He'd been given the option of leaving Percy at the hotel, but he figured that having the dog with him gave him an excuse to wander about outside a bit. He needed that time to clear his head, to give him some space to think. He still had the agent with him, but he knew they wouldn't intrude. They never said a word unless spoken to.

As they walked from Frick Chemistry Lab back toward Jadwin Hall, Michael thought for the umpteenth time about the card he'd found in his glove compartment. The lock of hair was definitely Maria's, but he still had no idea what the point of the message was. It wasn't even a *new* message. It was the same warning Maria had already voiced to him.

He hadn't told the FBI about it. He wasn't sure why. Something, some instinct, told him this was something he needed to keep to himself. The FBI had leads already, leads they needed to follow before he distracted them with something else.

He hoped he hadn't made the wrong call.

As they reached Jadwin Hall, Josh had just stepped outside. He spotted them and gave Percy a warm greeting. "Hey, Percy! How's the big puppy doing?"

Michael chuckled as he realized he was less popular than his dog.

"How's everything coming, Josh?"

Josh looked nervously around to make sure no one was nearby. Then he whispered, "Maybe in a few more hours we'll have enough tachyons for the beam you asked for. Do you want to take a final look at the setup?"

Michael nodded. "Let's do that."

Michael peered through the window of the vacuum chamber. A naked copper wire was stretched across the interior, and coming into the chamber through one wall was the shielded part of a standard ethernet network cable.

Josh pointed at the rack of computers it was connected to. "That's a 100G twinaxial cable with live traffic going back and forth. We have a transmitter on one end and a Wireshark trace on the other."

"Is the signal coherent as it stands right now? I'm worried about having such a large amount of unshielded wire in that chamber. Have we verified that the packet traces show no hiccups from the transmission to receive side?"

"The signal looks perfectly clean. We're in good shape. We're just waiting to collect the rest of the tachyons, and then I think we can run it."

"You said a few more hours?"

Josh checked a monitor. "Actually, maybe only another hour or two."

"Then that gives Percy enough time to finish his walk. There's a squirrel out there he wants to get to know."

At the word "walk," the dog barked, and several of the engineers in the lab looked up. It was weird having a dog in the lab, but everyone loved Percy.

Michael looked for the agent that had come in with him. Normally they sat at the entrance to the lab, but he wasn't there. Not that Michael was complaining. For once he was able to leave the building without an escort—other than Percy, anyway.

As they left Jadwin hall and walked across the grassy field, Percy's tail wagged aggressively.

"I agree, Percy. Just you and me is best."

Even as he said it, Michael felt a pang of guilt. These FBI agents were just trying to keep him from being kidnapped too. But in the back of his mind, he wondered if he *wanted* to be kidnapped. Because that meant he'd see Maria and Felicia again.

Maybe that was just wishful thinking.

No, it was *certainly* wishful thinking.

"Professor Salomon?"

He turned to see a student jogging toward him. She was petite, Asian, maybe a senior or a young-looking grad student.

"Yes?" he said.

She stopped in front of him and just stared, as if suddenly at a loss for words.

Percy was pulling on the leash, so Michael followed and waved the girl along. “If you want to talk, we’ve got to go where the German shepherd says.”

“Is that Percy?” the girl asked, sounding amazed.

“Yes. How do you know his name?”

The girl hesitated. “I guess I must have heard it somewhere.”

There was something very odd about this girl. And though it wasn’t surprising for an unfamiliar student to know who he was, how did she know his dog’s name, too?

Michael paused and turned to face the girl. “I’m sorry, miss. Is there something I can help you with?”

The girl’s eyes suddenly shimmered with unshed tears, and her face turned red.

“Miss, are you okay?”

“Michael, I’m—”

“Professor Salomon, thank you.”

“Of course. Sorry, it’s just, I know you’re just not going to believe me. This is totally nuts.”

Sunlight reflected off the girl’s gold necklace, drawing Michael’s attention. Attached to the necklace was a pendant—featuring a pyramid containing an unblinking eye.

The Eye of Providence. The same symbol that was on the business card.

“Mich—Professor,” the girl began again. “I’m here to warn you about Project Morpheus. It needs to stop. Or we’ll both end up ruining this world.”

The professor took two steps back.

How could she have even *heard* of Project Morpheus?

A wave of suspicion washed over him. "Who told you to talk to me?"

She stepped closer, tears streaming down her face. "My name is Alicia Yoder. You're not going to believe me, but ten years from now, you and I will work together on Project Morpheus. I'm responsible for the memory externalization process, and you're the one with the ability to send things across time and space. Together we ruin this world. Which is why I'm here. We have to stop this before it goes any further."

"Memory externalization?"

"We can't do it yet, but I figured out a way. Or I will." Alicia wiped her face. "You're looking at me like I'm crazy, and you have every reason to think that, but I swear I'm not. Even now I'm doing experiments with focused ultrasound over in the Neuroscience Institute. I'm taking genetically identical mice, training one to go through a maze, and then working on methods to transfer that training into the untrained one. And I've succeeded. The second mouse goes through the maze just as well as its twin, even though it's never even been in that maze before. And this is just the beginning. Ultimately I'll be able to take memories and turn them into transmissible datagrams."

Michael's eyes widened. "If you can take a memory and turn it into data..."

Alicia's tears flowed again. "You'll be able to take those memories and send them back in time."

Michael felt his mouth hanging open, and he quickly shut it. What was it the girl had just said?

"Ten years from now, you and I work together on Project Morpheus."

If what she said was true, then a future version of herself had somehow sent a warning… back in time.

He remembered the strange, lucid vision he'd had just before Felicia was born. A memory of himself looking down at Felicia's tombstone. A memory of a life without Maria. A life lived alone.

Feeling lightheaded, he crouched down and draped his arm over Percy, who was whining with concern.

Had he sent himself a warning about the baby's imminent death? Was that possible?

"Michael, someone's coming."

He looked up and saw an agent jogging their way.

Alicia held out her phone. "Quick, take a picture of my contact info and call me. We need to talk."

He fumbled with his phone and took a picture of her phone number, and Alicia walked away just before the agent arrived —not looking particularly pleased.

Before the man could say a word, Michael asked innocently, "Did you happen to bring any poop bags?"

The agent looked down at the fresh present Percy had just made. He shook his head.

"Well, then I'll just have to pick this up later, if it's still here." He started back toward Jadwin Hall. "I've got an experiment to oversee."

He moved confidently, not wanting the agent to think something was amiss and start asking questions. But suddenly he was filled with anxiety. There was a lot at stake with this experiment. If it showed promise, there'd be another day, week, month, or even year of research. If it didn't, that might be the beginning of the end of the project.

But that wasn't why Michael was anxious.

He wasn't afraid of the experiment failing.

He was worried about what would happen if the experiment was a success.

CHAPTER NINE

Alicia startled awake to the sound of someone stepping on the sand she'd sprinkled just outside the door to her dorm room—a trick her father had taught her years ago. It was three a.m., well past the time people normally walked the halls of the Whitman dorms. The room was pitch black, thanks to the construction paper she'd plastered over the window. She reached over to her nightstand and grabbed the flashlight her father had gifted her ahead of her freshman year.

Her father was an agent for some part of the government he refused to name, and he had instilled a cautious paranoia in her. She's always thought it was ridiculous, or at least pointless, but now, with the knowledge of what would happen to the world years from now, she had changed her mind.

She heard another grinding step—and then nothing. Someone was standing just outside Alicia's dorm room, and her senses screamed that there was something not right about it.

With a practiced shift of her finger, Alicia placed it over the flashlight's biometric reader and swung her legs out of bed. She detected the scent of metal heating as the bezel of the flashlight grew warmer without giving off any light. As she walked closer to the door with bare feet, she heard the slightest rustling of someone on the other side of the door.

She'd played this scenario through in her head ever since she'd first been given this flashlight as a means of defense against assailants. For it was a working flashlight, but it was also a hidden weapon. Purposefully hidden, because it would be illegal for her to carry such a thing in New Jersey, and it certainly wasn't allowed on campus.

She stepped back and to the side of the door, waiting, listening… and wondering if her senses were playing tricks on her.

Suddenly the lock clicked, the door swung open, and two shadowy figures rushed in.

Alicia struck from behind.

The first intruder received a flashlight smash to the back of the head, with a loud crack and sizzle. As he crumpled to the floor, his partner spun to face her, and she launched a side kick at his chest. The man grunted as he received the full impact, which sent him two steps back, but he grinned as he aimed some kind of spray can at her.

A cloud of mist erupted from the can. Alicia ducked below it, trying to sweep the man's legs out from under him. But he was prepared, so she lunged upward with the flashlight, its front end now searing hot, and connected with the man's chin.

To her shock, the metal penetrated the skin under her assailant's jaw and speared straight into his head. The air was filled with a sickening scent of burnt skin and something sweet.

Alicia staggered backward, dropping the flashlight. For a moment she lost track of time, and then she realized she was lying flat on the floor. She scrambled backward until she hit the far side of her dorm room.

Her stomach churned. She must have breathed in some of whatever it was that he'd sprayed.

She could see the dark outlines of the two men splayed across her tiny dorm room. They weren't moving. The second one was definitely dead; the first one, however, was probably only knocked out.

Though she felt disoriented and nauseated, she moved to her bed, grabbed her cell phone, and made a call she'd never imagined making.

It rang twice before she heard the familiar male voice on the other end. *"Yes?"*

"Dad, I need you. Something *really* bad happened."

"Where are you?"

"I'm in my dorm room. Two men broke in and attacked me. One had some kind of spray that I think was supposed to knock me out."

"Where are they now?"

"They're still here. I killed one of them. The other I at least knocked out, but I don't know how long it's been. I might have passed out for a while from whatever it was he sprayed at me. I'm scared, Dad."

"Alicia, listen very carefully to what I'm about to say. Get out of that room quietly. Don't run, just walk calmly out of the dorm and stay out of sight. I'm not in the States right now, but I'm heading back. I'm going to put you on hold, make some calls, and get back to you. Stay on the line, but get out now."

Alicia quickly got dressed and then fast-walked out of her dorm room, down the stairs at the end of the hallway, and exited the building. She wasn't sure where to go, just away from those men. She avoided streetlights as she walked, and all the while she kept her phone to her ear.

She suddenly realized that despite everything that had just happened, she had never felt short of breath, had never felt her heart race. She was mentally freaking out, but that reaction hadn't extended to her physical self. It was almost as if her future self was remote-steering the younger version.

"Alicia?"

"Yes," she whispered.

"I've got a friend named Brice on the line. I've told him what happened."

"Dad, there's more I need to tell you."

"Honey, one thing at a time. Brice, go ahead."

"Alicia?" The man's voice was higher-pitched than her father's, and he sounded tired.

"Yes."

"I know how scary this must be. I'll make this as simple as I can for you. I have people who are just now arriving on campus. They're going to take care of whatever is in your

room. Just stay away for ten minutes, and it'll all be taken care of. Do you understand?"

"I do. But what about if there are others?"

"I understand your concern, and it's being handled. First things first. We need to identify who attacked you so that we can better assess what threat you're currently under. You were targeted for a reason. We need to understand what that reason is."

Alicia grimaced. "I think I know."

"Alicia, let Brice do his investigation. We'll tackle it from there." Her father's tone was emphatic, as if giving her a clear warning. *"Brice, I've got thirty minutes before I get to the tarmac and board. I'll debrief her. You do your thing, and we'll talk before I take off."*

"Got it." There was a click on the line, which must have been Brice clicking off, because only then did Alicia's father say, *"What do you mean you think you know why they came after you?"*

"Dad, you're not going to believe me, but I'm not crazy. I suddenly have memories from fourteen years in the future—and I think there are people in the future trying to get people in the here and now to kill me. They don't want me to affect their plans."

She heard her father take a deep breath and then let it out slowly. When he spoke, it was with a surprisingly calm voice, considering what she'd just said. *"I think I'm going to need a bit more explanation before I know how to respond to that. Tell me what you think is going on. And start at the beginning."*

Alicia's father climbed the steps up to an unmarked gray military jet, the jet engines screaming across the tarmac. "Brice," he shouted over the noise, "you aren't serious."

"I'm very serious, Levi. Both were FBI agents, and they're both dead. Whatever she used on them evidently caused a huge mess. It'll be a closed casket funeral for one of them. The other is dead from a blow to the back of the neck. They suspect a vertebral separation of C2 and C3. I've scanned the high-side e-mail traffic that both agents have received in the last month, and there's nothing about Alicia in any of it."

"Then what the hell were they doing at my daughter's school, breaking in during the middle of the night?"

"Honestly, the situation stinks. I don't know. Our guys are sending the spray can to me in DC, and I'll test it, but they said it's labeled as sevoflurane. That's a powerful anesthetic."

"I know what it is, Brice. I've been using that in the field for years." Levi buckled himself into the sole passenger seat in what was mostly an empty cargo plane. "There's absolutely no reason my daughter would be a target for creeps with sevoflurane."

"I'm sorry to say it gets worse, Levi. Her phone? As of two days ago, it was authorized as an NSA target for indexing."

Levi frowned. "What does that mean?"

"It means that any conversation on the phone is being treated as if it's coming from a foreign agent. It's being recorded, her location is being tracked, and it's possible that someone heard us talking to her earlier. I wiped the official

records as soon I found it, but if someone had their ears on at the moment we were talking, they might already be moving resources."

"Son of a bitch." Levi gritted his teeth as the engines of the C-17 grew louder. "She's not safe at school. Brice, I need you to help me out here. The plane's taxiing on the runway, and it'll be at least ten hours before I land at Andrews."

"Don't worry. I'll make stuff happen."

Levi balled his hand into a fist. "I *need* to know who did this, Brice."

"I'll do what I can."

Levi felt himself being pushed against his seat as the plane accelerated down the runway. The cargo jet tilted upward and lifted off the ground.

He put his phone away. There was nothing he could do about whatever that gas had done to his daughter to make her think she was from the future. He could only hope that madness would wear off with time.

But his little girl being attacked…

He cracked his knuckles. *That* he could do something about.

It wasn't quite four in the morning when Alicia's phone buzzed. She had gotten tired of walking, and had found some bushes on the far side of Fisher Hall to hide behind.

"Hello," she whispered.

"Alicia, it's Brice. A phone has been left for you by one of

our people fifteen feet east-northeast of your current position. It's literally been placed at the base of one of the bushes."

Alicia hadn't heard a thing. "What? Which way is east-northeast?"

"You're on the north end of Fisher Hall. Put your right hand on the wall and you're facing east. Go fifteen feet, a little out from the building. You'll find it around there."

She didn't even bother to ask how he knew where she was. Given the kind of people her father associated with, they probably had a satellite tracking her phone or something.

"Okay, I'm looking." Alicia moved what she figured was about fifteen feet, then probed under the foliage. After a minute, her fingers found the phone. "I got it."

"Good. Turn it on and place your index finger on the middle of the screen."

Alicia pressed a button on the side to turn on the phone. It blinked once, and she put her finger on the screen.

"Okay, I'm getting your signal... got it. Tell me when you get prompted for a password."

Almost as soon as he said it, a soft keyboard popped up on the screen. "Got it."

"Type the following letters and numbers. Four."

"Four."

"A."

"A."

He continued dictating a surprisingly long string of characters. When he was done, the phone opened to a normal screen.

"The phone seems to be up and running now."

"Good. You won't have to do that again; it's now set to

your biometrics, and a fingerprint will be all you need. I'm going to call you on the new number."

Brice clicked off, and immediately the new phone vibrated. Alicia put it to her ear. "Yes?"

"Okay, Alicia. From now on, this is your phone. Drop your old phone and leave it where it is. Someone's been using it to track you."

Someone in addition to you, you mean, Alicia thought. But she dropped her old phone. "Okay, now what?"

"Now I get you somewhere safe. Walk north to the parking lot across from Dillon Court. It should be a set of buildings directly ahead of you."

Alicia pushed her way through the bushes and fast-walked north. "I know where it is."

"Okay, I can see your position. Go between the east and west buildings and hang a left. There's a blue Ford F-150 pickup parked on the west side of the parking lot. Tell me when you see it."

Alicia felt somehow naked to be walking across the pre-dawn campus with nothing on her but her school ID, which happened to have been clipped onto the sweatshirt she'd put on. No purse, no wallet, no driver's license or credit cards. But maybe that was all for the best.

The parking lot had only a handful of cars in it and she spotted the pickup. "I see it."

"Get in. The driver's-side door is unlocked. The keys are hidden above the visor on the passenger's side."

"Um, I don't have my driver's license on me. It's still in the dorm with my purse and everything else."

"Just don't drive like a crazy woman and you'll be fine."

Alicia panned her gaze across the parking lot, but there was no one around. She opened the door and slipped into the driver's seat. She flipped down the passenger visor, and a key fell into her hand.

"I'm in, and I have the key."

"Okay. I'm texting you an address—it's in New York, just across the Hudson. It's a safe house. I'll be acting as overwatch while you head there. Do you have any questions?"

"No. Thank you so much for this."

"There's no need for thanks. There will be two rather large gentlemen waiting for you at the destination. They might not look it, but they're part of our little outfit. You just get there in one piece, and we'll work out the rest."

"Thank you, Brice."

"No need for thanks, remember?"

As Alicia got off the call, she started up the truck and put it into gear. She felt proud of herself for not completely coming apart at the seams. Attackers, compromised cell phones, and safe houses… she'd never imagined being in the middle of this kind of mayhem.

And yet… all this craziness was going to make her mission that much more difficult. How was she going to convince Michael to end the project? If she couldn't get him out of the clutches of the government, she might as well have died in her dorm room.

Whoever it was that had attacked her, it was probably parts of the government. They were out to get her in the future, so why wouldn't they go ahead and short-circuit the threat she represented in the future by coming after her in her own past?

As she pulled onto US 1, Alicia decided to go along with whatever escape plan this guy Brice had hatched until she could talk with her father face-to-face.

Which raised another question. Her father worked for the government—some clandestine part of it. Could she trust him?

She thought she could. She always had. She knew he had her best interests at heart. But at the moment, it was hard to trust anyone.

Michael lifted his head from the control desk, rubbed his eyes and looked over at the wall clock in the lab. The vacuum pump was thudding as it normally did to maintain the near-perfect vacuum in the chamber and everyone was waiting for the dish to finish collecting the needed particles. "Josh!" He yelled over the sound of the vacuum pump. "We've been at ninety-nine percent for almost an hour. Go do something."

The grad student looked up from his phone and gave him a bloodshot stare. "It's not up to me to make your God particles get sucked up by the receiving dish any faster than they already are."

"I know, I just need someone to yell at so I can stay awake."

"Glad to be of service." Josh grinned and shook his head.

Michael stood and walked to the middle of the lab where the vacuum chamber was located. On one side of it there was a bank of computers attached to the chamber through a thick cable. He looked over at the bleary-eyed engineers manning the business end of the cable and asked, "We ready to pump those bits through the wires?"

Gino, the computer scientist with a big bushy black beard nodded. "You give a go and I'll be sending IP packets like nobody's business."

"Tell me again, how are we going to detect any changes in the packets?"

Gino began talking with his hands, a very Italian thing to do. "Each transmission packet ends up having lots of data, but because it's going to Susan directly," he hitched his thumb to the woman sitting at the opposite desk with a terminal in front of her, "most of that routing nonsense doesn't matter. There are only two things in the data payload for the IP packet. We have a monotonically increasing count, and we have a high-resolution timer value. That's all that's being transmitted."

"And that's where I come in." Susan spoke with an amused tone to her voice. "I receive the packet and spool it on the RAID storage, but at any time, I can go through those packets and search for hiccups in the count or if somehow the Ethernet frame or IP header got smooshed, I'd be able to detect it."

"Good stuff." Michael nodded.

"When are we going to be ready to go?" Gino asked.

"Should be any moment now."

"Yeah. We heard that a few hours ago." Gino sighed.

"Blame Josh," Michael said with a smile.

He had just walked back to his desk when the monitor

hanging from the ceiling ticked over to one hundred percent. A tired cheer went up from everyone in the lab.

They had enough tachyons to conduct the experiment.

With a sudden surge of adrenaline coursing through his veins, Michael felt his exhaustion vanish. He put on his headphones and dialed into the secure conference line.

"You are the first person on the bridge," the automatic attendant notified him. Beeps and announcements alerted him to the arrival of other callers, and then Josh's voice came through.

"I sent out a high-side alert, Professor. Everyone should be dialing in."

"High-side" and "low-side" were terms Michael had only recently learned. The government intelligence community communicated through two major networks, a high-side one, which was supposed to be for classified material, and a low-side one which was for unclassified material or things with a sufficiently low classification. He wasn't exactly sure where they drew the line, since everything related to Project Morpheus was only allowed on the high-side networks. Besides, since everyone here was a newbie to the security protocols, all the e-mail traffic went through Josh, who had been trained by the DC folks on how to act as a system guard. In effect he was the e-mail "hall monitor," and anything that went anywhere had to go through him first.

"Josh, let me know when everyone's on board. I think we're all ready to get this over with."

It took a couple more minutes before the last of the engineers dialed in. Evidently two people had fallen asleep at their desks and had needed prodding.

"Professor, we're all here. Everyone is on the secure channel and you're already sharing the control panel's screen."

"Thanks, Josh. Okay folks, let me just review once again what this experiment is attempting to show:

"We will have data packets streaming through a set of unshielded wires strung through the vacuum chamber and we're going to hit them with a tachyon beam. Knowing that the particles are charged, we are expecting that there's going to be some sort of blip in the data packets between the transmission side and the receive side.

"In other words, we're hoping for some packets to get corrupted. If they do get corrupted, then we know that the tachyons and matter as we know it can interact. If it *doesn't* get corrupted, it's on to Plan B."

He tried to sound matter-of-fact, but the truth was, there wasn't really a Plan B. If this didn't work, he wasn't sure what his next step would be.

"So, let's get started. Compute, how are we with the network transmission and storage?"

"Professor, we can transmit just under two-hundred million IP packets per second across the twinaxial wires. That gives us roughly a five-nanosecond granularity to the timer."

Michael leaned back in his chair and stared up at the ceiling tiles. "What kind of limits do we have on how much network traffic we can store?"

"We have a high-speed RAID storage system that should

keep up with the pace of the hundred-gigabit traffic. As to how much we can store, easily a few hours-worth of full-speed data before the storage even starts to complain."

"Great. Start the traffic and recording now. Verify once again that we have clean traffic."

"Roger that." Gino said. *"The packets are flowing."*

"I'm sampling the packets being spooled through the Wireshark," Susan's voice was loud enough he could hear her even across the lab. *"Everything looks good so far."*

"Engineering, you're up. How are we with the power curve profile I sent over? The beam will be a bit faster this time, which should be easier on your power grid, but it'll last for fifteen microseconds."

"Jan here, and I see no problems. We should be fine for this time around."

"Good. Anyone have any issues or last-minute opens before we hit launch?"

Michael waited a few seconds, then said, "Silence is acquiescence. Josh, start the countdown."

"Ten." A computerized voice spoke on the line.

"*Nine, eight, seven...*"

Michael leaned forward and with his mouse enlarged the shared screens coming from the transmission and received sides of the network.

"Three, two, one, launch."

A loud thwack echoed through the lab as the tachyon stream was routed from its containment and slowed to just above the speed of light.

"Susan, stop capturing traffic and let's see if you can find anything interesting."

"I've stopped the capture, and am now pulling up the spooled data. I'm now running a compare."

Susan sounded excited, but then again, they all were. As Michael looked around at the workstations, he saw none of the bleary-eyed stares everyone was giving each other just minutes ago. The whole lab was now wide awake.

A gasp sounded on the line, and Michael looked up at the monitor. It had been showing what Susan was doing, but now she'd stopped sharing her screen, and her icon on the Teams interface was now muted. He turned to look at her across the lab. She was huddled with Gino, both of them gesticulating at their screens.

After a moment Susan came back on the conference call, and she shared her screen once again. *"Professor, there's no doubt. At thirteen seconds into the spooled data, we have a series of packet corruptions!"*

The lab erupted with cheers loud enough to wake Percy from his doggie bed. He let out a confused bark, and Michael grinned.

"Professor... Professor..." Susan's voice was being squashed by the cross-talk on the conference call.

Everyone's icon was suddenly muted but Josh's. *"Guys, let Susan finish her report. She can't get in a word edgewise with you all talking over her. Go ahead, Susan."*

The lines were unmuted, and Susan began again. *"Professor, you should know that there were only about five packets that got corrupted in the entire stream. But they were all within that fifteen-microsecond burst."*

"Professor Salomon, it's Carl Sundenbach." Michael rolled his eyes. The red-eyed scientist from DARPA. *"I figure that the fifteen-microsecond burst likely produced about three thousand packets, and with five corruptions, that's about one-sixth of a percent corruption rate. Do you have plans on seeing if we can somehow create a 'brighter' beam to get a better tachyonic-baryonic interaction?"*

Michael was irritated, but he kept his voice even. "Carl, that's on my next step list. But remember there are a lot of things that we need to explore before any of this goes from lab experiment to tactical in any way." As soon as he said those words, he regretted them as Maria's warning replayed in his mind.

"I don't trust these people you're working with."

"Gino and Susan, I need your reports before you take off." Josh took over the conference call from there, and when it finally wrapped up, Michael stood and stretched his arms.

It was almost five a.m. and he desperately needed to get some sleep.

But as the FBI agent at the entrance to the lab stood, he remembered that he wasn't going home, wasn't going to see his family, didn't know where they were—or even if they were alive.

When he was at work, he could sometimes, almost, believe that everything in his life was okay. But the moment he stepped out that door, reality came crashing back down on him.

He was a prisoner in his own life—and it was a prison that was partially of his own making.

CHAPTER TEN

Alicia parked the pickup truck near the corner of Lenox Avenue and West 127th Street in Harlem. She'd never been in this area, but the streets were only just waking up as the sun began to rise. With almost no pedestrians or moving cars, she felt a weird sense of vulnerability as she walked down the street toward the address she'd been given.

As she approached her destination, she heard techno music humming from somewhere and noticed two bouncers standing outside a large door with purple neon lights.

It was a nightclub of sorts, but the place advertised no obvious name. Having been raised by her adoptive grandmother and growing up in an Amish community, she'd heard of underground nightclubs, but knew nothing of them.

In fact, she didn't have much experience with bars of any kind.

She paused and stared at the two men in front of the nightclub. They were huge, probably three hundred pounds each, and each had the thick build of a powerlifter.

Their dark skin and clothing helped them blend into the shadows cast by the awning hanging over the entrance to the club. One of them turned in her direction and blinked, showing absolutely no other reaction to her presence.

Alicia recalled Brice's words: *"There will be two rather large gentlemen waiting for you at the destination."*

Pulling in a deep breath, Alicia walked boldly up to the man who'd looked her way. "I was told that there'd be two large gentlemen waiting for me here. Are you them?"

They both stared at her for a few seconds before one of them spoke with a mild Jamaican accent. "That would be depending on who you are, Miss."

"Does the name Alicia Yoder help?"

"Is that who you claim to be?"

"It is."

One of the men bent lower and began squinting at her chest.

She took a step back.

The man who'd been staring at her frowned and shook his head. "Miss, I cannot read your ID if you move away."

"Oh!" Alicia flushed with embarrassment as she fumbled with the clip of her student ID, which happened to be pinned just over her left boob. "I'm sorry, here." She unclipped her ID and held it out.

The men nodded without reaching for it, stepped to the side of the door, and motioned for Alicia to enter.

Given the loud thumping of the strange music coming from

the other side of the door, Alicia braced herself as she opened it, expecting an auditory onslaught.

But the moment the door opened, the sound of techno music ceased and she found herself stepping inside a building that was utterly silent.

Only when the door closed behind her did the muted sound of the music start again—from the *outside*.

Or, apparently, from within the door itself.

Alicia was standing inside a wood-paneled lobby, fresh with the scent of wood polish and pipe tobacco. For some reason, the smells wafting through the air actually reminded her of her grandmother's home. A reception desk stood across the room, manned by a tall, thin, white-haired gentleman. She walked to the desk and even though it felt a bit silly to do it, Alicia held out her student ID.

"I'm Alicia Yoder. Brice sent me here," she said.

"Miss Yoder, it's so very good to see you. I'm Mr. Watkins, the proprietor of this establishment. You are expected." The man spoke with a very posh British accent, reminding Alicia of the butler from *Downton Abbey*. He waved her ID away. "Director Brice has given me specific instructions on how to handle your case. We will deal with your ID in a moment." He leaned across the reception desk and squinted at her. "Miss, that is a most unusual necklace you are wearing."

Alicia touched the pendant and smiled. "My father gave it to me when I started college. He said it was a charm that would keep me safe."

"Indeed." The man smiled and glanced at his watch. "We should get things started; I suppose. First things first…" He crouched down behind the desk and retrieved a black lacquered box, which he set in front of Alicia.

She picked it up and turned it over in her hand. She couldn't quite tell what it was made of. It felt kind of like wood, but it was heavy for its size.

"What's this?"

Watkins retrieved a card from inside his suit jacket, adjusted his glasses and began reading from it. "Miss Yoder, I'm afraid the technical description is a bit complicated, so I'll read what Director Brice's description card says."

"The enrollment box has a lacquer coating that is composed of an arrayed microheater fabricated on a silicon substrate. The electric resistance of the heater element will measure temperature differences between what is in contact and not in contact between each of the ridges of Alicia Yoder's finger."

Alicia frowned. "So, if I'm understanding that correctly, it's a fingerprint reader?"

The elderly gentleman nodded and squinted at the index card as he held it at arm's length. "It is a fingerprint reader, although I'd say it's a bit more in some ways. There is also a set of instructions as well as a bit of a warning written here, if I may."

. . .

"You are to press your index finger on the surface of the box, and keep it there for ten seconds. Use the same finger that you used to link yourself to the phone you received. Do not use a different finger, this is crucial.

"You might notice a puff of smoke—that's to be expected. Circuitry is embedded within the box to take the fingerprint data along with galvanic information and a few other proprietary pieces of biometric data. With that information, the ID within the box will be programmed to your body's signature."

Alicia extended her index finger and looked up at Watkins. Her eyes widened with obvious surprise.

The old man held a gun steadily in his right hand, aimed directly at her chest. He motioned toward the box. "Miss Yoder, it is time. Do as you were instructed."

Even though he was aiming a weapon directly at her, Alicia didn't feel scared. If she were in her right mind, she would be terrified, but there was something about all of this that triggered the opposite reaction. This sense of danger sent a thrill through her.

It was all very John Wick.

"You really don't have to point it at me. I'm not going to do anything wrong."

The old man smiled kindly. "One can never be too certain. You must still be properly identified." Watkins had smartly taken two paces back while still aiming directly for her. Despite his polite demeanor and elderly countenance, she could tell that he knew what he was doing with that gun.

Alicia placed her index finger squarely on the top of the box and pressed down. A wisp of smoke rose from the box, and a line burned across the top edge. She counted down from ten, then said, "Okay, it's been ten seconds. Now what?"

"It looks like the box has unsealed itself." Watkins placed his gun in a shoulder holster under his suit jacket. "Please lift the top of the box."

Alicia held the box in one hand and slowly wiggled the top off. Inside, on top of a velvet-lined bed, lay a silver coin emblazoned with an engraved logo: a pyramid with an eye in it.

It was the same image as the one on her pendant.

She fished the coin out of the box and turned it over. On the other side was an engraved eagle capturing a snake. Very unusual imagery.

She flipped the oversized coin in the air and caught it. "So what's this for?"

"If you don't mind," said Watkins, "with the Eye of Providence facing upward, hold the coin out toward me."

Alicia held the coin with the pyramid face up. Watkins reached out and grasped the other side of the coin.

"Keep holding on to it," he instructed.

For a moment, they both held on to the coin, and she wondered what the point was. But then, the coin grew warmer, and the eye in the pyramid began glowing.

"Whoa. That's cool as hell."

Watkins let go of the coin and gave her a curt nod. "That, Miss Yoder, is a confirmed identification between two people who are members of a brotherhood of sorts. The glowing of the eye is a confirmation that both are members." With a snap of his fingers, he produced an identical coin of his own. "This is what we use in lieu of any formal identification. There's no photo. There's no secret handshake. And if, God forbid, you have that coin stolen, it would not work for anyone outside of the brotherhood."

Alicia rubbed the face of the coin and stared at it for a few long seconds and looked up at Watkins. "Does my father have one of these?"

Watkins smiled. "That is something you would have to find out from him, now wouldn't it?" He motioned to his left. "Now, I'm to lead you to your next meeting."

Alicia looked in the direction Watkins had indicated. There was a hallway there that she could have sworn hadn't been there moments earlier.

Watkins walked out from behind the desk and motioned for her to follow. "Let's get you onto your journey, Miss Yoder."

"My name's Alicia by the way, you don't have to call me Miss Yoder."

"That's very kind of you, miss, but I think after as many years as I've been proprietor, I'd be more likely to spontaneously combust than to fall out of proper protocol."

The old man walked at a very brisk pace, and Alicia had to rush to keep up with him. Whoever this Mr. Watkins was, she liked him. There was something both mysterious and old-fashioned about him that so reminded her of an older version of 007. She wouldn't be surprised if in his younger days, he was exactly like Roger Moore, who to her was the quintessential James Bond.

The hallway was lit by old-fashioned sconces with lightbulbs that flickered as if they were aflame.

Watkins paused a few steps away from what she'd initially taken as the end of the hallway, but was actually the top of a set of stairs. The old man motioned toward the stairs and said, "Miss, the train awaits you."

"Train?"

Alicia stepped forward and looked down the stairs.

She heard a click somewhere in the building and turned back—only to find herself staring at a blank, wood-paneled wall.

"Holy crap! Watkins?" The hallway she'd just walked through had vanished, along with the mysterious Brit.

She knocked on the wall, knowing it had to be some kind of sliding mechanism or something, but it sounded solid and it wasn't budging.

"What the hell is going on?"

Alicia's mind raced as she briefly wondered if the walls in this place were on casters of some kind, but after a moment of staring at the blank wall, she turned back to the stairs.

With the spooky music at the front door and all the other weird stuff, this place definitely had a haunted house vibe to it.

With nowhere else to go, Alicia walked down the steps. A sleek railway car was waiting at the bottom, its doors open.

She stared at the one-car train. For a moment she wondered if a train could only have a single car and still be called a train. With a shrug, she shoved aside her mental grammarian and focused on the situation.

"I guess I have no choice in the matter." Alicia stepped on board.

A disembodied voice announced, *"The train will be leaving in ten seconds. Please hold on to a rail or you will likely be thrown backward. This is your only warning."*

Alicia rushed to take a seat and gripped one of the poles.

"Five seconds. Four. Three. Two. One."

Alicia slid backward as the train accelerated at a pace rivaling that of a race car. Within seconds, the wind was keening wildly as the train flew through the darkness.

Whatever tunnel it was that Alicia was in, it must have been very long, for despite the train's speed, Alicia traveled for nearly forty minutes before the train began to decelerate.

The disembodied voice returned. *"We will be arriving at Joint Base Andrews in approximately five minutes. Please disembark only after the train has come to a complete stop."*

Alicia frowned at the stupidity of that message. "Well, duh. It's not like I was planning on jumping off while zipping down the track."

Joint Base Andrews?

That was in Maryland, and she couldn't exactly be sure, but that had to be about two hundred miles from New York City.

She looked at her watch and shook her head.

How the hell had she gotten all the way here so fast? She did the math in her head and supposed it could be possible—if the train was going at the same speed as Japan's bullet train.

Andrews was a military base. She silently wondered if this train was something used by the military, or was it this weird brotherhood that she'd just evidently joined. Had she joined it?

She knew absolutely nothing about what was going on, but Alicia's curiosity was piqued.

She was more excited than frightened at this point, but in her mind, she couldn't help but dwell on her task.

Alicia was supposed to stop what would end up being a nightmare for everyone in this country, if not the world.

The train doors opened and Alicia spotted someone standing on the platform staring at her from about ten feet away.

He wasn't dressed like a soldier, instead he was wearing a suit and had a badge clipped to his belt. The man was short—not much more than five foot seven or so. Judging from the fine wrinkles around his eyes, and the frown lines, he was in his late fifties or early sixties. Light brown hair, with a slightly receding hairline, and very pale eyes that looked almost silver.

He smiled and suddenly something in her head clicked.

In her mind's eye, she saw an older version of that smile.

A scene flashed in her mind's eye as she saw herself in a darkened place that she remembered being deep underground.

Few people knew that fifty feet under Fort Meade was an old bomb shelter. It was left over from the cold war era, and had largely remained unused for decades. It was where Alicia had managed to hide enough of the stolen equipment they needed to try to undo what she and Michael had done. Somewhere outside their clandestine lab, she heard the splintering sound of a door being smashed open.

There was almost no time left.

Michael was lying on the gurney and held her hand with a

worried expression. "Just go ahead. They're going to kill us anyway, and you know it."

She plunged a full syringe-worth of the nanites into his carotid artery, and within seconds, tens of thousands of the microscopic automatons began transmitting data associated with everything they encountered.

Michael winced as his face turned bright red.

The capillaries in his eyes burst and the whites of his eyes turned crimson, changing his otherwise haggard appearance to one that was worthy of a horror show.

The LEDs on the mesh cap he wore began blinking in a series of patterns, indicating that the weak signal from the nanites was being received.

Michael squeezed her hand and whispered, "This isn't nearly as pain-free as we told everyone it would be."

Alicia looked up at the monitor and saw the program sorting through the data streaming from within Michael's head. Random images flashed on the screen. All of them were computer-generated interpretations of the neural pathways that had been translated from organo-electrical to digital form.

Michael's eyes closed. "I can feel them up there. It's almost like I can sense them crawling through everything that I am. This isn't a pleasant sensation. We've made so many mistakes going down this path."

"I'm sorry, honey." Alicia blinked the tears away. The nanites were her fault. Part of her contribution into what became phase two of Project Morpheus. "You'll be doing this to me soon enough."

The LEDs on Michael's cap all blinked green, signifying the end of the download of data.

Alicia smashed her hand down onto the transmit button, and several key messages splashed across the screen.

Satellite synchronization...

Completed.

Transmitting adjusted coordinates...

Completed.

Sending data...

The door to their room exploded inward as it was blown off its hinges.

Plumes of white gas billowed within the room as soldiers with gas masks raced, guns drawn as the world turned gray, and then black.

*** *Moments, hours, or days later...* ***

Alicia startled awake to the sound of a metal door squeaking on poorly oiled hinges.

Every muscle in her body ached as she sat up in what seemed to be a jail cell of some kind.

Her left arm was broken and hanging limply at a grotesque angle, with her elbow facing in the wrong direction.

The walls were made of bare poured concrete and it was barely big enough for her to lie down in. A metal door served as the only entrance or exit to the room.

She'd been put into solitary, which was a step above what she'd expected, which was to not ever wake up again.

For some reason, she couldn't feel any pain coming from her broken limb, which probably wasn't a good sign, but as she scrambled awkwardly to her feet she moved closer to the door.

There was a small slit in the metal door, just large enough to probably slide a tray full of food. Some pretty flat food.

Peering through the slit, she saw a soldier sitting on a chair, evidently tasked with guarding her.

His attention was focused on his cell phone.

There wasn't much she was going to be able to do, not in her condition. And certainly not from within the confines of her jail cell.

Had Michael's transmission completed? That was key to making this all stop.

Nothing seemed to have changed or had been fixed by what they'd just done, so it was likely that the transmission had failed, or was incomplete.

Maybe they hadn't killed Michael yet. There might still be hope.

Alicia heard footsteps through the slit, and the soldier immediately popped up from his chair and growled, "Who authorized you to come—"

His voice choked off into a high-pitched whine as she heard the sound of gas being deployed.

Alicia scrambled back into her cell, her heart racing and not sure what was going on.

She heard the sound of a body hit the ground. Something hard had also hit the metal door, possibly the soldier's head.

Alicia heard the jangling sound of keys and the snick of a lock being disengaged.

With some effort, the door swung open and she saw a short gray-haired man standing in the doorway. The soldier's unconscious body lay just past him.

The mysterious man wore a suit, and Alicia immediately noticed his peculiar eyes.

In this light, they seemed to almost glow with a silver hue.

"Miss Yoder, I believe you have something that needs to be finished, and it can't be done in this place." The man smiled and curled his finger at her. "Come with me."

Alicia shook her head as her mind returned to the here and now.

She stepped off the train and returned the man's smile.

Without even thinking about what she was doing, she said, "You're the younger version of the man who in the future gets me out of jail."

The man's eyebrows raised slightly and his smile broadened. "Excellent, Miss Yoder. I'm very pleased that the memory transfer worked for you."

Alicia gasped, and for the first time in quite a while, her heart raced and she felt her skin get clammy. "You know the future as well?"

The man stepped closer and put a steadying hand on her shoulder. "Only thanks to you."

He extended his hand and Alicia went to shake it, but realized he was holding out a silver coin.

"...this is what we use in lieu of any formal identification. There's no secret handshake."

Watkins' instructions replayed in her mind and she grasped the other end of the coin.

It took only about two seconds before the Eye of Providence began glowing and the man put the coin back in his pocket and again extended his hand. "Now we can shake hands."

He chuckled as they shook hands and then said, "Alicia, I'm Doug Mason, and we have a lot to talk about before your father arrives."

"Do you remember where we first met?" she asked.

Mason nodded. "I seem to recall a rather unpleasant jail cell was involved."

Alicia had a million emotions and thoughts racing through her at that moment, and the most intelligent thing she could muster was two blinks and a nod.

This man knew about the future.

She *wasn't* alone!

CHAPTER ELEVEN

Michael lay in bed as the midday sun peeked through the gap in the curtains of the hotel room. He'd managed to get a few hours of sleep, but that hadn't compensated for having pulled an all-nighter at work. Yet it wasn't his exhaustion that had woken him. It was that student who'd come up to him while walking Percy.

He'd seen her in his sleep.

"I'm here to warn you about Project Morpheus. It needs to stop or we'll both end up ruining this world."

He'd convinced himself that the girl was off her rocker, and somehow she'd managed to hear about the project. Too many people were now in the loop to completely bury the government-sponsored effort.

He'd caught some of the engineers talking in the break room and some of this stuff was bound to grow legs.

But the logo on the pendant she was wearing was identical to the image he'd seen on business card.

Turning on his side, he retrieved the business card from the top drawer in the nightstand and sniffed the hair.

Michael's throat tightened as he realized the lavender scent was beginning to fade. This was the only thing he had of hers.

He looked at the clock on the nightstand. It was two p.m.

He swung his legs off of the bed, and Percy lifted his head, ears alert and letting out a small yip, as if to say, "Are we going somewhere?"

"We're not working today, so let's go visit the house."

Percy got up and wagged his tail as Michael got dressed.

Without even bothering to even look in the mirror to brush his hair, he grabbed his wallet, keys, and Percy's leash and left the hotel room.

As he reached the end of the hallway, one of the FBI agents nodded at him. "Grabbing something to eat in the cafeteria?"

"Actually, no. Going to take a quick trip to the house. I want to see how the repairs are going and maybe grab some additional clothes."

The two agents looked at each other and shook their head. "We need to call that in. Nobody's authorized to leave the confines of the hotel other than via the shuttle, which is not currently in the parking lot."

Michael frowned. "No, it may not be, but my car sure as

hell is. If one or both of you want to come along, that's fine. But I'm going to get stuff from my house."

One of the agents pulled out a cell phone and put it to his ear while the other held out his hand, as if to stop him from moving forward.

The agent on the phone said, "Ya, it's Carter. Professor Salomon wants to collect some things from his house… uh, yes sir. Understood." He put the phone back in his suit pocket and held out his hand. "Professor, can you please give me your car keys. The SAC will make arrangements for whatever you need to be collected, but you are not allowed to leave the hotel, even under escort."

"Are you f'n kidding me?" Michael felt his face getting hot with anger as his voice rose. "I'm being detained?"

"No, sir. You are just limited to the secured perimeter of this hotel. We don't have the manpower here to spare anyone to go off site." The agent stepped closer; his empty hand extended. "The keys, please."

The other agent sighed. "Professor Salomon, don't make this unpleasant. We're all doing what's necessary to—"

"Yes, I know." Michael grabbed his car keys and dumped them in the agent's hand. "You're doing this for my safety. To be honest, I don't give a crap about my safety. I'd rather you guys find my wife and child."

"We understand—"

Michael turned away, seething with anger and headed back to his room.

As soon as he got in the room, he pulled out his phone, swiped several pages and grinned at the familiar icon.

Michael looked down at Percy and whispered, "They might have my car keys, but I don't need a car if I have an Uber. What do you think, big boy?"

Percy tilted his head and gave him a tiny wag of approval.

Grinning at the phone as he saw the nearest Uber driver was only seven minutes away. He sent in the order, turned around and walked down the hallway once again.

As he approached the FBI agents, he could tell that they were a bit tense, likely expecting round two of a confrontation.

As he got within arm's reach Michael smiled and said, "I'm sorry I gave you guys a hard time. You're right. We're all under a bit of stress. I was going to go to the bar and see if they're serving anything decent. You guys want to join me?"

They both shook their head and one of the agents said, "Unfortunately we're on duty, and like I said, there's only so many of us on site. We've got our stations."

Michael nodded. "Okay, maybe afterwards." He gave them a smile and walked past them, heading in the direction of the restaurant and bar.

As soon as he was out of their sight, he and Percy shifted their trajectory and went down one of the hallways that contained a series of conference rooms for events.

At the end of the hall was an unmanned exit he'd spied a couple days earlier, and with a quick shove of the pressure bar they exited the hotel and he aimed directly for the street, where a black SUV was idling.

As he approached, the driver hopped out of the car and looked at him and the dog. "Mr. Salomon?"

Michael nodded.

"Perfect." He opened the rear driver's side door and asked, "Any luggage or anything?"

"No, just a quick trip out and back. It shouldn't take much more than half an hour or so." Percy hopped into the back and Michael climbed after him.

The door closed and the driver hopped back into the car, put it into gear and began heading to the address the Uber app had already given him.

Michael smiled as he buckled his seatbelt and relaxed in the air-conditioned cabin.

Now to see if he could leave and come back before anyone even noticed.

Michael leaned forward in the Uber and asked, "Can you wait for me. I should only be about five or ten minutes."

The driver turned in his seat to face him and shook his head. "I'm sorry, but I already had a ride scheduled to pick up that isn't far away. If you want, I can come back."

"That's okay, I'll go ahead and call up another ride when I'm ready." Michael tapped on his phone to give the man a nice tip and he and Percy hopped out of the car.

He stared at his house and sighed. Other than a few calls with the insurance adjusters, he hadn't had any real contact with anyone working on the house. Some of the glass panes had been replaced, while other window frames were sealed with plywood.

At least all the shattered glass had been swept up. Michael

glanced at the lamppost across the street and spied the video camera still aimed at his house. Whether someone was watching or not, he had no idea, but he suspected that he'd be hearing something sooner than later.

Screw those guys, he hadn't done anything to deserve being confined to his room like a goddamn teenager.

He looked down at Percy and asked, "Ready to go in?"

The pup's rear wiggled back and forth as his tail became a blur.

The moment he unlocked the front door and stepped inside, Michael was hit with the aroma of fresh paint.

There were blue drop cloths laid across the furniture in the living room and Michael kept a tight grip on Percy's leash. "Be careful with your tail, some of the walls might still be wet in here."

Michael skirted past the living room, walking into the kitchen and saw that there were drop cloths everywhere. It looked like much of the first floor was being worked on at the same time.

The sliding glass door, which had been completely blown out earlier, had been replaced, although there were no replacement blinds installed yet.

He turned and climbed up the stairs to the second floor. His heart thudded loudly as he walked into the bedroom and spotted Felicia's crib.

They evidently hadn't yet done anything on the second floor. Everything was in disarray, just like he'd seen it on the day of the explosion.

He walked into the bedroom closet and stared at the empty room. "Where the hell are my clothes? Maria's clothes?"

The walk-in closet had been completely emptied of all clothes, hangars, and photo albums that Maria normally stored on the top shelf.

Feeling a sense of anger building up inside him, he walked through the rest of the room, and noticed that the bathroom and vanity area had been scrubbed clean.

No shampoos, none of Maria's makeup, his toothpaste, toothbrushes, everything was gone.

Even the magazine rack in the bathroom had been stripped bare.

"Percy, where is all of our stuff?"

The dog whined a bit and looked up at him with his head tilted as if to say he had no idea.

Michael walked into the bathroom and opened the cabinet just above the toilet.

It too was empty.

Normally they stored extra rolls of toilet paper in the cabinet, but there was one more thing they stored in the cabinet...

Michael pushed up on the middle shelf inside the cabinet and heard a click. The entire cabinet swung forward, revealing a hidden safe.

It was something he'd installed soon after they moved in, upon Maria's insistence.

With a few practiced turns of the dial, he opened the safe and his eyes widened with surprise.

He'd expected to see a gun case.

Even though neither of them were gun people, because of Maria's fear of the Colombian cartel that killed her family, they'd agreed that having a gun in the house was smart... just in case.

But it was gone.

He hadn't looked in this safe in months. There was no reason to. Only on rare occasions did they put some cash in the safe, and even then it was only a few hundred dollars. Neither of them liked to carry much cash.

Seeing a glint of gold, Michael reached into the safe and retrieved a small gold coin.

He stared at the strange figure etched onto the gold planchet and felt a dizzying sensation as he realized what it was.

The pyramid-shaped logo with the eye staring back at him forced him back two steps as he grabbed ahold of the doorway.

Suddenly he remembered seeing that logo one other time.

Michael walked through the winding hallways of the Pentagon to the cafeteria. It was just before ten in the morning, so the lunch crowd hadn't come in yet. Nor had his mysterious contact, Doug Mason. Mason was the chief of staff for the head of the Appropriations Committee in the Senate. Supposedly the guy wasn't a politician, he was some player in DC who knew just about everyone, but the man worked for a powerful politician, that much he knew. Michael had already been in DC for a handful of years, so he knew that when someone attached to a senator reached out, it would be wise to *not* ignore the invitation to have a conversation. Admittedly, he was a bit annoyed that the man wasn't very forthcoming on what he wanted to talk about.

Most of everything Michael was doing was highly classified, so he couldn't even acknowledge that he was working on anything that he was involved in. Whatever this guy wanted to talk about, the classified nature of what Michael had been doing would limit the scope of their conversation to the weather and Lord knows what else.

Michael decided to get a coffee from the Starbucks while he waited. He approached the counter, where a barista was grinding coffee beans, filling the air with the scent of freshly roasted coffee.

"Slow morning, huh?" Michael said.

"Usually is around this time of day. What can I get you?"

"I'll take a venti, plain coffee. No cream, no sugar, no squirts of anything."

"Venti black, coming up."

"What kind of breakfasty stuff do you recommend?" Michael asked.

"Well, a lot of people ask for a plain toasted bagel. But the menu board shows what we've got today."

"That works," Michael said. "A plain bagel, toasted light."

When Michael received his coffee and breakfast, he still saw no sign of his contact. He pulled out his phone and sent off a quick text. *I'm here, where are you?*

The response was quick. *Sorry. I'm in an all-hands meeting that got called last minute. I'm going to be late.*

For a moment, Michael brooded. Then he smiled as he had an idea. He texted a friend of his stationed in the Pentagon.

The last several years had given Michael a lot of clout in some circles, and with that clout came some useful acquaintances.

Are you attending a meeting with Doug Mason?

Probably. There's like two hundred people in the room. Why, you need him?

As quick as possible.

I'll see what I can do.

He sipped his coffee and waited. Only a minute passed before his phone buzzed with another text. This one was from Mason.

Something happened to the projector and we're taking a fifteen-minute break while it gets fixed. I can meet for a couple of minutes assuming you're still here.

Michael chuckled as he typed. *I'll be on the north side of the courtyard drinking an overpriced coffee.*

Then he stepped outside into the courtyard and parked himself on a bench along one of the walkways. A morning breeze blew through the trees and manicured lawn as he unwrapped his bagel and took a bite.

After a few minutes, a short man in a dark suit walked toward him. Doug Mason.

"So, how's life?" Doug asked as he sat down on the far side of the bench.

Michael raised an eyebrow. "I'm sorry, but do we know each other? All I know of you is that you work for a senator who is the head of the Appropriations Committee." He motioned to their surroundings. "I guess I'd ask you what brings a senator's staffer to the Pentagon?"

Mason was easily in his sixties, gray hair, and his eyes had a pale, almost silver color to them. But despite his obvious age, he seemed fit and very present. The man grinned and leaned forward a bit. "Professor Salomon, I know everything there is to know about you and your project."

Michael tilted his head and remained silent.

"I'm here to let you know that there's a time coming soon where some of the capabilities of PM2 will be used against the citizens of this country."

Michael's eyes widened at the mention of PM2. It was a shorthand that members of the project used when referring to phase two of Project Morpheus. They were in the beginning phases of merging two projects into one. His part, which enabled transmission of data across time, and another project which had something to do with decoding how the mind works.

Mason's voice was barely above a whisper as he said, "You will need to consider your options, and hopefully you'll do it before you bring forth a curse on our society through PM2's technology." The man retrieved a business card from within his suit jacket and handed it to Michael. "My number is on the back. If you need a way out, I can provide it."

Michael watched as the man stood and walked briskly away.

What the hell was that about?

He looked down at the business card and saw a strange logo. An eye peering from within a pyramid.

"What the hell was that lunatic talking about?" Michael wondered out loud as he tucked the card into his suit jacket pocket, convinced he'd wasted a better part of his morning.

The image of the Pentagon blinked out of existence as Michael found himself sprawled on his bathroom floor, the engraved image of that logo still in his hand.

Despite obviously having just fallen on his ass, he didn't feel dizzy like the last time he'd had a vision in this room, yet nonetheless he'd obviously had some kind of episode.

Percy whined and licked his face until Michael nudged the dog's nose away. "Percy, I'm okay. I just got dizzy; I suppose."

The memories of that logo, each and every time he'd seen it, they glowed vividly in his mind. Almost as if memories had been awakened in some way.

Percy sat in front of him, staring with his alert puppy eyes. He yipped.

"I don't know, big boy. How can I remember being in the Pentagon when I know I've never been there? But I remember some things…"

Percy placed a paw on his shoulder and yipped again.

"I'm not sure. I swear, I think I remember an apartment in DC that I was living in. Or will be living in. That all sounds crazy."

Michael's mind raced with the memory that had just awoken… or was it a delusion of some kind…

"Percy, this guy Mason said that I might bring forth a curse on our society. And that student… I don't remember her name, but she said something about her and I would ruin the world. And Maria…" Michael's throat tightened as he sat in their bedroom, alone. "Maria said I can't trust these people. Am I doing the right thing?"

Michael glanced at his watch and winced. "We have to get going."

He retrieved his phone, ordered up the car service, and grabbed Percy's chain after closing everything back up. He looked down at Percy and asked, "What do you think the chances are that the FBI is going to be hugely pissed when they figure out I broke their little security protocol?"

Percy barked twice.

Michael chuckled as the Uber pulled onto his street. "I think you're right, Percy. Almost certainly one-hundred percent chance of me getting some serious crap for this stunt of mine."

The driver hopped out of the car. "Mister Salomon?"

Michael nodded and he and Percy piled into the man's sedan.

As the driver put the car into gear and headed back to the hotel, Michael muttered to himself, "I guess I'll find out soon enough how much trouble I'm in."

Percy yawned and laid his chin on Michael's foot as the professor sat in front of the control console in the lab, staring at nothing in particular as he recalled yesterday's events. He grinned as he thought about how he'd snuck back into the hotel. It was almost like being a kid coming home past curfew, and not wanting his parents to catch him.

The FBI agents weren't much into letting anything slide, so they must not have caught on to his little episode of rebellion.

He picked up the phone and dialed up the head FBI agent's number. The so-called Special Agent in Charge said he'd handle whatever he needed, so this was going to be interesting.

The phone rang twice and a gruff voice crackled on the line. *"Yes?"*

"Agent Bernstein?"

"Yes, what can I do for you, professor?"

"Is there any way I can get more clothes from my house?"

"I'd rather you not make yourself a target by going to the house. I'll have an agent bring your entire wardrobe if that's what is needed to make you comfortable."

"Agent Bernstein, seeing my wife and kid safe would be the only thing that would make me comfortable. But having some other clothes at least helps."

"I'll have someone on it today. Is there anything else?"

"Not at the moment, thanks."

Michael heard a click, set the receiver back on its cradle and grinned.

If he gets his clothes, then that meant they'd likely offloaded it to some other location for storage.

But Michael had a sneaking suspicion that the FBI weren't the only people who'd been combing through his house.

Someone had left that coin in the safe.

But who?

"What's got you smiling like that?" Josh asked as he walked over and pulled up one of the lab stools.

Michael shook his head. "Nothing. I was just recalling a weird dream I had. What's up?"

Josh held a serious expression as he leaned forward, elbows on his knees and spoke in a quiet, conspiratorial tone. "Have you heard anything about DC yet?"

Michael frowned and shook his head. "Should I have? What's up with DC?"

"I heard from a couple of my contacts over in DARPA that there's talk about consolidating lab resources and bringing projects in closer to the mothership if possible, and our project was flagged as one of them."

Images of the Pentagon and other places flashed into his mind's eye as he shook his head. "It'll be a cold day in hell before I move to DC. Certainly not while Maria and Felicia are out there somewhere. The project can move, I'm not."

Percy lifted his head, looked up at Michael and let out another whining yawn.

Josh nodded. "Let's hope it all works out one way or another. I'm sure the police and FBI have to be on the verge of finding your family."

Michael shrugged and turned back to the computer. "Can

you go find out where we're at on the tachyon collection, and also about the larger dish we'd ordered. It was supposed to have come by now."

"I'll get on it."

Michael shifted his gaze to the receding image of the grad student-turned-project manager and clenched his jaw.

He wasn't sure when it happened, but somewhere along the way, Josh had gone from being *his* grad student to being an extension of one of the DC folks.

Maria's warning rang loudly in his head about not being able to trust these people.

At this point, Percy was about the only thing in his life that he trusted.

He retrieved his cell phone, pulled up its photo album, which consisted of only about four pictures, and he stared at the most recent one.

It was that girl's contact information.

Alicia Yoder.

Whoever she was, her crazy story was starting to seem less crazy.

He stared at the photo he'd taken with her number for a full ten seconds and got up from his chair.

"Come on, Percy. Let's go for a walk."

Brice tapped into the Utah Data Center computers, the same ones that the NSA used to monitor all phone traffic coming into and out of the country.

A little-known fact was that they actually monitored *all* calls in the country, but it was supposed to be only the foreign source or destination calls that could be flagged for keyword indexing. That indexing would flag words out of a registry such as "bomb" or "kill" and in days gone by, "Osama" was a popular term to flag.

Brice's focus was now on high-priority cases having to do with a Professor Michael Salomon. The details were especially hush-hush as to why and how the Outfit had gotten involved in this. Normally Brice was aware of *why* he was working on something, but this time around, only Director Mason, who was one of the top men in the entire clandestine organization, seemed to have an idea of what's up with some physics professor in New Jersey.

Brice had been tasked with monitoring the good professor's communications and understanding who he was in contact with, and likely listening in on what those people were up to as well.

Brice put on his headphones and leaned back as he listened to a conversation between a high-ranking FBI agent named Glen Bernstein and another man.

"What do you mean there's nothing in Professor Salomon's bedroom closet? Our crew inventoried the entire house before closing it up, didn't we?"

"Glen, I don't know what to tell you. I'm standing in the middle of the man's walk-in closet and there's nothing here. I don't have the original inventory list on me, but I'm pretty sure I'd remember a totally empty master bedroom closet coming up on the report. That stuff sort of stands out. And besides, this

entire bedroom has been wiped clean. Someone definitely came in and emptied it."

"What about the rest of the house?"

"The rest of the house looks fine. They're repainting and fixing windows and stuff, but there's knick-knacks where you'd expect them and other stuff. It's only the master bedroom that's been cleared."

Bernstein's voice sounded increasingly frustrated. *"Okay, then we need to run the surveillance tapes and see who came in and removed that stuff. I doubt a bunch of insurance-hired workmen are going to steal a man's clothing."*

"Um, yeah... about that. I sent you an e-mail about the surveillance a while ago. We'd only gotten a limited-time allowance on the surveillance, and you never responded, so nobody went to the judge to extend the order. I mean, the professor is under our protection elsewhere—"

"Are you freaking kidding me?" Bernstein sighed and Brice could almost imagine the man's shoulders sagging from frustration.

"Jason, this absolutely blows. We need that house re-inventoried, and compare it against what had been there. If someone's taken stuff, I want to know where it is, and why. We might have control over the professor, but his damned wife and kid are still a problem. Do you think he's a flight risk?"

"We don't think so. So far, he seems to be rather compliant."

Bernstein grumbled something unintelligible and then said, *"I really hate that this is all remote. If it was in DC, at least here there's a thousand reasons for us to get twenty-four-seven authorization on surveillance."*

"There are folks working on the DC angle already. So, what do you want me to do about the professor's request for his clothes?"

"Aw hell, when you see him, just tell him that his clothes are stuck in evidence and you can't get them. Get his clothing size and buy the bastard some of whatever the hell he wants to wear."

"You got it."

The connection ended and Brice frowned.

The FBI guys sure didn't sound like they had their stuff together.

Brice grabbed his cell-phone from his desk and dialed Mason's number.

It rang four times and went to voice mail.

"Doug, where in the world are you?" Brice muttered to nobody in particular.

It was very unusual for Doug Mason to be out of contact at any time, much less during the middle of the day. Hell, he'd been mostly out of contact for almost an entire week.

The last he'd talked with him, the man had dumped the task of gathering everything he could about this Professor Salomon and no further instructions.

Something serious was going on, and for maybe the first time in the fifteen years he'd been working for the Outfit, Brice was worried.

CHAPTER TWELVE

Sitting in Freedom Hall, the dining facility attached to Joint Base Andrews, Alicia studied her new ID and looked over at Mason, who'd just set down a tray of drinks and a large plate of french fries on their table. "Jennifer Smith? You couldn't get more creative than that?"

"It's probably not wise to use your real name in this case." Mason took a sip of his iced tea. "And besides, it's only temporary. Until we can figure out who exactly sent your attackers, and why."

Alicia bit down on one of the fries and panned her gaze across the cafeteria. About half of the people wore fatigues or some other form of military uniform, while the rest were in civilian clothes. "I guess I should thank you for arranging all of this, even though I wasn't exactly expecting to end up impersonating an officer in the Air Force."

Mason chuckled. "I think if you look more closely at your CAC, you're listed as an airman, not an officer."

"Cack?"

"C-A-C, Common Access Card. Your ID, it's usually referred to as a CAC." Mason leaned forward and spoke in just above a whisper, despite the relatively noisy environment of a bustling cafeteria. "You haven't been trained for any of this, so don't get the wrong impression. The ID is just to not have too much grief while we're on the base, waiting for your father."

"Is my father part of the military?"

"No." Mason laughed as he shook his head. "Like you, we sometimes pretend to be things that we're not. I swear to you, I'll explain a lot of things to you in due time, but let's focus on the next couple hours. Have you tried to tell your father about the future?"

"I did." Alicia nodded. "And he listened, but I doubt he believed a word of it. To be honest, I'm still in shock that you believe it."

Mason took on a serious expression and shifted his chair a bit closer, so that they were more side-to-side than facing each other. With his arms crossed, he leaned slightly to his side and spoke in a whisper. "I am a member of an organization that acts in many ways as a conscience for our government. The organization was founded around the birth of our nation, and we have resources across all of the continents, including a member or two on Antarctica. We often observe trends and try to steer things when we see them go awry.

"One advantage my organization has is that its access to data is almost limitless. And that's what led me into a bit of a problem. In the future, I learned of a project that on its face seemed to be a fantastic advance in science. It was headed by a professor out of Princeton, who you are very familiar with. And then I learned of a second phase of experiments, the combining of two research teams, one of which you were the head of. I looked into it and immediately saw the danger."

Alicia tried to remember when she first truly met Michael in the future, and she couldn't do it. Maybe those memories hadn't successfully transferred?

"If I had to name my best skill, I'd argue that it's probably being able to see the bad within the good, and vice-versa. Some might call me a cynic, others an optimist, but in the end I'm fairly pragmatic. I want what's best for our government and its people. Yet, everything about the projects you and this professor were involved in set off my alarm bells. Given that, I tried talking to this professor. I tried to warn him about some of what might happen. It was soon after that when the entire project team was sequestered. There were people in the government who were very interested in the promise of what your two teams might accomplish. For them, it was initially a military advantage. It was labeled a national security research project. In the end, it was an excuse to create a police state."

Alicia nodded as she remembered the feeling of paranoia on the streets. "I remember parts of it. I'm guessing my memory transfer wasn't nearly as complete as I hoped it would be. Police could actually arrest you on the suspicion of what you haven't even done yet …"

. . .

In her mind's eye, Alicia recalled the first time she'd been brought into court as an expert witness. She was listening to a prosecutor interrogate an elderly woman on the stand.

"Mrs. Patterson, your life hasn't been an easy one, has it?"

The frail, eighty-something year old woman sat on the witness chair and leaned into a microphone. *"Oh, I suppose everyone has their challenges now and again."*

The attorney raised his voice slightly. "Let me ask it a little differently. Your life hasn't been an easy one, living with your husband of fifty years. It has been a challenge living with that man, hasn't it?"

The woman's voice quavered a bit. *"All marriages have their challenges, Mister Jenkins. All of them."*

"Of course that's true, but for the last twenty years, your husband, who can't be in the court right now, because he's bedridden, he's been especially hard to live with. After the car accident, he never recovered his faculties. And the money from the settlement was never really enough to cover all of the expenses. Is that right?"

"I suppose that is true. In that sense things have been difficult."

Alicia's heart broke for the woman who began dabbing at her tears, smearing whatever cheap makeup she'd applied that morning. How could this woman be guilty of conspiracy to murder?

"And you have a neighbor, a Mr. Robert Kenyon. Do you recall Mr. Kenyon?"

"I do, he's been my next-door neighbor for almost a quarter century."

The attorney faced the jury as he said, “Mrs. Patterson, we have deposed your neighbor, Mr. Kenyon, and he admitted that he’s made an offer to you that was quite indecent, despite his claims of being a God-fearing man. Do you recall that proposal?”

Alicia noticed that the bored demeanor of the jury had suddenly changed to one that leaned forward in their chairs and looked much more engaged.

Maybe it was human nature to react that way to anything scandalous.

“No, Mr. Jenkins. I don’t remember Robert ever telling me anything inappropriate or indecent.”

The prosecuting attorney grinned as he read from an index card, “I believe Mr. Kenyon told you that he would be willing to take care of you financially if such a time came that you ever needed it. Mrs. Patterson, you don’t expect the jury to believe that such an offer isn’t an indecent proposal, do you?”

“Objection, your honor!” The defense attorney shook his head at the opposing counsel. “Argumentative.”

“Sustained.” The judge ruled.

“Mrs. Patterson, Mr. Kenyon’s offer of financial support, did you consider it indecent?”

“That wasn’t indecent. He was being kind, and you might take some lessons in that, Mr. Jenkins.” The old woman said with an outraged tone. *“Robert was just saying that if my Frank ever died, he would want to take care of me. It’s what a decent human being might say.”*

“Exactly.” That attorney said with a note of triumph. “I

would like to refer to document 3B that's already filed in the record. It comes directly from a government's authorized memory stenographer." The prosecuting attorney faced the jury once again, holding up a printout of the report, and without looking at Alicia, pointed in her direction and said, "I have an expert in memory stenography who will testify to the accuracy of this. It states unequivocally that Mrs. Holly Andrea Patterson fantasized about accidentally leaving out some of her husband's critically needed drugs from his daily dose of IV medicine. In fact, the memories go so far as to her calculating how long it would take for her husband to have a fatal seizure without those medicines. She further fantasized about sleeping late and the joy she'd have in finding her husband dead, giving her the freedom she'd long desired. And Mrs. Patterson has given a lot of thought to being in Mr. Kenyon's embrace. An embrace she knew was only possible if Frank Lloyd Patterson, her husband, was dead. This is all in the undeniable record of her memories."

There were a couple gasps from the jury, and the judge banged his gavel loudly, warning that any noises or interruptions would suffer severe consequences.

Alicia stared as the attorney continued rattling off the old woman's thoughts, and although unpleasant, it seemed like a moment of weakness, not of guilt. She felt nauseous with the idea that someone's moment of weakness, an ill-conceived thought, might result in severe consequences. This was never how it was supposed to be.

"Mr. Jenkins, I don't remember most of those things you just said, but I would never purposefully harm my husband. I

love him more than anything, and have taken care of him every day since his accident. I love my husband."

The attorney shook his head. "Maybe not more than Robert Kenyon, it seems. And as you know, per 18 USC 1117, you are currently charged with conspiracy to murder. Under the modified subsection dealing with memory data, and I'll quote: 'If two or more persons conspire to violate section 1123 of this title, and one or more of such persons do any overt act to effect the object of the conspiracy, the person committing the act shall be punished by imprisonment for any term of years or for life.'"

"Are you okay?" Mason asked.

Alicia shuddered, her focus turned back to the here and now. "My god, we actually tried people for murders they hadn't yet committed. The future is a horrid place, and it's my fault."

"It's probably worse than you remember. But realize that what you just described ended up needing not just what you came up with, it needed the professor's ability to send things back in time. Pre-crime prosecution became a reality on when a murder occurred, and a warning was sent back in time to a prosecutor."

"So it would have happened? The crime?"

Mason shrugged. "I think it can be argued many ways, but that's what the future government decided was what we'd do. It had a chilling effect on society as a whole."

Goosebumps grew on Alicia's arms as a chill raced up her spine. "I can't even imagine how that would work."

"The way you explained it to me was that when the memories are sent back, you're in essence using a shotgun blast to try and land pellets in an exact pattern in someone's head. It's almost impossible to do it completely right at a distance. For some reason, when you sent my memories across, either you hit a bulls-eye or you were exaggerating the difficulty, because I remember waking up about a week ago with the most horrible case of nausea, and for a moment I thought I was in the future. It took me a good hour to figure out what exactly had happened. I remember the future like it was yesterday."

Alicia shook her head. "I have no idea what's accurate or not about what you just said, but I can tell you that I had the same nauseous feeling about that long ago, but my memory is spotty. Some things I remember right away, like Michael… oh boy do I remember the professor."

"If I recall, you two became an item, right?"

She nodded. "And it tears me up inside to know that I saw him and he didn't even recognize me. Absolutely no recognition whatsoever." Alicia gasped. "But I guess that makes sense. Yes… I remember being in that room under Fort Meade, we were transmitting his memories when they broke in. Maybe he didn't get any of his memories. Or maybe just some of them. I don't know."

Mason drummed his fingers on the table as a loud group of airmen walked by, laughing about something. "Well, that's the thing. You'd said that memories can be transferred and the person wouldn't even know that it happened until something triggers one of those latent memories. You described memories as being a maze-like set of paths and only if you stumble into the entrance to the maze do you even realize it's there."

Alicia nodded. "That would make sense. I could go into the epigenetic controls on memory, the electrochemical processes and everything, but what does it even matter."

"It all matters, my dear. You see, I think I've been affected differently than you and your future lover has. I have a condition that is almost unique. I have an eidetic memory. I can remember everything I've ever seen, smelled, tasted, hell I can tell you that in the movie, The Hobbit, at exactly one hour and twenty-four minutes, twenty-nine seconds into the movie, Bilbo and his company first enter Rivendell. The city ruled by Elrond."

Alicia turned to Mason and grinned. "You're a total nerd, aren't you?"

"Hah!" Mason shrugged. "I suppose I have my moments. But my point is that I have a very different view of what's happening than I think anyone else. You and I have had this conversation four times in the past."

"What conversation?" Alicia asked with a puzzled expression.

"This one, the one we're having right now."

"Huh?"

"It's only a theory, I have…" Mason pursed his lips and breathed deeply. "Hear me out. I think that in the future, things can happen when you send a message back in time. Sometimes nothing. But sometimes it can have a ripple effect. This is no different than what would happen if you go back in time and killed Hitler when he was a baby. How would the world change? Or maybe if you helped Hitler succeed? Imagine how things downstream would change. I know I've woken up on four different occasions and had memories infused into me. I don't remember waking up four times, but I have the memories of four different times that my memories have been updated up here." Mason tapped on the side of his head. "I can tell, because each time the memories were a little different. I remember four different versions of our future. None of them are pleasant to remember."

"The multiverse." Alicia's eyes widened. "I've read about the theory. For each possible change in decision, a different universe exists. But you're implying that it's not a different universe per se, but all one single timeline, and I guess we've failed four times in trying to prevent what's going to happen. Is that what you're saying?"

Mason nodded. "That's my working theory. The only problem is that I have no idea what we did differently. How we failed. Or what we have to do to eliminate the threat." He scratched at his chin. "Tell me what you know of the professor."

"Well, I know he teaches—"

"No, not technically. Emotionally. You become lovers in the future. What do you know of him? His background. Does he have family? Parents? Is he religious? Anything…"

Alicia raised her eyebrows, surprised by the question. "I can't remember when we first met in the future. Gosh, it's weird to say that and yet it's the only thing that makes sense. But I remember us working together, and…" Her cheeks flushed warmly. "I think I seduced him. I got him drinking and I came onto him pretty strong. At the time, I wasn't sure if he was gay or straight, because I'd been flirting with him and he seemed oblivious." Alicia smiled. "He wasn't gay. As to his family, I don't know. He wasn't married, that much I know. And as far as I could tell, he spent all of his time at work. He was obsessed. I remember we had sex in his office. And in my apartment." She looked at Mason and shook her head. "I can't believe I just admitted that out loud. Anyway, I don't remember if I'd ever seen his apartment. I'd say he was a very private person, but I don't know if he had a private life at all. He was always at work. Why do you ask?"

Mason pressed his lips tightly into a thin line and shook his head. "No real reason. What are your feelings now with regards to this professor?"

"I shouldn't have any, right? I'm only a grad student and never met him." Alicia sighed. "Since I received these memories, I saw him once and tried to warn him about the future. That was a miserable failure. I'll be honest with you, I want to go back and get him out of there. Pull him away from the project and change the path of how things go."

"But did the feelings you have for him transfer over?" Mason stared at her. "I think you are emotionally attached, aren't you?"

Alicia's throat tightened and she couldn't say anything, so she nodded instead.

"You realize that the easiest thing to do would be to have a sniper take him out and it would be over."

"No!" Alicia exclaimed and then clamped her hand over her mouth as the world seemed to turn toward her.

Mason laughed.

Alicia took a big swig of her iced tea and tried to smile away her outburst. "Sorry, I didn't mean that."

Everyone around them quickly seemed to lose interest and focused back on their own meals and conversation.

"You see?" Mason said. "What if that's the only answer we have left?"

Alicia felt the oppressive weight of the future on her shoulders and knew that she sent her memories back because it was her fault. Maybe both of their fault that the world had turned into a dystopian version of itself. She leaned to her right, and with her head almost touching Mason's she whispered, "If it comes to it, I'll pull the trigger on him myself. We can't let the future I've seen happen."

"Fair enough," Mason nodded. "But how would you describe the professor with regards to his loyalty to his employers?"

"In the future, or now?"

"Either or both would be great."

"In the future, I had the distinct impression that something had broken his spirit and he'd become a creature of the lab. I'm only guessing at that, because I only knew him as a lab rat, someone who spent all his time working. I only glimpsed the real Michael the few times I had him in bed." Alicia pressed her hands against her warm cheeks. "I can't believe I'm speaking like this. Anyway, I think somewhere deep inside he hated the government, but he never said a word against them. It was just that I glimpsed an occasional eye-roll or some of the words he said at the very end… almost fatalistic statements. He knew they wanted to kill us because we weren't team players anymore. That was mostly my fault, I'm afraid. But he went along. He knew that we'd done something unforgivable and there was no way to undo it. Pandora's box had been opened."

"Yet you came up with the idea of undoing things by warning your earlier selves."

Alicia shook her head. "Actually, that was his idea. I just helped put the pieces together. He was actually pretty animated about it once I'd suggested that we could try to undo what we'd done." She turned in her seat and looked Mason in the eye. "I think it's the right idea for me to go back to New Jersey. If anyone's going to trigger any memories of his and convince him to leave, I think it'll be me."

"We'll see." Mason glanced at his wristwatch. "Tell me, what are you trying to get out of this?"

"This?"

"Going back to New Jersey, seeing the professor. What's your real motivation?"

Alicia sighed as she let the question stew for a moment. "My motivation for going back? I've seen what my end looks like in the future, and I'm sure Michael's is the same. The only way I know to avoid that is to get him out of the project."

"And you realize in so doing, you may never see him again."

Alicia held her palms up as if weighing two options. "On the one hand die gruesome deaths after maybe having some pretty awesome sex a few times? Or save the world and see what happens? I'll take save the world. What idiot wouldn't?"

Mason smiled. "Young lady, I think we're on the same page." He stood and picked up the tray with the half-eaten plate of fries and partially-consumed drinks. "Your father is about to land, let's get you two reunited and we'll see what happens afterwards."

Alicia followed Mason and asked, "Do you think I should try to explain to my father what's going on? The whole multiverse thing?"

Mason put the tray on a moving conveyor belt that slowly fed into the kitchen area and turned to her. "I'll leave that up to you, but realize that he might find it very hard to believe. I barely believe it and I've lived this four times already."

Mason was right. There's no way he'd understand, even if he wanted to, there's no way.

Mason pushed through a door that led them onto the tarmac, the sound of jet engines washed over them.

"I think I'm going to play the confused college student and make it easier on him."

They began walking north toward a set of buildings and he yelled over the noise, "That might be the easiest."

Alicia had a plan, and it was one her father would never approve of.

Brice scribbled furiously in his notepad as he listened to the intercepted conversation happening at that exact moment between the Special Agent in Charge Glen Bernstein and someone in the Utah Data Center.

"What's up Sandi? Anything new out of the UDC?" Bernstein asked.

"Actually, yes. Remember that cell phone number you had me add to the list? The one for Alicia Yoder."

"Yes." He said with an excited tone, *"What do you have?"*

"Well, it looks like your Michael Salomon tried to call from his cell to hers just a little while ago. It did register because the voicemail on her service picked up."

"Excellent. And this just happened?"

"Yes, about five minutes ago."

"Perfect, anything else?"

"Nope, but you asked me to call you if that number ever got triggered and not to wait for my daily report."

"You did great, I owe you big time. Thanks."

The phone disconnected and Brice watched the monitor as the SAC's cell-phone signal triggered another connection, this time with someone located in New Jersey.

"Jason, what's the story with this Alicia Yoder? Your guys were supposed to get her, so what gives?"

"Nothing good on that end. The girl hasn't been seen in a couple days, and the folks I sent over... well, I don't know. I've tried reaching out to them, but their phone must be off."

"Damn it all to hell, why can't I catch any kind of break?" Bernstein fumed. *"We've got a direct connection now between our professor and this Alicia chick. Somehow they know of each other and he tried calling her."*

"Listen Glen, we've been watching him like a hawk. I have no idea how she might have gotten her hooks into him."

Bernstein sighed. *"Fine, keep trying to find that girl. We need her under our control and out of the way. I think I have an almost air-tight case for accelerating the move to DC—"*

"Glen, you might want to double check that plan. I have direct from the horse's mouth that says our guy won't go to DC."

"Why? What the hell's his problem with DC?"

"He's still holding out hope for his wife and kid reappearing."

There was silence on the line for a good five seconds, giving Brice enough time to catch up with his scribbling.

"I see. Well, maybe I'll have to break the news to him."

"What news?"

"Never mind, I'll handle it."

The signal disconnected and as Brice scribbled, he glanced at the screen, seeing no further cell activity and silently cursed his lot in life.

"Why do we care so much about this damned professor?"

Michael stared bleary-eyed at the screen as he put the finishing touches on his latest report. The one thing that he could say that was good about working with the government folks was that it was forcing him to write stuff down and fully explain things. It was a good discipline to keep, one that he hadn't really had to do before, since most of the people reading his work were peers.

Nowadays, he had to make management types who had a computer science or mechanical engineering background understand advanced physics topics. It was almost like writing for students—stupid ones.

There was a buzz at the lab and Percy hopped up from his bed as several agents walked in.

The dog began growling.

"Percy! Come here."

With Percy's nails scratching the lab floor, he rushed past the agents and sat next to Michael's chair.

Michael stood as soon as he saw Agent Bernstein was at the head of the group.

He hadn't seen the man since that first day at the house. Why would the FBI lead agent be here?

Could his little escapade with the Uber driver have come back to haunt him… or maybe—"Agent Bernstein, any news on my wife and kid?"

The man held a grim expression and motioned for Michael to take a seat as he pulled up one of the tall, three-legged stools nearby. "Have a seat, professor."

Michael's heart thudded loudly in his chest and the other two agents hung back, neither of them looking particularly happy.

"I don't know an easy way to say this, so I'm just going to be plainspoken about it. There was a car accident, which resulted in the vehicle going up in flames." Bernstein sighed. "Your wife and child are dead."

The man continued talking, but all Michael heard was a buzzing sound in the air. He was no longer even aware of the lab around him. He was somewhere else. Standing on an embankment, looking down at a charred SUV. Fire engines dousing the smoldering remains. Helicopters overhead. Body bags being carried away on stretchers.

The sound of the fire engines receded, and he heard Bernstein's voice again. "The kidnappers were foreign agents. We were closing in on them, and when they suspected they had been compromised, they raced across a highway during bad weather, which led to the crash. There were no survivors. The bodies are damaged beyond recognition, so we won't be asking you to try to identify them if you don't want to. We've already begun a DNA analysis, but the medical examiner has your wife's dental records, and they match the deceased adult. I'm sorry."

Michael felt numb. Something was wrong about this. He'd just had a memory of the accident. How was that possible?

He felt a surge of anger well up inside of him. But he took a deep breath, let it out slowly, and then said as calmly and firmly as he could: "I want to see their bodies."

The SAC got up from the stool. "I expected you might. We're ready to take you, if you want to go now."

Michael was in a daze as he followed the agents to their car and suffered through a police escort to the office of the Mercer County Medical Examiner.

It seemed like they were expected, because within three minutes of entering the building, Michael was standing in front of two extended body drawers with sealed body bags on them.

A man in a white lab coat looked at Michael, then at Bernstein. "Are we ready?"

The agents looked at Michael. He nodded.

He braced himself for a horror show. Blood, guts… he didn't even know what to expect. But somehow, what he saw was even worse.

The bodies had been burned so thoroughly, they were now little more than skeletons with charred skin. No hair. No lips. No facial features.

Felicia's little body had nearly been consumed. All that was left was her torso, head, and stubs where limbs should have been.

The only two people he'd loved in this world were now nothing but charred remains.

Michael let out an uncontrolled sob and turned away. It was too much for him to take.

The agents gently escorted him from the room.

As he climbed back into the sedan, Percy whined and put his head in Michael's lap. The professor stroked the dog's head numbly.

She's dead. They're both gone.

He felt a tightness around his chest, like a metal band that didn't want to let him breathe. He knew the agents were talking to him, but he couldn't hear them. His thoughts were still back in the morgue. Looking at the bodies. And in his mind, he imagined both corpses turning their heads to face him. Their empty eye sockets stared and their lower jaws opened, screamingly silently at him.

Percy yelped with pain. Michael realized he had squeezed

the dog too tightly, and he quickly loosened his grip. His heart was racing, and the world lost color. For a moment he felt himself losing consciousness.

And then everything snapped back.

He breathed more comfortably and Michael reached over to Percy, who stared back at him with a level of distrust.

"I'm sorry, Percy. I had a nightmare. You're a good boy."

The dog lowered his ears and Michael petted him once more. The oversized puppy came closer and whined in his lap.

"I know, big boy. It'll be okay. It's just you and me now."

His throat tightened and he repeated the statement again. This time with a bit less emotion.

"It's just you and me."

CHAPTER THIRTEEN

Sitting in a private conference room located on Joint Base Andrews, Alicia sat across the table from her father as he stared at her with those blue eyes of his. She could tell that he was angry by the way his jaw muscles clenched. Even though she knew he was simmering with anger, he maintained the placid expression of a Zen master. It was the clenching of the jaw muscles that gave him away. "Dad, I'm going to be involved with this. Doug and I talked about it already, and I know you don't want to hear it, but this is something I need to do."

Her father turned to Mason and raised an eyebrow. "Doug…" he said with an overly sweet tone that promised destruction. "What is this about an agreement that she's going on a mission? It's one thing that I come back early to find out my eldest daughter has been inducted into the Outfit, and she doesn't even have a clue what it's really about. But a mission?"

He tapped his index finger loudly on the table for emphasis. "She's a student."

"Levi, I'm very well aware of her being a student." Mason grinned, unfazed by her father's intimidating glare. "As to her going on a mission, we have yet to decide what the parameters of that might be. I still haven't talked with Brice, who's been gathering intel for me on our illustrious professor. Nothing is happening right away."

Levi turned to Alicia and pointed at her. "What in the world kind of training do you have that makes you think you're ready for a mission? Just because I taught you basic martial arts, and you can shoot a gun, that's what qualifies you? Alicia, you're just a student. Honey, you don't know what kind of business this is. You're not ready, trust me."

Alicia felt the hairs on the back of her neck stand up as her father's angry frustration poured out of him. "Dad, for this, I'm ready. I might be a student, but for this I can help where most agents cannot. I can elaborate, but you might not like the answer."

"Hell yes, tell me." Her father leaned back in his chair with a grin. "I can't wait to hear this."

Alicia took a deep breath and let him have it with both barrels as she began talking in Mandarin, a dialect of Chinese that her father was fluent in. "Well, I'm not exactly twelve anymore, and even when I was twelve, you know I wasn't an innocent little thing on those streets when you adopted me. I'd been abused and used by men and women for years on the streets, and I'll forever thank you for saving me and my sisters.

But what I'm about to tell you is going to remind you of who I am, and what I'm capable of."

She switched back English. "We are trying to get this professor away from his work. Away from the government who is trying to get him to do something that will ruin this world.

"I'm the best qualified person to get this professor's attention and convince him to leave."

Her father opened his mouth but she showed him the hand, halting whatever he was going to say.

"Dad, I told you about how I have memories from the future. I'm sure you don't believe me, but you have to believe one of these two things, because one of them is true.

"I either know this professor intimately sometime in the future, or I've had sex with this professor while I was student in the same school. One of those is true, and regardless of which is true, the fact is that I know him much better than anyone else and I'm convinced that I can at least get him to come away so that we can talk." She turned to Mason. "If I can't knock some sense into him or seduce him into it, do we have the ability to hold him against his will?"

Mason furrowed his eyebrows and gave Levi a look.

Her father stared at Alicia and shook his head. "Young lady, your attitude very much reminds me of Lucy, and that's not exactly a good thing. She's reckless to a fault."

"Hah!" Alicia scoffed. "You've been with Lucy off and on for years, so I take that as a compliment. And besides, you need women in your life that challenge you."

Her father snorted and then sighed. "What in the world am I going to do with you?"

Mason stood and looked back and forth between father and daughter. "You can work out between the two of you whatever you want, we're not making any calls just yet anyway. Levi, I need you to take Alicia to the local safe house, transport is ready for you in the garage attached to this building." He turned to Alicia. "It's best you aren't seen on the streets until we get a better idea of what's going on and if those FBI agents who tried to take you are just the tip of the spear." He shifted his gaze back to Levi and said, "I'm going to talk with Brice and see what kind of intel he's picked up. Tomorrow morning at nine a.m., let's meet at the Rooster and Bull. I'll have you introduce your daughter to what the Outfit is all about. And we'll have a mission meeting at headquarters. Any questions?"

They both shook their heads.

"Good." Mason hitched his thumb toward the door and said, "Get going, so I can tell General Owens he can have his conference room back."

Alicia got up and her father offered her his arm. She took it and grinned. "You're not mad at him, are you?" She asked in Mandarin.

"Of course not, you've always been bull-headed, yet generally responsible." Levi glanced at Mason as they walked to the door. "You should probably know something about Doug Mason."

"What's that?"

Mason called out in perfect Mandarin, "I also speak Mandarin."

Michael sat in the small conference room in the lab, it had been constructed as a private sound-proof alcove where Michael or Josh would have conversations with folks in DC. It was particularly useful when topics would come up that weren't appropriate for everyone else in the lab to listen in on. More often than not, the topics would be discussions about personnel, funding, or prioritizing next steps on research. Today, the DC folks had set up this meeting only with him.

"We currently have thirteen full-time salaried engineers and scientists on Project Morpheus, and we've gotten approval for scaling our efforts out, per your plan, Professor Salomon. This is going to be an inflection point on the evolution of the project. With the large expansion, and the multiple facilities and ground stations needed, the DoD has requested a consolidation of key personnel to the DC metro area."

The DoD was the Department of Defense, the ultimate holder of the purse strings for DARPA and this project.

Michael frowned at the speakerphone. "Before we go into the whole DC metro discussion, can someone tell me why in the world we think there's a need for a huge scale out effort? My plans didn't require it. What's this expansion going to accomplish?"

"Dr. Salomon, it's Carl—"

"Hold up, Carl." Carl "Red Eye" Sundenbach was one of Michael's least favorite people on the DARPA side of the team. He was quiet, the opposite of a people person, and there was something about his personality that irked him. Nonetheless, he was at every single meeting, without fail, and even though he said almost nothing during any of those meetings, the few times he spoke, it was clear he'd been paying careful attention. "Carl, explain what the purpose is of this expansion. One of your folks on the call even spoke of ground stations, that implies—"

"Yes, we're going all the way." Carl replied. *"We're committing space probe launches for the upcoming tests."*

Percy's ears perked up as Michael's eyes widened. "Woah, you guys want to go straight to in-space testing? That was like phase five of my plan. We haven't yet proven out that the time shifts are directly related to the speed of the tachyon stream. It's just a working hypothesis from my first set of experiments."

"I realize that this might be a surprise, but all I can say is that the higher-ups have a lot of faith in your direction. But that also gives you an idea of why there's a move to coalesce resources in DC. Center of operations will be out of Quantico, since they have a lot of what's already needed. As to the mission control and space probe setup, there's work afoot already out of Cape Canaveral. That will be our sole remote location for this highly-sensitive project. Also, some of us have been working on a design for the space probe we plan on launching for a couple months now. We'd like you to come to DC, that way we can brief you on some of the work we've done and have you go over things. Obviously you'll want to take a tour of the facilities, and I can make arrangements for a house hunting trip."

Michael sighed as his mind drifted to his house. It had been a couple days since he'd learned of his family's death.

The FBI guys had filled in some of the blanks of what had

happened. Evidently the kidnappers were some kind of foreign agents, and the FBI believed that their location had been compromised, they raced across a highway during bad weather, crashed and rolled their SUV down an embankment, where the vehicle and its occupants caught fire, with no survivors.

Michael hadn't given a moment's thought to the state of his house, he frankly couldn't care less at this stage. The idea of going back there with all of the memories within those walls, and the indelible mental image of his wife and child being taken forcefully from it… it made him nauseous. "Carl, a trip to DC sounds fine. However, forget about the house hunting trip. When we move the project, I'll just rent an apartment. There's no need for me to have anything more than that."

"Okay, I'll pass that along to the girl who's going to book your flight. When can you come down?"

"How long do you think I'd need to be there initially? A couple days?"

"I'd say let's plan for you to be here for three days. That gives you time at the facility, you can meet some of the team you've only talked with on the phone, and you never know, you might change your mind on the house thing."

"I won't change my mind, but that's fine. Since I'm running another tachyon burst test tomorrow, how about any time after that? Also, when are you guys going to message the DC move to the rest of the team?"

"I'll talk to my management to make sure, but I think the e-mail is scheduled to go out some time after your test."

"Does anyone else on the team know yet? I don't like the

idea of knowing something that's going to mess with people's lives and them not knowing about it as well."

"Josh knows, but he's the only one local to you who does."

Of course, Josh knew. He'd probably known for a while and those hints of his about DC were just him not being very good about keeping a secret. "Okay, is there anything else for today?"

"Jennifer is going to call your cell phone when she's making the arrangements for your flight. Is your dog coming as well?"

"Yes." Michael glanced at Percy, who was sitting on one of the chairs as if he were part of the meeting. His ears swiveled a bit as he let out a yawn. "I prefer that he's with me."

"That's fine, I know how it is. Our pets are part of the family. Realize that because of the security concerns, you'll also be accompanied by a couple of plain-clothed US Marshals. They'll be the ones to not only take you to the airport, but they'll accompany you on the plane, and I'm sure there'll be some kind of hand-off occurring at the destination airport, but the Marshals can fill you in on that. That's obviously not my area of expertise. I look forward to having you local, it'll make things a lot easier. Talk to you later, professor."

Michael tapped on the speakerphone's end-call button and looked over at Percy. "Percy, what do you think about moving to DC?"

The dog's upper lip came up slightly as he bared his teeth.

In his mind he heard himself say, *"It'll be a cold day in hell before I move to DC."*

"I know, I know. I guess hell might be getting a cold front coming in."

Percy growled, baring his teeth and his jaw snapped loudly at the empty air as the puppy teetered and fell off the chair.

The world tilted as Michael was hit by a sudden bout of vertigo.

In his mind's eye he saw a cascading set of numbers scrolling across his vision, almost like a scene from the Matrix.

Dates… random numbers… and suddenly Michael found himself climbing out of the back seat of an Uber in some rural place he didn't recognize.

He'd been given a business card with this address. An unlikely place in the middle of nowhere, but the thing that had made him come—the thing he couldn't ignore—it was the two locks of hair taped to the back of the card. One dark, the other finer and lighter in color. Both had smelled of lavender.

Percy shook his head rapidly, making a jangling noise with his chain.

Michael panned his gaze in every direction and spied a small gathering of people standing about a quarter-mile away in an empty field.

His wife and child were still alive, he knew it, and with a surge of energy, Michael raced toward the group, his heart practically beating itself out of his chest.

Percy barked and ran alongside him.

Halfway to the group, Michael heard the screech of tires

and a set of loud thumps as two sedans swerved off of the road, aiming in his direction.

Gunfire erupted from the group in the field and Michael felt two impacts to his chest. One from behind, the other from the front.

Percy let out a cry of pain.

The world slowed as his long stride faltered.

A deep burning sensation bloomed from within him and he sensed the coppery taste of blood in his mouth.

The world tilted as more gunfire erupted.

Michael tried to look at the group, to see if Maria and Felicia were there, but he somehow found himself laying face up on the ground, staring up at the sky as the world darkened and went black.

Michael gasped as the conference room reappeared in front of him.

He lurched upward, smacking his head on the conference room table, and spied Percy lying on the floor, convulsing.

Ignoring the dizziness and nausea he felt, Michael scrambled to the dog and whispered, “Percy, it’s me.” He clamped his hand onto the dog’s rear haunch and shook him lightly. “Come on, big boy! What’s wrong?”

Suddenly the dog’s body stiffened and he threw up whatever had been in his stomach, scrambling to his feet, dazed and wide-eyed.

As the nightmarish sensation of his last moments on Earth replayed in his head, Michael focused on the dog as it staggered over to him, whining in doggie words as if trying to communicate what had happened. "Did you have a vision as well?"

The dog made a non-committal huff as he carefully sidestepped where he'd been sick all over the carpeting, and tried licking him on the face.

"Ew, Percy, you're going to make me throw up as well." Michael stood on shaky legs and said, "This room is starting to stink. Let's get some fresh air, I think we both need it."

As he opened the conference room door and breathed in the relatively clean air of the lab, Michael couldn't help but shudder at the strange dream. A mixture of nightmare and wishful thinking.

Grabbing ahold of the edge of one of the computer racks, Michael steadied himself as a flood images and emotions washed over him.

What the hell did he just see?

He'd heard of psychotic breaks in people who had undergone trauma. Whether at war or even the death of a loved one. But he never imagined that he'd experience something like what he'd just seen.

The tombstone of his baby girl loomed large in his mind, and even though it hadn't come to pass, it could have.

Had he actually seen a glimpse of the future?

A possible future, maybe…

No, it couldn't be. He had seen their charred remains.

It was probably some kind of psychotic episode.

Michael suddenly felt a chill as he imagined that admitting he'd had such a thing might be cause for him to lose his security clearance. Would these people still trust him if he was having nightmarish visions in the middle of the day?

He pulled in a deep breath and let it out slowly, trying to loosen what felt like a tightening band of steel around his chest

Maybe a move to DC was exactly what he needed. Get away from everything in this state. It all reminded him of his family. There was one thing he knew that would get rid of these thoughts, and it was pouring himself into his work.

It might be the only way to keep him from going crazy.

Having only been in DC once before, Alicia stared at her surroundings as her father drove his rental past Lincoln Park, through the National Mall, past Foggy Bottom and finally she saw a sign saying they were entering old Georgetown. "Where exactly is it that we're going?"

Levi glanced at her and shook his head. "Pull your hoodie up. There's cameras everywhere and the last thing we need is your face appearing on some computer's pattern matcher."

Alicia pulled forward on her hoodie and adjusted the air vents for the air condition so that it blew directly into her face. The idea of wearing a hoodie in the summer wasn't exactly Alicia's idea of sensible attire, but even if her father didn't realize it, she knew in her bones that there were people in the intelligence community looking for her. She was most definitely persona-non-grata in the future and she'd been caught illegally transmitting thoughts to unauthorized times and locations.

"As to where we're going, I explained it before… this is where things started for me. And I suppose Mason thinks it's a good idea that you be involved with this particular case—at least while we're trying to figure out who is after you."

Her father pulled into an open spot on the side of the road and they both hopped out of the car.

As she pulled the hood of her sweatshirt forward, he put coins in the parking meter and motioned for her to follow him.

An old man in dirty threadbare clothing yelled across the street, "Do you have any food I can have?"

They both continued walking south on 31st Street and she spotted a sign up ahead featuring a profile of a rooster on the left, the head of a longhorn bull on the right. The area wasn't exactly upscale, to say the least. Her father paused underneath the sign, opened the door and motioned for her to enter.

Alicia walked into the dive bar and was hit with the smells of stale beer and wood polish.

The place was like any other dingy bar, not that she had that much experience in such things, but it fit the description of the few that she knew about. The place was dimly lit, had a few tables and booths, and there was a gray-haired man behind the counter toweling a glass dry who looked in their direction and nodded.

It was obviously a slow time of the day, as there was nobody else in this place but the one man sitting at the bar, wearing a suit. He turned and Alicia immediately recognized the pale eyes and short stature of Doug Mason.

He hopped off the stool and motioned for them to approach.

Mason offered her his hand and just as she was going to shake it, she noticed the glint of metal and grabbed the edge of the challenge coin.

It took only a second for the Eye of Providence to light up and Mason repeated the motion with her father, yielding the same results.

Mason shifted his attention to Alicia and grinned. "Welcome to our headquarters, young lady. What do you think?"

Alicia looked around at the less than impressive environment and grinned weakly. "Okay, I suppose. I guess I would have expected something a bit more…" She wiped her finger on the edge of the bar. "Oh, I don't know—clean?"

He chuckled and motioned for her to follow. "Come with me, your father has already been through this, so this will be fun."

Alicia glanced at her father who was wearing his practiced emotionless expression, but she could tell he was amused. His facial muscles were relaxed, except at the top of his cheeks, a sure sign that he was trying not to smile.

Mason opened the men's bathroom door and motioned for her to enter.

With a confused expression, Alicia walked into a men's bathroom for the first time in her life.

Three closed stalls and two urinals were lined up on one wall, with an "Out of Order" sign taped to the door of the farthest stall.

She stared at the urinals, never having seen one before and said, "So is that where you guys pee, instead of urinating in the toilet like a civilized person?"

Her father chuckled and shook his head.

Mason held an amused expression as he watched Alicia take in the details of the restroom.

She shifted her gaze to the sinks, where a white-haired man sat on a stool, dressed in tan slacks and a plaid button-down shirt. He nodded at Mason, then looked over his John Lennon-styled spectacles at Alicia.

"Is this the new girl, the one that's replacing the Black Widow?"

Levi shook his head. "No, she's just here for a temp assignment."

"Temp assignment?" The old man snorted and shook his head. He muttered something about Molly Maids and gave her a withering stare.

"What is this?" Alicia asked. "Why are we gathered in a bathroom with an old guy giving me the stinkeye?"

"Who you calling old?" said the white-haired man, crossing his arms.

"I wouldn't recommend pissing Harold off," said Mason. "He might give you the wrong one."

"The wrong what?" Alicia asked.

"The wrong towel. It's only happened once or twice," Mason said. He accepted the towel that Harold was holding out to him, then went into the stall marked "Out of Order." "At least, that's what I've heard," he added as the door closed behind him.

From inside the stall came a loud metallic click followed by a long whooshing sound.

"Those rumors were never substantiated," Harold said

loudly over the din of the flushing toilet. He held out another towel.

Her father motioned for Alicia to take it, so she did. It was heavier than she expected, but otherwise it was soft and fluffy and… well, a towel.

Her father pushed open the door to the out-of-order stall. Mason wasn't inside. The stall was empty.

"What in the world?" Alicia said. She glanced at her towel. Was this place some kind of bizarre entrance?

"Put the towel on the lever and flush," her father said. "But make sure the towel is in contact with the lever when you press down."

Alicia stepped into the stall and shut the door behind her. She inspected the toilet, looking behind the tank and around the underside of the bowl. It looked like an ordinary toilet. She felt the towel in both hands, running it through her fingers, feeling for anything out of the ordinary.

"Put the towel on the flushing lever," her father said from outside the stall.

Alicia did as she was told. "And just flush like normal?"

"That's the idea. I'll join you as soon as you're done."

"She's kind of slow, isn't she, that daughter of yours?" said Harold.

Alicia shook her head and pushed down on the lever.

CHAPTER FOURTEEN

The instant the toilet flushed, the floor dropped—taking Alicia and the toilet with it. She put her hands on the tank to steady herself as she dropped down some kind of elevator shaft.

Her stomach lurched and her eyes widened as the brown walls of the toilet stall had been replaced by a blur of slate-gray concrete marked with alternating yellow and black stripes.

Then the walls fell away and the toilet-elevator slowed nearly to a stop, forcing Alicia to focus on her balance as she descended into a featureless room about as large as the restroom above. The entire rig settled into a recess in the floor, and stopped.

"Surprised?"

Alicia turned to see Mason smiling at her. "You could say that."

"Step over here."

As soon as Alicia's feet cleared the platform, it launched

itself upward, toilet and all, disappearing into the ceiling. A series of clicks echoed down the shaft as it locked into place above.

Alicia shook her head and looked around. She stood in an empty, featureless room. There was a wastebasket filled with hand towels, but that was it. The only exit—other than back up the shaft, if that was an option—was a plain steel door. A panel beside it featured a stenciled outline of a hand.

This entire place reminded Alicia of a fallout shelter one of the neighboring farms had built back during the 1950s. The air carried a musty scent and the aroma reminded her of an abandoned warehouse.

Hydraulic pistons hissed, and the toilet platform descended once again, bringing her father with it.

Alicia frowned. "Okay, I'm starting to get a definite top secret 007 vibe out of this place." She gave her father a sidelong glance and smiled. "Kind of cool."

"Young lady, you have an interesting reaction to challenging environments. It does remind me a bit of your father." Mason looked over at Levi and grinned.

Her father shook his head. "She has a bit too much influence from Lucy, I'm afraid."

Before Alicia could say anything in response, Mason motioned for her to follow as he walked toward the large steel door. "You're about to see something that very few people have ever seen before. That would be the Outfit's inner sanctum."

"The Outfit?"

"That's the name of the organization Director Mason and I work for."

"Not a particularly snazzy name, if you ask me." Alicia frowned, showing a bit of disapproval. "You need to hire some marketing people to come up with a better name."

"Yes, well not everything can get a sexy name—"

"What about that Black Widow person Harold mentioned. That's a sexy name. Is that like some kind of call sign?"

"Let's keep the spiders out of this for now," her father motioned in the direction of the steel door. "Let's not stand around here with our thumbs up our butts."

Alicia watched as Mason stepped up to the door and placed his palm on the smooth panel. A blue line passed back and forth underneath his hand, a green LED flashed, and a click echoed from inside the wall. The director stepped back, and three massive locking bolts slid out of their retaining blocks on the right side of the door.

"Stand clear," a digitized voice warned, and the door slowly opened outward.

Alicia stared in awe at the immensity of the object moving, seemingly of its own accord.

Mason rapped his knuckles on the side of the door as it swung open. "Four feet thick, tungsten-steel alloy. This thing will stand up to a nuclear blast. Just don't get your fingers caught in it while it's closing. You'll be using your toes to paint with for the rest of your life."

Alicia looked past the door and saw a plain concrete corridor that seemed to run straight for at least one hundred feet.

"How in the world did you get this giant door down here? Alica asked.

Mason led them through the door and down a plain, concrete corridor lit by bright LED lights. "There's another shaft dug solely for the purpose of heavy transport. Still, it was no simple task. And I know, because they had to replace the original door about ten years ago. The thing weighs eighteen tons."

"How long has this place been down here?"

"It was all dug out of the bedrock in the late nineteen fifties."

They turned the corner, and the hall ended at another door. Mason put his eye up to a box on the wall, and after a green light flashed, the door clicked.

Mason pushed it open. "Welcome to the Outfit's US headquarters, Miss Yoder."

Alicia stepped through.

She found herself standing on a metal walkway twenty feet above the floor of a room larger than most warehouses. Cubicles were arranged in a grid below her, stretching as far as she could see, with men and women working busily at computer screens or talking among themselves. Up here, at Alicia's level, metal walkways led to offices positioned all around the edges of the room, looking down on the central work area. Through the office windows, Alicia saw more people working at computers.

In the very center of the room, four huge display screens, each easily fifty feet across, hung from the ceiling, displaying information, maps, photographs, satellite feeds, and more.

"Why do I feel like I'm in the movie Men in Black and I'm the Asian and female Will Smith looking down into the headquarters? Next, you'll be telling me there really are aliens, and they work for you guys."

Her father furrowed his brows, and said, "What in the world are you talking about?"

"Your father probably never saw the movie." Mason laughed. "I totally see your point of view. Sadly, there's no aliens that I know of working in the Outfit."

Levi shrugged. "I don't know about aliens, but my reaction to this place was that it looked like a villain's lair out of a Bond film."

"You would, Dad. That's because you're old." Alicia said with a lop-sided grin. "If not MIB how about imagining that Mission Impossible had a headquarters, this is what it would probably look like."

"Yeah, whatever." Her father stepped around Alicia, and motioned at the expanse of activity ahead of them. "Whether it's aliens or bad guys, it might be a little weird at first, but you get used to it."

Alicia's eyes widened as she spotted a painted image of a giant eye on the ceiling. "What's the deal with the big eyeball surrounded by words in Latin? It looks like the logo we have on our paper money."

Mason nodded. “That’s the Eye of Providence. When our little organization was created, the founders created that logo since they felt it embodied who and what we are. Novus Ordo Seclorum means ‘New Order of the Ages,’ and Annuit Coeptis means ‘providence favors our undertaking.’”

“Hold on,” Alicia stared at the image and was certain she’d seen it all over DC in one form or another. “Are you saying the Outfit preceded the founding of this country?”

“Is that such a shock?” The director said with a note of amusement. “The original members of the Outfit were the Agents of the Revolution. It was actually the original name of our organization.”

“And what do the Agents of the Revolution do?” Alicia said it with as even a tone as she could muster despite her rising skepticism.

“Originally, the Outfit was formed around the time of the Revolutionary War,” Mason explained. “Hence the name. It started with a group of British officers that weren’t particularly loyal to the Crown, along with the members of the original Continental Congress. They saw the need for an organization that could do things that needed to be done… but which couldn’t be done in the view of the public.”

“Like what?” Alicia asked.

“Like assassinate the king of England.”

Alicia raised an eyebrow. “I’m pretty sure the king of England was never assassinated.”

Mason nodded. “The war ended before they got into position to pull it off. But it was in the works. At the time, it was believed that King George the Third was mentally ill. His son, George the Fourth, was old enough to take the throne, and he was a much gentler soul—a regular patron of the arts. Washington himself signed off on the operation.

“But that was just the beginning. After we’d won the war, the founding fathers knew they’d continue to need the Outfit. They’d seen how much arguing went on in Congress over even the simplest issues, and they realized that if they ever needed to act quickly, they’d have to be able to get around that bureaucratic nonsense.”

“So even back then, there was too much red tape.”

“Exactly,” Mason said. “The Outfit is a way to cut through all the nonsense for the betterment of all.

“But this is the US capitol. Everyone wants their hands in everything; they all want their say in decisions. So we have one mandate: if it’s actionable, we act. It’s as simple as that. We don’t need to build an airtight case for court, and we don’t need to convince politicians somewhere on some golf course that a particular target needs taking out. We just do it.”

A sense of curiosity welled up within Alicia. “That sounds dangerous. Like an anarchist’s wet dream. What about if you’re wrong, or one of your people goes rogue and abuses his power?”

"Do we really need to go into this with Alicia?" Her father's furrowed eyebrows were an easy tell for anyone that he was getting annoyed.

Mason shrugged. "Alicia and I have talked. She understands the need for secrecy, and since she might be helping us with our problem with the professor, so I'd rather she be aware of what it is she's temporarily involved in."

"Dad." Alicia turned to her father and felt a surge of emotion. "Please, I just want to understand. You don't know how long I've wanted to know what it is you do, and this is just so damned cool. Please, I'll stop asking dumb questions, but let me soak it in."

Her father lightly grabbed the back of her neck, and for a second, playfully roughhoused with her like he used to when she was little. "Fine, but remember… when this is all over—you have another life to live. This isn't it."

"Dad, I know…"

"You asked about a rogue agent?" Mason shook his head. "It's never happened. As to whether we make the right call, of course we need to be positive that we're on the side of the angels before any action takes place. The difference is we don't need to convince layers and layers of bureaucrats. We just get clearance from within the group."

Alicia stared wide-eyed at Mason. "It's hard to imagine you never had a bad egg in the group."

"Well, it's true." Mason motioned to the far end of the cavern-like interior. "On the far side we have conference rooms. I've reserved conference room C3, your father will take you over there and I'll gather Brice so we can get this started. Any questions?"

Alicia shook her head.

Her father led her down the stairs as Mason walked off in another direction. He was talking to her, but Alicia barely acknowledged what he was saying as she felt a tingling sensation from head to toe. If there was a way to measure excitement, she knew hers was off the charts, and the idea that she was in this secret place with her father was so beyond anything she'd imagined, it took everything she had not to burst at the seams.

The only thing that tempered her excitement was the idea that Michael may never believe anything she said if he hadn't received his memories from the future.

Would she have to kill him herself to stop what was coming?

Alicia had been sitting patiently at the conference room table for what seemed to be almost half an hour. She looked over at her father who'd closed his eyes, and she could tell from his deep breathing that he was meditating on something. She'd seen him do it countless times. He'd one time said that his technique of meditation felt almost like an out-of-body experience, and he usually used it when he needed to concentrate on a problem. She'd asked him to teach her how to do it before she went to college, since it seemed like might come in handy for her classes, but those lessons were one of the few he'd given her that hadn't stuck.

Alicia had seen him sit and focus for an entire day without even so much as twitching a muscle. She had no idea what problem he was noodling on, but maybe it was as simple as a cheat for letting the time pass more quickly.

Just as her patience was waning, she heard a beep at the door and a slightly overweight man wearing glasses walked into the room carrying a laptop. Immediately behind him was Doug Mason.

Her father's eyes opened and he said, "Brice, are we ready to start?"

Brice plugged his laptop into the electrical outlet on the center of the table, and then plugged another wire into his computer. "Let me share my screen, it'll be easier that way."

As a projector from the ceiling lowered into position, the forty-something year old leaned across the table and shook hands with Alicia. "Hi, I'm Marty Brice. You must be Alicia, that daughter I've heard so much about."

"Brice is our chief technologist." Mason said as the projector began beaming an image on the far wall of the conference room. He turned back to Brice and said, "Levi and Alicia need a quick intro into what I asked you to do before we dive in."

"Right." Brice sat down and pulled up a document on the computer.

Alicia focused on the image projected on the wall, it looked like a bunch of typed up notes.

"I was asked to gather as much intel as I could about a Princeton professor by the name of Michael Salomon. Setting aside his normal CV stuff about what colleges and papers he's written, I focused more on the most recent stuff. Who was he acquainted with and who were they talking with, and about what.

"Let me go ahead and summarize what I learned. Our man is under FBI protection, but that protection is not on any of the official high side or low side e-mail traffic."

Alicia raised her hand. "High side? Low side?"

Her father turned to her and said, "Think of the high side as the place where all the top secret type of stuff resides, and the low side is where you'd find more mundane things that aren't necessarily a government secret."

"Right." Brice nodded. "Like I was saying, I searched on all of the internal networks, regardless of classification, and I found no orders of protection for the professor. However, I have surveillance footage that confirms he's being accompanied by FBI agents practically twenty-four-seven, and they've sequestered him in a nearby hotel with several other members of his team.

"This is where things get murky. Whatever this guy is working on, it's not on the system. I've managed to listen in on some conversations coming out of the DC area from the professor's DARPA associates, and none of the stuff they talk about is ever written down anywhere I've been able to see. It's very weird. Because you know that professor is generating some kind of e-mail or document traffic. My suspicion is that they are working on something that's on an isolated network, and none of my spiders crawling the web have found entry points into their network. At least not yet. It may be that the network is completely cut off from all other internet traffic, and that means even the intelligence community's network backbone. That's possible, but I'll say this, I've only once ever run into such a project, and it was having to do with a rogue intelligence agent who really knew what he was doing. He'd set up his own network and was manually migrating things from high side secure content to his own private network. If the people involved are doing that again, we'll need someone with physical access to their network to figure out what these people are talking about."

"Wouldn't Michael have access to that network?" Alicia asked.

Brice nodded. "I'd expect so, and before anyone jumps the gun and starts talking about acquiring our professor, let's peel the onion a bit.

"There were a couple of interesting tidbits I learned. Two main players are a SAC named Glen Bernstein and—" Brice shifted his gaze to Alicia. "Sorry, an S-A-C, or SAC is a Special Agent in Charge. Basically a high-ranking FBI official. He's evidently in charge of the professor's physical security, but from what I can tell he's mostly working through others. There's another involved person named Jason Whitley, also an FBI agent. He's interesting, in that Glen seems to use Jason as his eyes and ears when it comes to the professor." Brice scrolled down the document until he reached what looked like a transcript of a conversation and pointed at the screen. "Here you can see an annotated transcript of a conversation I caught between those two."

. . .

[SAC Glen Bernstein] *"What do you mean there's nothing in Professor Salomon's bedroom closet? Our crew inventoried the entire house before closing it up, didn't we?"*

[AGT Jason Whitley] *"Glen, I don't know what to tell you. I'm standing in the middle of the man's walk-in closet and there's nothing here. I don't have the original inventory list on me, but I'm pretty sure I'd remember a totally empty master bedroom closet coming up on the report. That stuff sort of stands out. And besides, this entire bedroom has been wiped clean. Someone definitely came in and emptied it."*

...

[SAC Glen Bernstein] *"Are you freaking kidding me? Jason, this absolutely blows. We need that house re-inventoried, and compare it against what had been there. If someone's taken stuff, I want to know where it is, and why. We might have control over the professor, but his damned wife and kid are still a problem. Do you think he's a flight risk?"*

[AGT Jason Whitley] *"We don't think so. So far, he seems to be rather compliant."*

Alicia gasped. "Wife and kid? He has a wife and kid?" Noticing her father's look at her outburst, she took a deep breath said in a calmer voice, "I didn't think he had family at all."

"He does." Brice nodded. "But there's a missing person's report filed a couple months back."

How could she have not known? How could Michael have kept that from her? But if his wife and child were missing—and presumed dead—then after a decade, maybe his lack of candor made sense?

"Hold up," Levi pointed at the screen and frowned. "First, why the hell does this professor even need protection? What triggered that? And I assume the FBI has this professor's house under surveillance, and if someone took stuff out of that house, does that mean there's someone else involved in this other than the FBI? Is that boogieman the reason the wife and kid are missing as well? Any suspicions on who that boogieman might be?"

Brice grinned. "All good questions. As to why he needs protection, I wasn't able to dig up a solid answer, and that in and of itself is an answer. Any orders of protection go through channels, and it's usually not the FBI that would do that, it would go through the US Marshals service. The same path as witness protection might go. Either way, there's places where I have access to that would register that data. I found nothing. So either they have a new place to register protection orders, which I doubt, or this is being done in some unofficial capacity."

"Is that normal? An unofficial protection?" Alicia asked.

"Not in the least is it normal." Brice said as he squinted at the screen. "So Levi, I don't *know* why he's being protected is the simple answer. I can guess that if the wife and child are missing, the FBI could have used that as a pretense to put him under protection. That, however is complete speculation on my part.

"I can say that the agents around the professor are legit agents of the FBI, so whoever is enabling this is someone higher up the food chain than this SAC I caught on the phone. As to who emptied the house, I have no idea. There's no surveillance data on the house, and any trail I looked at came up empty. It might have been robbed, or there is a boogieman, and he's gotten very lucky and managed to evade the FBI."

"Or she's gotten lucky." Alicia grinned. "Women are quite capable of doing some of these things."

Her father laughed and pointed in Brice's direction. "Alicia, Brice knows very well what women are capable of. He's married to that woman you thought had a cool call sign."

"The Black Widow?" Alicia asked.

Brice's face turned a bit pink as he nodded. "Nowadays she prefers the name, Annie." He cleared his throat and scrolled to the next page of notes and more transcript. "This one mentions you, Alicia."

[SAC Glen Bernstein] *"Jason, what's the story with this Alicia Yoder? Your guys were supposed to get her, so what gives?"*

[AGT Jason Whitley] *"Nothing good on that end. The girl hasn't been seen in a couple days, and the folks I sent over... well, I don't know. I've tried reaching out to them, but their phone must be off."*

"Those guys who tried to get me in the dorms were from the FBI?" Alicia asked, her eyes getting wider.

Brice nodded. "I'm afraid so. And this also confirms not only that we correctly ID'd them, but that this thing they have with you is absolutely off the books. I've scoured every government computer for information on those two clowns that they sent after you. No orders for them to go anywhere near New Jersey, much less get custody of a student. They were both out of the Arlington, Virginia area."

Alicia noticed her father staring at the screen, his jaw muscles bunched up, but he remained silent. He was fuming. She'd never seen her father outwardly angry in her life, but she could imagine what it might be like. A cold and calculated fury. When she was still on the streets as a little girl, before her father came into her life, she'd dreamt of killing the men and women who'd taken advantage of her. At the time, she was too small to have acted on those desires.

She imagined that, like her father, she was capable of great destruction when properly motivated.

[SAC Glen Bernstein] *"Damn it all to hell, why can't I catch any kind of break? We've got a direct connection now between our professor and this Alicia chick. Somehow they know of each other and he tried calling her."*

[AGT Jason Whitley] *"Listen Glen, we've been watching him like a hawk. I have no idea how she might have gotten her hooks into him."*

. . .

"He tried calling me?" Alicia stared at the screen. "Oh, my old number. I made him take a picture of my contact screen. He probably tried to call my old cell phone which I dumped back at school when you guys gave me the new one."

Her father leaned back in his chair. "The FBI is definitely monitoring our professor's communications. I didn't think you could do that without a warrant." He looked in Brice's direction. "Any warrants?"

Brice shook his head. "Nothing I could find. The whole thing stinks. This isn't the way things are ever done."

Alicia looked over at Mason and they both smirked. Both of them knew that in the future, this was the only way things were done. There was no privacy, not even for your own thoughts.

[SAC Glen Bernstein] *"Fine, keep trying to find that girl. We need her under our control and out of the way. I think I have an almost air-tight case for accelerating the move to DC—"*

[AGT Jason Whitley] *"Glen, you might want to double check that plan. I have direct from the horse's mouth that says our guy won't go to DC."*

[SAC Glen Bernstein] *"Why? What the hell's his problem with DC?"*

[AGT Jason Whitley] *"He's still holding out hope for his wife and kid reappearing."*

[SAC Glen Bernstein] *"I see. Well, maybe I'll have to break the news to him."*

[AGT Jason Whitley] *"What news?"*

[SAC Glen Bernstein] *"Never mind, I'll handle it."*

"*'I'll have to break the news to him'* What the hell does that mean?" Levi asked. "Is there any data on his wife and kid?"

Brice shook his head. "Those two have become ghosts. I don't know what happened, or what he meant by that. But there is something interesting about this Agent Whitley. The guy clearly stated that he has direct interaction with the professor. I pulled up Whitley's file and since I have some voice prints, I verified that someone who looks a lot like the agent was seen coming and going from Jadwin Hall on the Princeton campus.

"That same agent is also listed as a grad student at Princeton University under the name Joshua Whitley. The same Joshua Whitley who a handful of months ago got himself assigned as a grad student assistant to none other than Professor Michael Salomon. I'll note that he was embedded with the professor before the birth of his only child, so it was certainly ahead of any of the possible missing persons events. These guys have had their eyes on the professor for a while. In fact, I did some digging and I think this Josh guy ended being what brought the DARPA guys into this project. Even though the transcript statement of the person talking claims to be someone named Ken Lee, it turns out the voice print I listened to matched that of Agent Whitley."

[DARPA - Dr. Carl Sundenbach] *"Ken, are you sure about this?"*

[AGT Jason Whitley] *"I'm one-hundred percent sure. We have managed to detect tachyon particles in our vacuum chamber by their Cherenkov radiation. I figured you're the person who should know. I think if you reach out to the Professor Salomon at Princeton, he'd be amenable to working with the US government on furthering the research."*

[DARPA - Dr. Carl Sundenbach] *"And you are who, again?"*

[AGT Jason Whitley] *"Ken Lee, I'm a post-grad researcher on Professor Salomon's team.*

[DARPA - Dr. Carl Sundenbach] *"Well, I will be sure to take this up with some others and you might be hearing from us. Thanks for the call."*

"I'd also add," Brice said, "that I looked up Ken Lee to find any association with the professor and it turned out he was a post-grad researcher working for Professor Salomon. He'd died in a car crash sometime in the last couple months."

"People keep disappearing and dying around this professor." Mason noted. "I'm sure our professor would just love to hear that he has FBI spies among his engineers." Mason noted. "What do we know about the professor's whereabouts and protection?" He shifted his gaze to Levi. "And based on what we know, what are we dealing with if we wanted to get an extraction team going?"

Alicia looked back and forth between her father and Brice. An extraction team sounded like a military operation. Was that something her father actually did?

"I'd say we have a pretty easy route if we don't mind friendly fire on the FBI. He's best protected coming to and from his work. Full police escort, leading and trailing cars, as well as a contingent of FBI agents in his vehicle. I'd say his time at the hotel might be the least protected, because from what I can see, there are routes where you'd only have to deal with a handful of agents in a stealth extraction. But there's a problem and maybe an opportunity. Just a little bit before this meeting, our professor had a flight to DC confirmed for the day after tomorrow. Even though I see nothing official, you'd have to imagine there's an armed escort involved."

Alicia's father leaned forward in his chair and focused on Brice. "Can you have eyes on him at the airport when he lands?"

Brice nodded.

"I suppose it depends on who's accompanying him, we have to presume the worst and say he's got FBI or US Marshals as an escort, but maybe he won't. I can probably shadow him as long as you're my overwatch. I need eyes in the sky so I can see what's going on as things unfold."

Alicia looked over at her father, but Mason shook his head. "Alicia, before you even ask, it's my responsibility to keep you safe. We don't know the extent of the government's interest in you, so we have to assume everyone's got a little picture of you and is waiting for you to pop up somewhere."

"Wait a minute," Levi said with grin.

Alicia was staring at her father when their eyes met, and she could almost hear his thoughts as they shared a father-daughter connection. He understood her better than anyone ever had. She was doing everything in her power not to be unreasonable, but she *really* wanted to get involved in getting Michael out of his situation.

Her father winked at her and shifted his gaze back to the other two men. "Mason, I'll have a list of a couple people I'd like on an extraction team. I don't know if we'll use them, but I'll need them at the ready."

The director pursed his lips for a second before nodding. "I can do that. Just send me the list of who you need."

Levi pointed at Brice. "Obviously if you manage to hear anything about itineraries or anything that implies where he's going in the area before he gets here, I'll want to know. But as long as you're in my ear feeding me decent intel, then we'll see what can be done. I have an idea or two and I'll keep Alicia out of harm's way." He turned to Alicia and said, "Are you ready to see what I really do for a living?"

Alicia nodded, and it took every ounce of her will-power not to clap excitedly like a little girl at the prospect of watching her father in action… and maybe even helping out in some small way.

She angrily wiped an unbidden tear from the corner of her eye and her father shook his head.

"Honey, don't get mad when your humanity peeks out from behind the curtain. It's a good thing to know it's still there. I think you'll be surprised by what I have planned."

"What are you planning?" Mason asked.

Her father harrumphed as he stared at his boss. "It's a surprise."

CHAPTER FIFTEEN

Alicia sat on the edge of the bed as she listened to her father talking on his cell phone.

"The Air Force Memorial in Arlington at three in the afternoon? Brice, are you sure?"

Alicia heard a muffled "Yes" and the rest of the response was too faint for her to hear as her father paced back and forth in the small apartment the Outfit provided him, which was just outside of the DC area.

"Have you been there? That place is wide open. There's no sneaking up to the memorial nor is anyone going to sneak away. We'll be two steps from the Pentagon and Arlington Cemetery. If anything goes sideways, that place will be swarming with Feds in no time." He nodded to something Brice must have said. "Okay, that works. Hey, have you heard from Mason at all today? No, he's ghosting me as well. Don't worry about it, I have what I need. You know how to get me if anything changes." Her father tossed his phone onto his bed and shifted his gaze to her. "Are you sure you still want to do a ride-along with me?"

"Absolutely." Alicia nodded. "What are we doing? How can I help?"

He pointed to the bathroom. "Go shower, and scrub whatever makeup or anything else you've got on you. We'll go from there."

"Dad!" She frowned. "I just spent thirty minutes putting my makeup on, why—"

"You'll see." He raised an eyebrow and shook his head. "Go get all that stuff off."

"Fine." Alicia huffed and pointed at the clothes she was wearing. "What about my clothes, is this okay?"

"Don't worry about the clothes, I'll come up with something more appropriate. Hey, did my mother ever show you how to make those figures out of sheets of paper?"

"You mean origami, Dad?"

"Yes, origami."

"She did. In fact, she said that you learned how to do it in Japan and taught her how to make all those different animals and shapes." Alicia said with some hesitation. "Why do you ask?"

"You'll see in a bit." He grabbed a large duffle bag from his closet and tossed it on the bed. "Go get yourself cleaned up, you'll see why I'm asking."

Alicia held a perplexed expression as her father began pulling out vacuum-sealed bags of clothes, a set of what looked like cases of makeup, and other things she'd never have expected to find in his apartment.

He gave her a sidelong glance. "Alicia, get washed up now or you're not going with me. I'm serious. Do it now."

Alicia grabbed a fresh towel and practically tripped over her own feet as she rushed to the bathroom to get washed up. She absolutely wanted to understand why her father had makeup kits, wigs, and hair extensions in that duffle bag.

What in the world were they going to be doing?

Mason peered through a set of high-powered binoculars at the building on Randolph Street. The target had men on all four sides of him as he was transferred out of a vehicle and walked the fifty feet to the nearest building entrance. It would have been a difficult shot, but not one that couldn't be made.

Very few people in the Outfit were still around from when he'd first been recruited to join. One of the things he'd brought to the table wasn't just his managerial skills, but his background as a military sniper. Buried somewhere up in his head, he replayed a memory of pulling out his trusty old M40 sniper rifle and making that very shot.

Through his scope, he could almost see the beginning of the bald spot the professor was developing as he walked from the parking lot toward the building.

He'd loaded his rifle with 200-grain rounds for a subsonic

flight downrange. That coupled with the suppressor and the noise from the mid-day traffic would give him a modicum of anonymity regarding the origin of his shot.

He glanced at the flags near the target, they were hanging limply against their flagpoles.

Go time.

Peering through the scope from his elevated position, he placed the buttstock firmly against his shoulder and rested his finger on the trigger.

The professor was a wide-open target as he walked along the sidewalk, the crown of his head lined up perfectly for a clean head shot.

He placed the crosshairs on the back of the man's head, adjusting slightly for the distance and pace of movement. It almost felt like time had slowed.

Each beat of his heart pushed blood through his body, imparting the slightest wobble to his aim. To compensate, he waited. Waited for the pause between heartbeats, and when his aim recovered from the almost imperceptible wobble, the crosshairs settled on the target.

He squeezed the trigger. The rifle bucked back against his shoulder.

It took less than two seconds for the bullet to travel through the barrel, over the city streets and rush hour traffic, and slam into the back of the professor's head.

He dropped as if he were a marionette and someone had cut his strings.

. . .

That memory was from another time. Things were different this time. There were forces at play in the future who were adjusting strategies and sending back different tactics.

The multiverse he was in had shifted.

The memories he carried of having killed the professor were only a hint of what had been in one instance of an alternate reality. And a future reality was still trying to compensate. Trying to keep the status quo, while Mason and others in the future were trying to remedy the sins of the past.

The professor was no longer a sitting duck.

Today's elements of the FBI knew of the future, they must, otherwise things would still be as he remembered.

Someone from the future had reached out to the past and warned them.

Either way, him killing the professor hadn't done the world any good last time… the man's death was clearly insufficient to stop what was going to happen.

What were they missing? What else needed to be done to prevent the hellscape that the future would turn into?

There was only one person who actually had the answer to that question… and he had just walked into that building.

Sitting in the DARPA headquarters building in Arlington, Virginia, Michael watched with some level of amusement as Dr. Sundenbach, good ole Red Eye, showed a short video clip from a projector. It was giving a visual representation of a future stage of Project Morpheus. Even though the voice broadcasting from a hidden speaker on the projector had a metallic quality to it, it was obviously Carl's voice narrating the film.

"Today, lasers can be used to carry digital information from one point to another at the speed of light, but what if we could use our newly harnessed tachyon beams to transmit data from one time to another?"

A cartoon showed a modern scientist sending an e-mail, and the words on the e-mail were digitized and beamed from a satellite dish up into the sky, and suddenly the contents of the e-mail appeared on a scroll, in the hands of someone in Ancient Egypt.

It was a silly nonsensical thing, but it clearly showed a concept, not the reality of how it would work. A papyrus scroll obviously wouldn't suddenly appear out of nowhere with the e-mail's content, like shown on the cartoon.

Michael kept his sense of annoyance to himself, but the video was obviously a sign of what would happen to real science if you let the marketing people try to spin it for management's sake. The idea of dumbing things down for easy consumption was fine, but he hated the idea of giving inaccurate messages. Clearly others didn't have the same sensibilities.

Several graphics appeared on the screen with launch dates and coordinates peppering the illustration.

"For this reality to be achieved, we need to verify what has already been seen in a controlled lab environment. The relationship

between the speed of the tachyon beam and its ability to traverse time is understood, but not verified. To truly verify and fine tune our ability to control not only where the beam goes, but to -when- it goes, we need to launch a space probe to receive the beam. If we predict that the beam can travel back one year, the probe will need to be located where we were one year ago to receive it.

"Since our world is traveling through space at well over 300 kilometers per second, experiments with time greater than tiny fractions of a second could never be done on Earth. And that's why we must include these probe launches in our capital expense forecasts.

"Project Morpheus has an aggressive plan of five probe launches in the next four years. With each progressive test refining the calculations and enabling a way forward for us to possibly have the ability to reach back into our own time. Our own history.

"There are parallel efforts underway to explore how such a thing can be leveraged, both for national security purposes as well as humanitarian causes such as the eradication of modern diseases in the past.

"The possibilities are endless."

The film ended and Michael stared at the logo of the Defense Department. His mind drifted back to that college student and what she had said.

"I'm the one responsible for the memory externalization process, you're the one with the ability to send things across

time and space. Together we ruin this world. We have to stop this before it goes any further."

How could she have known? The only thing that made sense was that she was some kind of foreign spy. Someone who maybe was associated with his family's kidnappers. Or maybe just a student who'd heard one of the engineers talking and she had a wild imagination.

A while back, during a moment of weakness, he'd tried calling that number she'd shared with him. Nobody had answered, though the voice on the voice mail was the same girl's voice.

"Together we ruin this world."

Michael shook his head. It didn't matter. At this stage, whatever was happening was going to happen. There were enough people on the team and he'd documented enough of this so that even if he stopped work today, it would only slow things down. There was nothing he could do to stop the motion of progress.

The best thing he could do was to be involved and do the right thing. And the right thing was to pursue the science, and by earning everyone's trust, help influence how things got used.

It was the only way.

One of the men in the conference room said, "Now that we've seen the sales pitch for the higher-ups, how about we break for lunch?"

An FBI agent standing near the door to the conference room looked over at Michael and asked, "Professor, I think the schedule has you in Quantico this afternoon. You still want to visit the Air Force Memorial before we head out there? It's only a few minutes away from here."

Michael nodded. "I do. I long ago promised my grandfather I'd pay respects to his friend and fellow pilot if I was ever in the area."

"Roger that." The agent pulled out his phone and put it to his ear as everyone else got up from their seats.

Percy sat up and yawned as Michael pushed back from the table.

He gave the puppy a scratch on the top of his head and whispered, "Are you hungry, big boy?"

The dog thumped his tail loudly against the conference room furniture and let out a huff, as if to say, "Of course."

Grabbing his leash, Michael followed the other engineers out of the conference room, and looked forward to getting some fresh air.

He and Percy both needed it.

With a large array of makeup and costume paraphernalia on the bathroom counter, Alicia stood in front of the bathroom mirror, her hair still damp from the shower, wearing just her bra and pajama bottoms. She looked over at her father who'd stripped naked to his waist and was also in front of the mirror. She grinned, "Dad, you're the last person on Earth I was expecting to get a makeup lesson from, ever."

He chuckled and shifted the angle of an illuminated magnifying mirror he had on a gooseneck attachment. "Baby girl, a person in my field sometimes has to mask his Hollywood good looks and charm and be something he's not."

Alicia snorted and rolled her eyes.

"You'll see what it's like to take on a new persona, and it starts with the easy part—how you look."

"That's the easy part?"

"Sure," he responded. "You wouldn't believe how hard it is to take on someone else's identity. Imagine trying to act and talk like someone in their seventies. Including holding a conversation and using language that's appropriate for a different age. It's not as easy as you might imagine. But for now, we'll just focus on how you look. That's the only thing the FBI has to go on at this moment, and since we have to assume they might know you and I are related, then we're both going to end up looking and sounding a bit different when we're done."

Alicia stared at all the unfamiliar things on the double-sink counter and she felt a bit nervous. This wasn't as simple as a little eyeliner, blush, and lipstick. "Okay, where do we start?"

"As a girl, you probably wouldn't do this, but watch what I'm about to do."

Alicia stared wide-eyed as her father wet his hair in the bathroom sink, and then smoothed it back so that it lay tight against his scalp. Even though he was in his forties, he had the physique of someone in their prime, well-chiseled and a bit annoying how symmetric his musculature was. With her having one breast a cup larger than the other, symmetry, or lack thereof was a thing that she'd become a bit sensitive to. She stared at him and noticed something for the first time: unlike most white guys his age, he didn't have a single gray hair that she could see. "Dad, do you dye your hair?"

"No, and I won't for this disguise, you'll see."

"I mean, normally. You don't have any gray hair at all."

"I guess I'm just lucky. My mother has plenty for the both of us." He ripped open a package and pulled out a floppy flesh-colored piece of latex. "This is an untrimmed latex skullcap." Her father gazed into the bathroom mirror and carefully laid the thin, flesh-colored cap on his head. He took a small sharp pair of scissors and began explaining things as he did them. "Now I trim the edges, leaving just enough overlap with my skin to apply spirit gum and glue the edges down."

He tilted his head back and forth and side to side, examining his work in the mirror. "I'm looking to make sure the cap fits well and doesn't bunch up unnaturally anywhere. So far, so good. As soon as I'm done with my hair, you and I will both do our faces at the same time."

Alicia stared at her father, fascinated by the transformation happening in front of her. "So we are both aging up for this mission?"

Her father looked over at her and grinned. "Listen to my baby girl talking about missions. Yes, we're going to age quite a bit. Just watch. This stuff is called crepe wool." He opened another package and began teasing apart a braid of some sort of hair. "Actors tend to use the cheap stuff that's made of vegetable fibers, but I always look for a more realistic look, so this is actually plaited wool. As in from a sheep." He applied adhesive along the crown of his bald cap, cut a four-inch segment of the teased wool, and carefully placed the cut end against the tacky glue. "Now I wait a moment for this stuff to dry." He repeated the process until he had a semicircle of hair on the crown of his head.

With a makeup applicator he began patting himself with some powder. "This is translucent powder that I'm putting on any of the exposed glue. It'll help hide the edges of the cap. Now for a bit of styling."

Alicia watched as her father carefully combed the horseshoe of hair sticking up from the cap and, using an electric shaver, contoured it a bit so it lay correctly.

He turned to her and smiled. "So, what do you think?"

With her mouth hanging open, Alicia shook her head. "You look like a young Farmer Jenkins. It looks weird that you're bald but with a relatively young face."

"It can happen. I remember Mr. Jenkins began losing his hair when he was twenty. But you have a point. Now is time for both of us to start aging." He opened a jar and said, "We start with some foundation."

Alicia picked up the same jar next to her sink, opened it and looked over at what her father was doing.

"Take a wedge-shaped sponge and place a thin coat across your forehead, cheeks, and along your throat."

Alicia watched what her father did with practiced motions and she tried her best to follow along.

He looked over at her and said, "Hold your chin up." Her father began dabbing foundation onto her skin. "This changes the opacity of your skin and acts as a base layer to apply our changes." He looked at her from various angles and nodded his approval.

Alicia continued to watch and follow along as she grabbed a makeup brush and a plum-colored shader. With light taps, she tapped the brush against the powder-based makeup, and applied shadow to her temples, the hollows of her cheeks, her forehead wrinkles, under her eyes, and along some lines on her neck.

Her father glanced at her and evidently not seeing an issue continued applying makeup, without even looking at the mirror anymore.

"Dad, slow down, you've I guess done this a million times. I can't keep up."

"Sorry, honey. Now onto the highlights…"

Alicia applied highlights to her cheekbones, nasal folds, and forehead wrinkles.

"Now you softly blend the wrinkles to ease the contrast between the highlights and the shadows." He dabbed on a maroon effect and said, "This gives the illusion of broken capillaries on the nose, upper cheeks, and forehead."

She continued mimicking him and to her shock, saw herself slowly transforming into an older Asian woman.

"Now for some aging spots. Alicia, turn to me."

She did and he dabbed something on her face, and then focused a bit more on the back of her hands.

"This helps highlight the blood vessels on your hands, which will definitely be seen by others, so you want to have the subtle signs of age show even there."

Alicia looked in the mirror and didn't recognize herself. She turned to her father who was doing something to simulate bushy eyebrows and he'd completely changed his appearance.

The arguably good-looking, in-shape forty-something father of hers, was replaced with a ridiculously in-shape seventy-year-old. "Dad, this is so weird to see you like this."

He turned to Alicia, tilted his head as he looked at her and grinned. "I like it. We have some teeth discoloration work to do, and clothing adjustments, obviously, but I think we can pull this off."

Alicia frowned. "Um, Dad. You never really explained what it is we're pulling off."

He glanced at his wristwatch and said, "I'll explain in a bit. However, while I'm getting our wardrobe straightened out, you've got some airplane origami to work on."

"Airplane origami? Really?"

"Yes, really."

Alicia stared in awe at the three stainless steel arcs rising a couple hundred feet into the air. Her attention shifted past the structure and on the horizon she saw an immense building with an unmistakable five-sided design. The Pentagon wasn't quite a stone's throw away, but it was very close.

A man nearby was talking loudly to an older woman next to him who must have been hard of hearing since he pointed at the structure and said quite loudly, "Mom, those steel arcs remind me of the contrails from Dad's plane. Remember how he'd described how he and his buddies would do the bomb burst maneuver?"

There was a reasonable crowd of people milling about at

the memorial, maybe about two or three dozen people, most of them fairly silent in their own thoughts as the place seemed to be the kind of place for quiet contemplation.

"Kumiko, help me give these out as a thank you to coming and honoring our vets."

Alicia turned to her father, whose back was bent forward so much that he was forced to crane his neck to look straight ahead. They'd practiced their roles in the apartment, and as the elderly Japanese wife to a veteran, they made a very unobtrusive couple, and certainly not a pair of people that would set anyone on alert. He was wearing a U.S. Air Force Vietnam Veteran hat and had a grocery bag full of the gray paper planes they'd folded into intricate facsimiles of jets. She scooped up a handful of the planes out of the bag and watched as he shakily approached strangers.

"Thank you so much for coming, please, take a souvenir." His voice had a reedy and gravelly tone to it that was distinctly old-man style. "My wife and I are so happy you've come to visit and honor our fallen."

A young couple hesitated and finally accepted one of the planes. The young woman gushed as she studied the intricate paper art. "These are so beautiful. Thank you for your service."

Alicia followed her "frail husband" and helped give out some of the planes.

One man gave her father a crisp salute and smiled as he accepted the gift. "May I ask what unit you were with?"

"388th tactical. But that was a lifetime ago."

"Really? My father was in the 388th flying Phantoms out of Korat. Were you a pilot?"

Her father nodded. "The Phantom was after my time, young man. I mostly flew the Thunderchief back in '67. Please enjoy your time here." He glanced in Alicia's direction. "Come with me, Kumiko. It's getting warm."

Watching her father struggle with his walker, it reminded Alicia to take shorter, more hesitant steps as she followed him toward the memorial wall.

He whispered, "To the left."

She glanced in that direction and spotted a group of well-dressed men heading toward the memorial. Her eyes widened as Alicia spotted the familiar gait of the man she'd known for years. "It's him," she whispered, "he's the one wearing a light-colored polo."

"He'll probably head toward us. I'll start with his guards; you work toward the professor. Whether it's you or me who gets to him, do what you need to do."

Alicia had marked the nose of the specially-prepared paper plane and it was in the voluminous pocket of the shapeless gown she was wearing.

Her heart began thudding loudly and she felt butterflies in her stomach as the group headed straight for them.

Michael walked along the path up to the Air Force Memorial and smiled as he saw the three steel spires seemingly bursting out of the ground. The image immediately brought to mind the few times he'd gone to an air show where three Thunderbirds would zoom up into the sky, smoke trailing behind them and burst outward in an amazing display of aerial acrobatics.

One of the agents leading the group motioned toward the far end of the memorial and said, “The Medal of Honor recipients are inscribed on the wall over there.”

They moved as a group and he remembered his grandfather’s stories of the Vietnam War. He’d been a pilot, had run quite a few missions, and had downed a couple MiG-17s during his time out there.

There were several people reading the granite-etched inscriptions on the memorial and Michael walked up and began reading them as well.

One hit him particularly hard as he read it out loud, “Tell them that we gave our todays for their tomorrows.”

Michael felt his throat tighten at the sentiment and his mind drifted to his wife and child. Not everyone would have any tomorrows…

“Thank you for honoring our fallen.”

He glanced to his left and saw an older gentleman stooped over from age, holding himself up with his walker. He was a veteran. “Sir, I’m glad you made it home, and thank you for your service.” He moved to his right and spotted the name of Leo Thorsness. Michael’s eyes widened at seeing the name of the friend his grandfather had always talked about. His grandfather had described the man as “the damned luckiest, bravest, no-sense bastard hero he'd ever known.”

That was high praise from his grandfather, a man who didn’t think much of anyone’s accomplishments, including his own.

Michael hadn't realized that his grandfather's friend had been a Medal of Honor winner. That was a huge deal.

If only grandad was still alive, he would have loved to talk to him about that. Nevertheless, seeing his friend's name gave Michael a warm feeling of contentment.

"Sir."

Michael looked over at an old woman as she handed him a piece of origami in the shape of a jet. It was a small piece of paper artwork. He waved the offer away and smiled. "Thank you, but that's okay. You keep it."

"Please, as a memento of your friend who died. So you can remember being here." She offered once again the paper.

One of the agents approached and was about to shoo her away when Michael accepted the airplane with both hands and gave the Asian woman a small bow. "It's beautiful. Thank you." The woman's eyes teared up and her face contorted with barely contained emotions. He approached her and put his hand on her shoulder. "Is this plane something you made?" She whispered something he couldn't hear, so he leaned down and whispered, "Say again?"

The woman looked over at him and whispered, "Unfold it when you are alone. There's a message written inside that you must see." The woman shrugged off his arm, turned and hobbled over to the old man using a walker.

He looked at the paper plane and carefully placed it in his pocket as an agent came over and asked, "Are we done?"

Michael nodded and the four agents escorted him past the old couple, who were still giving away more of the pieces of origami to whoever was nearby.

He patted his pocket and wondered if the old woman was crazy or something important had just happened.

His heart began thudding loudly in his chest as he knew it would be many hours before he'd be alone.

"There's a message you must see inside it."

What could that message be?

CHAPTER SIXTEEN

Michael waited in the car at Gate Four, one of the entrances to Marine Base Quantico, as the agent in charge of his security paced back and forth, arguing with someone on the phone.

"Are you shitting me? The Inn is full? It wasn't full this morning... yes, but we didn't know for certain if we needed it, and now we do." The agent continued pacing and frowned as the crickets chirped loudly in the ever-deepening darkness of the evening.

Percy whined and put his chin on Michael's shoulder as he too stared out of the rolled down window, wondering what was going on.

The agent held a sour expression as he pocketed his cell phone, hopped into the front passenger's seat, and told the driver, "Let's turn around, go back up Russel Road and hang a left on Richmond Highway. Supposedly there's a Marriott about a mile away. It'll have to do."

The driver put the car into gear and remotely rolled up Michael's window as he did a U-turn, heading away from the Marine Base.

The agent in the front seat turned around and said, "Professor, it's late and we'll just have to make due with what we have. Tomorrow we'll figure out where we can get more controlled quarters for everyone on the detail."

Michael shrugged. "As long as they have a hot shower and a decent mattress, I'm good."

The agent pointed in Percy's direction and the dog immediately let out a low growl. "When the dog needs a bathroom break and you need to go walk him, make sure you call me."

Michael nodded and ran his fingers through Percy's fur, trying to calm him as the dog stared at the agent, ears lowered, and fur standing on end. Something about the way the agent had pointed at him had set the puppy on edge. The last thing Michael needed was a seventy-pound canine wanting to get a piece of the guy who's trying to keep him safe.

It took them no more than five minutes before Michael was handed a keycard for his hotel room and the agent said, "I'm in room 205. Remember, call me whenever you need. I or one of the other agents will be at your room right away to walk with you. You got it?"

"Sure." Michael nodded, fist-bumped the agent and walked in the direction that the lady at the front desk had told him his room was located.

He swiped his card into the lock, a tiny LED flashed green and he felt the crisp cool air of the air condition as he entered his room.

He and Percy were finally alone in the hotel room.

And despite being exhausted, he hadn't forgotten the odd encounter at the Air Force Memorial as he dug into his pants pocket and carefully extracted the folded-up piece of paper.

Taking a few seconds to find the light switches, he pulled the curtains to his room, locked the door and as Percy climbed up onto the bed and settled in for a nap, Michael carefully began unfolding the intricately constructed airplane.

Within seconds he noticed hints of some writing and what looked like money that had been used in the jet's construction.

It took him a full minute or so before he'd discombobulated the separate pieces of paper and realized the old woman had weaved a one-hundred-dollar bill into the plane's construction. As he turned over the blue piece of paper on which he'd spied some writing, he noticed it also had some tiny print from a laser printer.

The print looked like a fragment of some kind of transcript of a conversation.

[FBI Agent - Jason Whitley] *"We have managed to detect tachyon particles in our vacuum chamber by their Cherenkov radiation..."*

[DARPA - Dr. Carl Sundenbach] *"And you are who, again?"*

[FBI Agent - Jason Whitley] *"Ken Lee, I'm a post-grad researcher on Professor Salomon's team.*

[DARPA - Dr. Carl Sundenbach] *"Well, I will be sure to*

take this up with some others and you might be hearing from us. Thanks for the call."

Voice pattern analysis between Agent Whitley and Princeton graduate student "Josh Whitley" is a match.

Michael stared at the paper, his hand shaking with anger as the answers to questions he'd encountered months ago were suddenly revealed.

Of course Ken hadn't called Red Eye, he was physically incapable of it, yet Sundenbach wouldn't have had a clue about the deceased researcher's speech issues. It was Josh who'd alerted DARPA about his discovery.

An FBI agent posing as a grad student?

Percy sat up, sensing the anger building within him. He yipped a question at him.

"I don't know, Percy. I just don't know." He looked over at the dog and asked, "What if Ken's death wasn't an accident?"

Michael stared at the paper and noticed a handwritten address and time on the paper.

Three a.m. tonight.

The hairs on the back of Michael's neck stood on end as he thought of the likelihood of this being some kind of setup.

But the information made too much sense.

Josh's seemingly smooth transition from meek graduate student to confident navigator of government bureaucracy was too easy. And the whole Ken communicating to the DARPA folks had never been resolved to his satisfaction until now.

It made sense.

Who was going to be at this address?

He looked at his watch and grimaced. It was almost ten p.m., and from what he could tell, the address was somewhere in Arlington, which was about thirty minutes away.

The agents would never let him go.

Surely the old woman was just a way to get a message to him. It wasn't her or her elderly husband that he'd be meeting.

Who could it be? Someone trying to give him heads-up about something bad going on, more than likely. And if they knew about undercover agents and the conversation with Ken, these people had to work for the government. There was no other possibility.

Two factions in the government? Maybe…

And the FBI guys were not his friends, that much he'd already suspected, but the Josh thing clinched it.

Knowing about Josh, it seemed an impossibility that he could ever work with him again. There was no way.

He glanced at the paper and stared at the handwritten portion.

If he left at two in the morning… the FBI guys wouldn't know. He could scout out the area and see what it was about. And he had Percy with him, who'd tear chunks off of anyone who approached him with ill-intent.

Using an Uber had been stupid back in New Jersey. It would involve a credit card charge and he might not get lucky two times in a row. For all he knew, his credit card was being monitored at all times… was that even a thing? He had no idea. He'd only seen stuff like that on TV.

He held up the hundred-dollar-bill and grinned. Whoever

this was, they were probably thinking similar thoughts. He could call a cab and this would more than cover the round trip. And it would probably be untraceable.

He turned to Percy. "We could go out and come back before dawn. Nobody would be the wiser. What do you think?"

Percy looked at him, his tongue lolled out in a panting grin as he wagged his tail.

It was agreed.

Michael gazed longingly at the bed and reached over for the clock on the nightstand so he could set an alarm. "A couple hours of sleep and let's see what we can find out."

Sitting cross-legged in the back of a van during the wee hours of the morning with her father and Brice wasn't something Alicia had imagined herself ever doing. However, this was definitely starting to feel legitimately like some kind of secret spy mission. Her father had put in his "ears" and had an elastic band around his neck with a flat microphone sitting flush against his throat, as did she.

To add to the whole mysterious John Wick feel of everything happening around her, Brice resembled a mad scientist as he was mixing some concoction in a clear plastic cup. He looked over at her and asked, "Are you ready?"

Alicia prepared herself to be fitted with a custom earpiece. With her head tilted to the side, she brushed back her hair so her right ear was exposed to the roof, then held her breath. "Yes."

Brice approached with a bulb injector in one hand and a set of tweezers in the other. "Alicia, this stuff will feel weird as it fills your ear canal. Just don't move until I say so. We need this receiver to be aligned properly as the silicone sets. Understood?"

"Yup." Alicia responded, even though she was a bit freaked out about some goop being poured into her ear.

"Don't worry, this'll be over quickly."

With tweezers, Brice held a tiny electronic device in her ear while he injected the flesh-colored liquid silicone around the device. Alicia felt the goop expand, filling the gaps and crevices in her outer ear. The stuff was getting warmer as it lay there, feeling not unlike a bunch of bubbling snot that threatened to dribble out of her ear and into her hair.

"Okay, now just stay still for two minutes and you'll be set. Not too horrible, right?"

"It feels hot, and I can't hear anything through it. Are you sure it's working right?"

Brice chuckled. "Don't worry, that's normal. The silicone probably just oozed over the far end of the auditory tube. In another minute or so, the concoction will cure, I'll pull it out for you, shave the edges, and we'll test it out."

As the earpiece solidified, Alicia watched as her father popped out the magazine from his gun, chambered a round, and then seated it into his shoulder holster. Brice was also busy rummaging through a toolbox that was welded into the floor of the van. He pulled out a bag filled with oddly-shaped bent metal tubes whose ends were sharpened. "What's in that bag?"

"Oh, these?" He held up the bag. "They're caltrops.

They're for what I like to call 'oh crap' moments. Since these are made of hardened steel tubing, they're particularly good at blowing out tires."

"They're often used for area denial campaigns in wartime. Dump a bunch of those things and anything with normal wheels is going to have some issues trying to cross. It prevents regular vehicles from advancing on your position, and admittedly, it's less problematic than mines."

"Dad, how do you know about wartime uses of..." she forgot what Brice had called them. "Have you been to war?"

Her father shrugged and she knew he wasn't going to answer. Brice on the other hand approached her with a set of tweezers and said, "Assume your father has done a little bit of just about everything, and you'll probably be more right than wrong. Let's get that ear piece up and working so we can do a comms check."

"Is this a bit overkill for what you'd described as a pick-up/rescue mission?" Alicia asked.

"Honey, you can never be too prepared." Her father harrumphed as he drew a knife out of some sheath hidden under his dark-colored fatigues, and he examined its edge.

"You never know." Brice said in a calm, matter-of-fact tone. "The professor may resist coming with us, his dog might be an issue, he could be followed, any number of things might cause things to go awry and the last thing we need is to lose communication with each other, and if there's an enemy about, we don't want to telegraph what we're doing."

Brice popped the plug of form-fitting silicone out of

Alicia's ear, shaved off the excess, and handed the earpiece back. "Put it in, and let's test it out."

Alicia put the earpiece back in, and was surprised to find that she could barely even feel it in her ear.

Her father raised his voice and said, "Hey Walt, give us some comms chatter."

Walt was one of the Outfit's men and he was sitting up front in the driver's seat of the van, acting as this morning's driver.

"Testing one, two, three."

Brice touched his throat mic and said, *"Got it, testing four, five, six."*

"Mary had a little lamb, it sure was tasty." Her father said with a look of amusement.

All of their voices came through clearly in her earpiece.

"Do we have a thumbs-up on the chatter?" Brice asked.

Alicia gave a thumbs-up as did the others and Walt said through her earpiece, *"Imagine a big hairy Italian thumb sticking up."*

"Give me a mic check, Alicia. I haven't heard you yet." Brice pointed at Alicia and motioned for her to press the button on the elastic band that held her microphone flush against her throat.

Alicia press on the button and she felt it click. *"Am here."* Her voice crackled through her own earpiece, and the others nodded.

Her father's back stiffened and he put a cupped hand over his right ear. *"I just got word. Our professor is on the move."*

Alicia felt butterflies in her stomach like a school girl with a huge crush, which pissed her off. She knew that her feelings needed to be swatted to the side. This whole thing could go sideways in any number of ways.

Her father's brows furrowed as he focused on whatever was coming into his comms unit.

"He's been picked up by a yellow cab and nobody seems to be following the vehicle. So far, so good. However, our professor has a large German Shepherd with him." He looked over at Brice. *"Got anything, just in case. I'd rather not have to shoot it."*

Brice held up what looked like an unmarked shaving cream can and tossed it to her father, who snatched it in mid-air and attached it to his utility belt. *"And now we wait."*

"Mr. Jones," the cab driver glanced backward. "Are you sure this is the address you want to go to? I don't think there's any houses over there."

Percy whined next to Michael in the back seat of the cab, probably smelling the anxiety oozing from him as he studied their surroundings. "I'm sure."

He'd told the cabbie that his name was Jake Jones, thinking John Smith would obviously trigger some fake alert in the cabbie's mind. Mr. Jones was just as laughable, and Michael was having all sorts of self-doubt about heading out toward no man's land to meet someone who knew things they shouldn't know.

He'd turned his cell phone off, to make sure there was no

way for the FBI to find him, but as his doubt grew, he wondered how big of a mistake this all was. Maybe he should turn it back on?

As he was contemplating the wisdom of his choices, the cabbie said, “It looks like you’ve got a friend waiting for you.” The cab slowed to a stop and the driver put the car into park. “That’ll be thirty-two bucks.”

Michael paid the man and stared out the front window.

There was a large panel van parked alongside the road. A tall woman was standing by the vehicle, her arms crossed and it looked like she was staring directly back at him.

Michael stepped out of the cab, holding tightly to Percy’s leash, and before he could even close the rear passenger’s door, the cabbie took off with gravel kicking back from his rear tires.

Had something spooked him?

“Michael, I’m really glad to see that you came.” The woman called out and took a few steps forward.

Percy let out a low growl and that was enough to put Michael on alert.

The back of the van popped open and a man hopped out. He held his hands out to likely show he wasn’t actively seeking to harm anyone, but Michael saw the gun strapped to a shoulder holster, and knew that these people weren’t your run-of-the-mill government secretarial staff.

“My name is Levi, and we’re all here to get you and Percy to safety.” The man crouched down and held his hand out for Percy to sniff.

The dog’s ears were down low as he sniffed the air between them. The initial sniffing yielded no growling. Percy pulled at the leash, wanting to get closer, and at this stage, Michael figured the dog knew what he was doing better than he did.

The girl took a few steps closer and Percy shifted his attention to her, his hackles raised and he growled loudly.

Levi waved the woman back and spoke with a warm tone, "Percy, none of us mean you or your dad any harm."

The dog pulled and Michael slowly walked closer, all the while wishing he'd turned his cell phone back on. None of this seemed legit.

As Percy got within sniffing distance of the man's hand, the dog began wagging his tail harder and harder. After a few seconds, the dog cried and whined with excitement.

What the hell?

Michael's eyes widened as he watched his guard dog flipping out over the stranger. He sniffed, and then licked repeatedly at the man's hand as if it was made of some kind of treat.

Percy cried and nuzzled Levi's hands and shoes as the stranger stroked his head and looked up at Michael. "I represent an organization that looks out for when things go wrong within our government. Professor, I believe you want to come with us, for many reasons I can't yet get into, but primarily to stop what agents within our government are trying to do. If you come with us, I'll show you some things that will really tell you who you've been dealing with, and the lies they've been telling you."

Michael took a deep breath and let it out slowly. "Do you know what happened with Ken Lee?"

"Your former assistant?" Levi asked.

Michael nodded.

Levi stood and motioned for Michael to follow. "I read the report. He was killed in a car accident. Evidence seems to indicate that he'd been run off the road, but I saw no suspects listed. It's a case with nobody assigned to it."

Michael closed his eyes and recalled the moment when the head of his department told him what had happened to Ken.

"There's no good way to say this. He's dead...

"The police had told the school that there'd been a car accident and the wreck had been found at the bottom of the Delaware Raritan Canal off Old Lincoln Highway." Michael said it with a note of revulsion.

The woman came closer as they approached the opened back of the van. She was Asian and there was something very familiar about that face. She held out her hand and Percy didn't seem to have too much of a reaction. He still seemed to be preoccupied with the armed agent.

They shook hands and she asked, "Michael, do you remember me at all?"

The girl was young, too young for someone with such a serious expression, and then his eyes widened. "You're the girl from the school... Alicia, isn't it? You tried to warn me about the project I'm working on."

The girl suddenly had a teary-eyed expression as she nodded. "That was me."

An overweight man popped his head out from the back of

the van and motioned to the group. "Hi, I'm with these folks, but let's stop socializing and get going to somewhere that isn't in the middle of nowhere."

As soon as he said that, Michael panned his gaze over to his left and noticed the large empty field. His blood ran cold as a vision replayed in his mind.

He spied a small gathering of people standing about a quarter-mile away in an empty field.

Michael raced toward the group, his heart practically beating itself out of his chest.

Percy barked and ran alongside him.

Halfway to the group, Michael heard the screech of tires and a set of loud thumps as two sedans swerved off of the road, aiming in his direction.

Gunfire erupted from the group in the field and Michael felt two impacts to his chest. One from behind, the other from the front.

Percy let out a cry of pain.

Michael stared at the field and felt his chest tightening as he experienced the dread sense of déjà vu. He'd died in that field… or at least he had in that vision.

Seeing no other options, Michael rushed toward the back of the van and Percy hopped up into van as he climbed in, the others right behind him.

"Brice, we've got visitors!" Someone yelled from the front

compartment of the vehicle. Levi pulled the back door to the van closed as headlights appeared in the distance.

"Walt, get us out of here." Brice yelled as everyone grabbed ahold of a strap attached to the side of the van.

Michael grabbed Percy's metal collar as the van accelerated, fishtailing a bit before getting traction on the road.

Levi growled in his direction, "Do you have a phone on you?"

Michael handed it over to the intimidating man with the gun strapped to the side of his chest. He then handed it over to the pudgy guy.

Brice dumped the phone into a metal box and approached him with what looked like a handheld metal detector. "These guys have to be tracking you. Maybe the phone, maybe more than the phone."

Michael held up his arms and as the van swerved mightily to the right. Brice seemed unfazed by the chaos all around him as he continued to move the wand over him from head to toe, all the while his frown deepened. "I had the phone turned off, I thought that would be good enough."

"Clearly it wasn't," Levi said as the van took another sharp turn. The engine's whine echoing through the rear compartment.

Brice approached the dog with the detector, and Percy growled, not particularly happy about being unexpectedly thrown back and forth.

"It's okay, Percy. He's just checking you."

Brice extended the wand over Percy's head and the moment it got near the collar, it let out a tiny shriek. "Get that collar off. It's transmitting something, likely a tracking device."

Michael tried undoing the latch to the collar, but it seemed locked into the closed position.

As the van turned yet again, Brice reached forward with a set of wire cutters he'd pulled from his belt and with a grunt of effort snipped the metal collar off the dog.

The collar slid to the front of the van as the driver applied his brakes and negotiated a crazy set of turns.

Brice managed to snatch the collar as it raced past him and tossed it into the metal box that seemed to be welded to the floor of the van. Someone yelled "We're being fired on!"

Alicia knocked Michael to the floor of the van, whatever air was in his lungs whooshed out as he slammed onto the metal floor with her full weight on top of him.

Tiny holes peppered the back of the van and Michael gasped for air as the chaos intensified all around him.

Somewhere in his peripheral vision, he saw Levi opening some hatch on the floor of the van and another voice said something about caltrops, whatever they were.

With Alicia's entire body weight on top of him, Michael breathed in her scent and images flashed in his head.

Alicia was on top of him, naked, and older by quite a few years, and they were making love.

He saw the older Alicia in the lab, working with mice, and then working with people.

Images of the countless dinners and late-night snacks

shared in the break room of a lab he'd never seen before, yet it felt as familiar as the one back at school.

And again, the overwhelming guilt as he succumbed to temptation. Waking up to the woman who wasn't his wife, it was something that had eaten him up inside.

Michael blinked as he heard someone say, "We're in the clear. I think you got them with the caltrops."

"Is everyone okay?" Levi yelled. "Any holes we need to know about?"

Alicia climbed off of Michael as everyone took inventory of their situation.

Michael couldn't help but stare at the girl who looked back at him and asked, "Are you okay?"

He nodded. "I don't know how. I don't know why, but I *now* remember everything."

Alicia's eyes widened and Levi took her by the arm and motioned to the front of the van. "Go keep Walt company."

"Wait, I—"

"Alicia." The man's eyes took on a hard look and the girl wilted under his stare. "Go, I know you want to talk to him, now is not the time. Make sure Walt doesn't run us into a ditch or anything."

Alicia walked away and climbed into the front compartment.

Michael turned to Levi, who seemed to be somewhat in charge. "We have to stop these people."

"That's why we're getting you to safety—"

"No!" Michael felt his heart thudding as his mind raced through memories that must have been lying dormant for some reason. Without even questioning it, he knew it was memories of things that hadn't yet happened. Alicia triggered something in him that overcame whatever had been blocking those memories. "They don't *really* need me anymore. Even if I vanish, it might slow them down, but it won't stop what they're going to do. We have to stop them."

"What do you mean?" Brice asked.

Michael winced as his mind drifted to the only conclusion he had left. "I have to go back. Go back and somehow figure out a way to kill all of the records they have on the inside. They have a separate computer network just for my project. If we don't get rid of all of those reports and documentation that I've painstakingly written down, someone else will be able to continue down the path I was going." He motioned toward the front. "Alicia as well. But her work hasn't yet really started. It really only becomes a nightmare when both of our work is combined. Mine is the more dangerous of the two, without a doubt. I'm telling you, it needs to be stopped or we're all screwed. I'm one-hundred percent convinced it can only be stopped from the inside."

Brice turned to Levi and nodded.

Levi shifted his gaze to Michael. "What are you going to tell them that isn't going to just get you in trouble?"

Michael frowned. "I was supposed to call one of the agents when Percy needed to go to the bathroom so he could accompany us. I suppose I can say I dialed a room and didn't get an answer. I'll play stupid and accidentally remember the wrong room number. Given that, I had to go and then got stopped by folks with guns."

"The cabbie who dropped you off might get into a pickle over that." Levi noted with an arched eyebrow.

"No." Brice shook his head. "That hotel's security video for the outside is garbage. I checked. And I can fix it so that the records from the cab company don't even show a pickup in your area. I can cover all of this up."

Levi pursed his lips for a moment and then put his finger to the band on his neck. "Walt, get us somewhere so that we can let the professor and his dog off. Near civilization."

Michael felt at the swelling bruise on his cheek from getting slammed to the floor by Alicia and smiled. Grabbing the collar on his polo, he yanked hard and ripped it along a seam. "Between the bruise and this, it at least lends some credence to a story of me jumping out of the van and managing to outrun you folks."

Levi gave him an approving nod as Brice sat down next to him. "That shiner will go a long way toward some credibility and a demonstration that you have some serious balls on you, but you and I need to talk about next steps. Their private network and what we're going to do. I have a few ideas, but I need to know a few things."

From his peripheral vision, Michael had seen Alicia glance back into the rear of the van several times. Each and every time his stomach flipped as his emotions flared between the guilt and the longing of being with her. Michael adjusted his sitting position so that he faced Brice and the back of the van.

Collecting his thoughts he asked, "Are you familiar with the Princeton campus?"

Brice nodded. "I am, at least from a military satellite view perspective. Why?"

"Well, assuming this whole thing doesn't change how we're proceeding back home, I'll be heading back to New Jersey in another day or two. I have a good place that you could send me something and nobody would be the wiser."

Brice smiled. "A dead drop, eh?" He glanced at Levi and winked. "The professor is starting to talk our language."

Michael grinned, and his cheek flared with pain. "If that's what you call it, then fine. But did you have something in mind I can do? I can probably get physical access to a machine on the network. I just need to know what to do. Computers are not my thing."

Brice pulled out his own phone and showed Michael an image of the campus. "Let's focus on the dead drop, and I'll come up with something you can do."

It took them only a minute of zooming into the map for them to agree upon the location of the dead drop.

Michael pointed at the tool box. "Can I get my phone back?"

"Sure," Brice responded and said, "Just don't turn it on until we're gone. As to that dog collar, do you know where it came from? I'm going to take it back with me to the lab so I can analyze it."

Michael shook his head. "Someone had given it to my wife. Supposedly an old couple. Do you think… of course. I guess I'm naïve about such things. Maybe they recruit older people for simple assignments like handing off things like the dog collar."

Levi chuckled, the first hint of a smile coming from the otherwise serious man. He opened the back door to the van and in the distance was dark, empty street with a twenty-four-hour convenience store on the corner.

Brice handed Michael his phone and said, "It'll probably be a couple days before I get something worked out. Be on the lookout, okay?"

Michael nodded. He shifted his gaze to Percy who'd settled down next to him. "You ready, big boy?"

The dog yipped to the affirmative.

Michael hopped out of the van, with Percy by his side, and within seconds the van had vanished into the darkness of the early morning.

He looked down at Percy and said, "Don't rat me out to the feds when I start stretching the truth."

Michael turned on his phone, got a solid signal, and dialed Bernstein's number.

CHAPTER SEVENTEEN

"Come in." Mason yelled through his door and saw a bleary-eyed Brice walk into his office, plop himself down on the chair in front of his desk and hold up a USB dongle with a look of triumph. "Is that it?"

"Yup." Brice leaned forward and placed the tiny storage device on the desk. "That right there is going to cause a whirlwind of problems."

Mason leaned forward and made a rolling motion with his hand. "Okay, tell me more. How's it work, and what's the plusses and minuses."

"Well, how it works is simple. There's a zero-day flaw that every government computer is susceptible to and I'll be exploiting it in a very nasty way."

A zero-day exploit was in effect a vulnerability in something running on a computer that the virus software was unaware of.

Mason nodded. “What’s the virus do?”

Brice winced. “To be honest, this could easily get out of hand. The virus will take advantage of a couple things, one is a vulnerability that is pretty much on every modern system out there, on the same scale as the Spectre and Meltdown vulnerabilities from 2018. So, that’s enough for most systems out there. But since we can’t know where some of this data has gone, and you told me it needs to be eradicated everywhere, well this is where it gets ugly.

“You know how the government machines are all IT-managed and get regular security updates, right?”

Mason nodded.

“Well, I’ve introduced an exploit as part of a security patch going out tomorrow. When I hit ‘go’ every machine managed by IT will suddenly lose its mind. There will be silent data corruption at first, and I’ve made sure that the backup systems are poisoned all the way back to before any of this stuff with Morpheus started."

Mason felt a moment of apprehension. “This could bring everything down.”

“Yes and no. It’s going to wipe almost everything that’s happened in the last four months. None of the backups are going to work right ahead of that initial start date you gave me. I’ve inoculated the older backups so they can’t get perturbed. And any of the newer backups that might have been shifted to tape, our restoration software is going to have their hashes precalculated so that it’ll think that the backup is corrupt as well. Nothing’s going to work. It’s sort of a doomsday scenario.”

Mason drummed his fingers on the table and furrowed his brows. "Are you sure we'll be able to restore back to the older backups? And what about Wallstreet and this going outside the government facilities?"

Brice smiled. "It won't infect anything that isn't running government-issued versions of the software. That's the beauty of it, there are a couple things the virus checks for to make sure it's running on either government hardware or government-licensed software. Either of those will make the machine fair game. I don't think it'll cause too much trouble outside the walls."

Mason pointed at the innocuous-looking storage device. "Have you worked out how you're going to get that to the professor? I heard he's back at Princeton."

"We've got that worked out." Brice grabbed the finger-sized source of computer doom and tapped his finger on it. "The way I figure it, it'll only take about forty-eight hours between the time the professor installs the first copy of the virus and it propagates across the private network. When he does a couple of preplanned things, that will call for the cavalry, and it'll kick off the extraction and infection of the main set of government computers."

"Okay, it sounds horrible, but we'll deal with the fallout as needed." Mason leaned back in his chair. "I have some people who are going to handle the hardcopies of the professor's research.

"There's going to be quite a few fires in Arlington in a couple days."

With Percy's leash in hand, Michael walked the same path as he always did. It had been particularly tense for the next couple days after his "kidnapping." The FBI was pretty good about the so-called rescue, and the bruise on his cheek must have passed muster, because other than doubling his security detail and having someone stationed outside his door at the hotel—not much had changed.

The two FBI agents accompanying him on the walk on campus still trailed slightly behind him, but on either side.

Michael walked past a set of shrubs, noticed something which made his heart race and he made a point of quickly finished his small lap, returning back to the bushes and coaxing Percy over to them. "Come on, big boy. I know you have to poop."

And with a surge of barely-contained elation, Michael watched as Percy sat at an awkward angle, and to the untrained eye, it would have looked like the dog was trying to crap. He wasn't.

The countless times Michael had worked with Percy in the hotel room had paid off as the dog got up and wagged his tail.

"Good job, Percy." Michael crouched down near the base of the greenery, and with a plastic baggie, grabbed the cold and hard chunk of poop that had been left there.

With a show of sealing the Ziploc bag, he put it into his windbreaker's pocket and they continued walking their normal path.

Percy suddenly stopped, and this time he really did have to poo.

One of the agents commented, "That dog of yours must eat a lot."

"I think it's the brand of dog food. It seems to go right through him." Michael grabbed another baggie and handled Percy's business like he always did.

And as they returned back to the physics lab, Michael dumped the real poop into a waste can, leaving one bagged up poop in his pocket.

Sitting in the bathroom stall at work, Michael broke open the "poop" inside the Ziploc bag only to find what looked like a USB device, a plastic dropper filled with some kind of liquid, and a bunch of purple powder. He carefully extracted the device and remove a piece of paper wrapped around it. It had written on it a very simple message.

"Stick the device into a machine. Wait for the green LED to flash. Remove the tip from the dropper and pour the glycerin on the purple and brown 'poop' then pull the fire alarm and run."

He stared at the contents of the plastic bag and wondered what in the world that guy had given him.

Pocketing the USB dongle, Michael sealed the Ziploc bag and carefully put it in his pocket. The last thing he needed was for whatever it was to blow him into pieces.

Sitting on the toilet, Michael wiped the sweat from his forehead, realizing that he was about to utterly ruin his career if he went through with whatever it was these people were having him do.

He really didn't know what any of this was going to accomplish, so maybe he had some defense?

He shook his head and knew there was no turning back. The memories of the future haunted him. The images of what society would turn into, they loomed large in his mind and he knew it was his fault. At least in large part, he'd enabled a future dystopia.

With all of the thoughts and memories floating in his head, he no longer held any doubts about his role in all of this.

Thinking of the future as a thing he'd done in the past seemed bizarre to anyone who was sane, but that's literally what he was doing. His future self had come back.

That incident with Alicia had awoken fragments of memory that he had no idea were up there. For all he knew, he might have all sorts of other memories up there somewhere, but it didn't matter. The more he dwelled on what was coming, the more depressed he became.

He was no longer who he'd been just days ago. In his mind, he was much older. A somewhat broken man. He couldn't get out of his head the tragedies that his life's work had brought to the world.

And even with the unimaginable chance of maybe undoing

some of the harm, he felt that same festering wound he'd lived with for years. The loss of his family… if nothing else, this strange set of events had given him just a little more time with his wife. And he actually got a chance to hold his child. Small miracles in what otherwise felt like a cursed life.

Michael blinked the tears out of his eyes and knew that if nothing else, those miracles were worth whatever penalty he'd face from the actions he was about to take.

He took a deep breath and blew it out with some force. It was time.

He flushed the toilet, washed his hands, and left the bathroom. As always, an agent was waiting for him and escorted him to the lab.

Things were about to go in a very unexpected direction.

As Michael walked back into the lab, Percy yipped at him as Josh came from the back of the lab with a clipboard in his hands.

"Professor, I'm taking orders for lunch. Today everyone seems to be in an Indian mood, so Cross Culture over on North Harrison is where we're ordering from. Do you need the menu?"

"I'll take a chicken vindaloo."

Josh's eyes widened. "You know that's spicy, right?"

"I do. It was my wife's favorite, so I'm doing it for her."

"Awesome. I'll go see if the agents want anything."

Josh walked out of the lab and Michael felt a sense of relief as he walked past the control desk and headed to the back of the lab where Josh normally sat.

With the USB dongle in his hand, Michael didn't hesitate to plug the device into one of the exposed USB slots.

Josh's computer was locked up, but even so, he saw a red LED turn on.

Was the device doing something?

He couldn't tell.

Michael stood at the back of the lab, a place he almost never went, and felt the sweat drip down the back of his neck as he probably had guilt etched all over his face.

He heard the beep at the lab's entrance just as a green LED began flashing on the USB device.

Michael snatched the device from the computer and walked away as one of the engineers walked into the lab and went to their desk.

Michael halted mid-stride as it dawned on him that there was more for him to do.

He didn't even really know what the bag of stuff in his pocket was going to do. Would it explode? He veered off to the area where nobody's desk was nearby, retrieved the Ziploc bag, opened it and stared at its contents.

He crouched low, near a bunch of cabinets filled with office supplies and lab equipment, and carefully extracted the plastic dropper from whatever it was that was in the bag.

He pinched off the tip of the plastic dropper and braced himself as he put the baggie on the floor, dripped the contents of the dropper into the baggie, and hurried toward the front of the lab.

He heard a loud hissing sound just as he pulled the fire alarm and a near-deafening alarm bell echoed through the building.

Someone yelled "fire" as Michael glanced in the direction of where he'd been and saw billowing smoke.

"Fire, everyone get out!" Michael yelled as he pushed open the door, grabbed Percy's leash and everyone exited from the building.

Percy barked loudly at anyone who was too close in the stairwell. Agents managed to find Michael in the chaos and accompanied him out of the building. Everyone had been through fire drills before, so they all took their places a good hundred feet away from the nearest cars.

Somewhere in the distance Michael heard a siren and as the sound of a fire engine approaching grew louder, he wondered what would happen next for him.

Would whatever that USB device was supposed to do actually do its job? What would happen to the lab?

Was he now on his own, given that he'd done what those people had needed?

Michael closed his eyes at the first sign of a fire truck approaching and realized that maybe he'd be able to just go on as if he hadn't done anything.

There weren't any cameras in the lab as far as he knew… but maybe he was wrong. He might be screwed no matter what.

All he knew was physics and research. This was all feeling like a poorly planned escape strategy.

"Did you guys smell the smoke?" Someone in the crowd asked.

"I didn't smell or see anything. It's probably another one of those fire drills."

"No, I smelled something pretty heinous down in the basement."

The large fire engine drove past the crowd of people as it headed straight for the building. Almost as soon as the vehicle stopped, one of the men with a large bundle on his back raced inside and it was less than a minute before he came running back out, motioning crazily with his hands as the fire engine reversed toward the group.

"What's going on?" Someone asked.

"Crap, that guy looks like he's freaking out. Why is the fire engine heading back towards us? Should we back up?"

Michael overheard one of the agents say, "Call Bernstein and see what he wants us to do."

The crowd parted as the fire truck reversed back up the path it had taken.

One of the students nearby said, "Did you notice that that fireman carried something big into the building, but he ran out without—"

Michael felt the shockwave from where he was standing as gouts of flame burst out of every part of the ground floor.

One of the agents gagged as his neck seemed to sprout a feathered dart and suddenly someone grabbed Michael from behind as they placed a damp cloth over his mouth and nose.

He heard Percy yelp and the world went dark.

Doug Mason sat in his office with his computer frozen, unable to access the network. Brice's virus overshot just a bit, which was a concern of his. The only computers in the entire headquarters building that seemed to be able to connect to the internet were people's phones.

He stared at his phone and turned up the volume as a new reporter gave the latest news, with the chyron spelling out "Trouble in DC."

"This is Tom Nusbaum with the ABC News Desk and we have on the line Jennifer Griffen who is reporting out of Washington DC. Jennifer, can you tell us what's happening down there with this mysterious virus. Is it true that it's only affecting the DC Metro area?"

"Thanks Tom, yes, this is Jennifer Griffen reporting out of DC, and I can say that unlike the Corona virus, which affected nearly everyone's lives and livelihoods, this virus seems to be focused only on the DC area.

"I talked with Admiral Greg Richardson, who's the National Security Council Coordinator for Strategic Communications here in the Pentagon, and he said that he couldn't comment on the whether the military has been affected by the virus. He did want to assure the viewers that the virus has not jeopardized our state of military readiness, and that the U.S. is ready to respond to any threats to the homeland.

"However, when I did talk with some people in the Pentagon, off the record, many of them believe this is a

targeted cyberattack from the Russians or maybe even the North Koreans.

"Also, I can say that there's a lot of confusion in the halls of Congress. It seems like the House and Senate have had to resort to manual roll call votes since the computerized voting system is not working at the moment.

"Tom, that's about all I have for now here in DC."

"Thanks a lot Jennifer. In possibly related news, IRS spokesperson Claudia Thomas said that due to some computer glitches, they would be announcing one-month delays in the tax filing deadline, meaning that taxpayers can expect their filing deadlines to move from April 15th to May 15th of this year."

Mason grinned. "It seems to be working."

His phone vibrated, he looked at the number and tapped on his ear bud. "What's up, Levi?"

"Hey, I've got the meeting set up. Alicia is in the conference room and knowing what you told me, I think she'll need to see this."

Mason got up from his chair, and began walking toward the conference room. "Levi, do me a favor and give me a few minutes. The computers here are all sorts of screwed up and I'm going to need to use my phone as a Wi-Fi hotspot to get onto the video feed."

"Roger that. You want me to call or—"

"No, just give me five minutes and I'll text you when we're ready."

Mason rushed down the metal staircase and after a few

quick "hellos" and a "don't have time for that right now" he walked into the conference room with Alicia sitting there, looking at her phone.

She looked up and smiled. "My dad said I needed to be here for something important. Are you it?"

Mason shook his head and immediately felt sorry for the girl. She wouldn't be smiling when they were done.

It was dark by the time Michael stepped out of the car with Percy by his side. They were somewhere near the ocean, he smelled the salt in the air and wondered where exactly he was.

He didn't remember much after getting exfiltrated from his school.

Exfiltrate, it was the perfect word to describe what happened to him: to withdraw (troops or spies) surreptitiously, especially from a dangerous position or situation.

Whoever these people were, they knew what they were doing. The next thing Michael remembered was waking up in the back of a van with Levi looking over him.

The man was kind enough to try and fill in the blanks for him: evidently the initial fire truck that arrived wasn't a real one. Somehow they'd managed to reroute the alarm call and it gave them an opportunity to in effect blow up the entirety of Michael's lab with an incendiary device.

All his little poop bomb had accomplished was to cause enough smoke and fire to cause a bit of panic, the rest was on them.

This morning, he was given a new set of identification. Gone was Michael Salomon, respected professor of particle physics at Princeton. He was now Michael Gantry, a teacher of physics, who was currently unemployed.

Evidently whatever deal he had didn't include fame and fortune, but it was anonymity that he needed. Especially if he wanted to truly vanish like he knew he needed to.

Levi stood next to him and motioned for him to follow. "Let's get this over with."

Michael followed him into the warehouse, which was almost pitch black and he could barely see a foot in front of his face. "What exactly is this that we're getting over with?"

Percy sniffed the air and his tail wagged just a couple times, almost as if he wasn't sure about something. His ears were perked up and he was definitely taking in whatever he saw.

"You'd asked what you were going to do with your life now that you're no longer who you were." Levi pressed his hand against a metal door and a green LED lit as the door clicked open. "I'm not the right person to ask that question, as you might imagine."

Michael followed him into a well-lit room. The room was wood-paneled and smelled faintly of wood polish.

Percy sniffed loudly and pulled at the leash, which Michael held onto tightly.

"No, Percy. Sit." The dog whined piteously and sat. It was an odd room to have inside of what looked like a dingy storage warehouse somewhere near the ocean. "Okay, that's fine. I think I have all that I need. You guys already gave me a new identity and a modest bank account and ATM card so I don't starve. You guys have done more for me than I could have hoped for. I can figure it out from there."

Levi tossed him a smile, which was a bit unnerving given the man didn't make a habit of smiling. "There's one more thing." He stepped to the room's opposite wall and placed his hand on it. After a couple of seconds, machinery sounded in the wall, and a crack appeared.

A hidden door.

Percy began barking and going nuts. He yanked at the leash, wanting desperately to get at whatever was behind the door.

Levi stepped to the side and motioned for Michael to step through.

Percy led the way, and Michael had to shoo him aside so he could pull the door open. Beyond it was a tiny space, hardly bigger than a walk-in closet. Inside, sitting in a puffy leather recliner, was a woman. And beside the recliner was a bassinet.

Michael couldn't believe his eyes.

"I… I thought you were dead," he said, his throat tightening.

Maria launched herself into his arms, and they embraced each other for the first time in months.

"*Ay, mi amor*!" Maria's muffled cries were the most beautiful thing he could have imagined hearing. "With you here, the baby and I are perfect."

As he held his wife, he looked down at the bassinet. Felicia—now so much bigger than when he last saw her—fussed as Percy sniffed her all over.

Without letting go of Maria, Michael turned back to Levi, who stood in the doorway. “How? How is this possible?”

Levi shrugged. “Some things you don’t ask why. You just live in the moment and be thankful for what you have.”

Michael buried his head in Maria’s mop of hair and began crying. Levi was right. The reasons didn’t matter.

Being together was the only thing that did.

Alicia wiped the unbidden tears from her face and she had to remind herself to breathe as she watched the video feed of the joyous reunion between Michael and his wife.

Mason watched her as she watched the video feed from the warehouse. He spoke with a soft voice and said, “Let’s turn this off—”

“No!” Alicia gave him a glare. “I need to see this. It makes so much sense now that I know. He thought they were dead?”

Mason nodded. “Those bastards at the FBI had no idea where they were, but they knew that Michael had hope. They ended up showing him some poor family who’d gotten burned up in a car wreck.”

Alicia’s eyes widened. “They told him his family died? Why?”

“They had no more idea what had happened to his family than Michael did, but uncertainty over their whereabouts was what was keeping him at Princeton. They wanted him to move to DC, so…”

“That’s cruel. It’s beyond cruel.”

Mason shrugged.

"So… where were they all that time?"

Mason winked. "That's where I come in. Remember, I've seen this play out several different ways. One of those times, the FBI did kidnap and hold his family as veritable hostages. Another time the baby died, which caused strife between Michael and his wife, and the FBI eventually got rid of her so he could focus on the program. So this time, I decided to head off all of that. I got them out of harm's way as early as possible. I was too late to get Michael, that sure would have short-circuited things, but I still managed to get the wife and child."

"You did the right thing," Alicia said. "When it's actionable, you acted. Isn't that our motto?"

"You do listen very well." Mason nodded at the video feed, which was still playing. "You told me once in the future—one of the possible futures—that you were pregnant with his child. So how are you dealing with this? Seeing the love of your life in the arms of his wife, with a child of their own?"

"I'm okay." Alicia shook her head and even though she never would have imagined it to be like that, she truly felt okay about what had happened. "What happened in the future wasn't real." She tapped the side of her head. "It might be real up here, but it didn't happen. At least it didn't happen in the normal sense of the word. I need to make a new reality and not dwell on a future that won't happen… it isn't going to happen, is it?" She gave Mason a hard stare. "It won't, right? How can we be sure we've fixed things?"

Mason smiled. "I'm feeling confident. We can't be sure—you can never be sure about the future—but things are trending in the right direction. We've already collected everyone that we suspected of having been made aware of the future. And what's interesting is that some of those people—Bernstein and Whitley among them—are already finding that their 'memories of the future' are beginning to fade.

"Which makes me think that yours should as well. And that's the biggest proof I've got that our efforts were successful. Because if there is no dystopian future like we saw, then there's no way to send those memories back. It never happened, so you should no longer remember it."

Alicia frowned. "But you can't be sure."

"There's only one way to be sure," Mason replied. "And that's to live our lives and see what happens."

Alicia nodded. That was exactly what she intended to do.

Then she asked the question that had been on her mind for some time now. "Can I work here? Permanently, I mean." Before Mason could say no she held up her hand and added, "I've given this a lot of thought. Going back to school on the path I was on could still yield things that are terrible to contemplate. I think I can do more, and do better, by taking action on things that are actionable."

Mason grinned. "You're using our motto in your pitch. Nice touch."

"Please say yes, Doug. I really want this. More than anything."

Mason eyed her thoughtfully. Alicia wished she could read minds, because she was terrified of what he might say. She feared a "Maybe later" or a "You're too young." Or any excuse that was actually a sugar-coated version of "No."

“Well, I’m afraid that…” Mason paused, a grim expression on his face, and Alicia steeled herself. “I’m afraid that I wouldn’t have allowed you into our headquarters if I hadn’t already scouted you as an ideal prospect,” Mason finished with a grin.

Alicia barked out a laugh. “You bastard.”

Mason’s eyebrows raised. “Don’t forget you’re talking to your new boss. And you’re going to need a lot of training. But I think things are going to work out for you here.”

He offered his hand, and she shook it.

“Welcome to the Outfit, Miss Yoder.”

“Thank you, Mr. Mason.”

Alicia looked back at the video feed once more. Michael was now holding his baby, his wife at his side. And all Alicia felt at that moment was joy for him and his family. He was one of the best people she’d ever met, and he deserved happiness.

EPILOGUE

It had been six weeks since Michael's life changed forever. They lived in Guilford, Connecticut, which was a suburban coastal town not particularly near anything of note and for the moment, Michael was still unemployed. He still had money from the agency that had rescued his family and they were doing okay, but today was a day to celebrate.

He'd just left a second interview with the principal of Guilford High. It turned out it wasn't exactly a second interview, it was an opportunity to meet some of the other staff members and he was told that if the job of science teacher interested him, it was his.

With a starting salary that was about one-third what he was used to getting in New Jersey, it was a hard pill to swallow. Especially after working most of his life for what he had, things would be very different at home.

But no matter how different it was, he and Maria had had a

long talk. There was nothing in the world that mattered as long as they were together. So, starting over is what it would take.

And starting over meant a one-bedroom apartment, a used car, and pinching pennies where they could.

Nonetheless, he stopped off at Kauszer's Food Store next to the apartment and walked to the flowers section and picked out a single red rose. He needed something… anything for Maria, it was something he had to do. A tiny celebration, no matter how much it would cost. It was worth it to him.

As he stood in line at the cash register, the customer in front of him ordered fifty Power Ball lottery tickets at two dollars each. The jackpot was almost $300 million, and everyone was buzzing about it. Michael suppressed an urge to roll his eyes. He'd always called the people who played the lottery failures at math.

The odds were never in your favor to win.

Yet as Michael waited for the man to get his tickets, he suddenly remembered seeing a cascading set of numbers, it was almost like a scene from the Matrix. Within those numbers was a date. Today's date.

And the numbers cascading across his vision were all within the allowed limits of the lottery choices.

Was he fantasizing something that amounted to wishful thinking? Probably.

But it was only two dollars.

Without allowing himself to think about how ridiculous it was to waste two dollars on such terrible odds, Michael plugged in the numbers he saw from that vision. He paid for the ticket and the rose, and he walked out of the Krauszer's feeling like a fool.

But hey, it was part of today's celebration. And after all, it was only for fun.

Later that night Michael and Maria sat watching TV on their "new" sofa—they'd bought it at a garage sale just a few days earlier—with the rose on the coffee table before them, in a vase that Maria had picked up at the very same sale. The baby was asleep, and Percy was in his normal spot next to her crib, keeping watch.

The TV news was wrapping up, and Michael was just about to turn it off when it switched to a view of a blonde reporter standing in front of a grocery store.

Maria patted him on the leg. "Look, honey, our Krauszer's sold the winning lottery ticket."

She turned up the volume.

"The winning ticket in tonight's Power Ball was sold at a Krauszer's Food Store in Guilford, Connecticut. We don't yet know who the lucky winner is, but they have one hundred and eighty days to claim their prize."

The winning lottery numbers appeared on the bottom of the screen.

Michael gasped.

He nearly ripped his pocket open retrieving his wallet, and showed Maria their ticket. "Check that for me?"

Maria took the ticket and went back and forth from the TV and the ticket.

The screen switched to a commercial and he looked over at her.

Michael tried to remember the numbers he'd used and even though he remembered seeing numbers dripping down his vision, he couldn't remember what they were anymore.

"Hold on, it left the screen too fast." She rushed over to their bedroom and brought back their cell phone. With a few swipes and taps to the screen she pulled up today's winning numbers and they both compared the ticket's numbers to what the web site showed.

Maria's eyes widened. "Oh my God."

They stared at each other, stunned.

"We won."

Jason Whitley walked into the room he thought of as his underground lair. This bunker was probably last used during the Cold War, but he treated it as his refuge, the place where he was able to get things done without anyone interrupting him with calls or messages. His computer was off the grid, and cell phone signals couldn't even reach down here.

He sat down at the computer and typed in his password to unlock the screen. A PDF file had been left open from the last time he was here, but that was a while ago, and he no longer recognized the report. He scrolled up to the top to find the project name: Morpheus.

Morpheus?

Something about that name rang a bell…

With a shrug, he closed the PDF and opened up Microsoft Office. He had some PowerPoint slides to create for tomorrow's meeting with the generals. He didn't have time to look at some old PDF.

Maybe later.

AUTHOR'S NOTE

Well, that's the end of *Multiverse*, and I sincerely hope you enjoyed it.

If this is the first book of mine you've read, I owe you a bit of an introduction. For the rest of you who have seen this before, skip to the new stuff.

I'm a lifelong science researcher who has been in the high-tech industry longer than I'd like to admit. There's nothing particularly unusual about my beginnings, but I suppose it should be noted I grew up with English as my third language, although nowadays, it is by far my strongest. As an Army brat, I traveled a lot and did what many people do: I went to school, got a job, got married, and had kids.

I grew up reading science magazines, which led me into reading science fiction, mostly the classics by Asimov, Niven, Pournelle, etc. And then I found epic fantasy, which introduced me to a whole new world, in fact many new worlds, it was Eddings, Tolkien, and the like who set me on the path of appreciating that genre. As I grew older, and stuffier, I grew to appreciate thrillers from Cussler, Crichton, Grisham, and others.

When I had young kids, I began to make up stories for them, which kept them entertained. After all, who wouldn't be entertained when you're hearing about dwarves, elves, dragons, and whatnot? These were the bedtime stories of their youth. And to help me keep things straight, I ended up writing these stories down, so I wouldn't have it all jumbled in my head.

Well, the kids grew up, and after writing all that stuff down to keep them entertained, it turns out I caught the bug—the writing bug. I got an itch to start writing… but not the traditional things I'd written for the kids.

Over the years I'd made friends with some rather well-known authors, and when I talked to them about maybe getting more serious about this writing thing, several of them gave me the same advice: "Write what you know."

Write what I know? I began to think about Michael Crichton. He was a non-practicing MD, who started off with a medical thriller. John Grisham was an attorney for a decade before writing a series of legal thrillers. Maybe there was something to that advice.

I began to ponder, "What do I know?" And then it hit me.

I know science. It's what I do for a living and what I enjoy. In fact, one of my hobbies is reading formal papers spanning many scientific disciplines. My interests range from particle physics, computers, the military sciences (you know, the science behind what makes stuff go boom), and medicine. I'm admittedly a bit of a nerd in that way. I've also traveled extensively during my life, and am an informal student of foreign languages and cultures.

With the advice of some New York Times-bestselling authors, I started my foray into writing novels.

My first book, Primordial Threat, became a USA Today bestseller, and since then I've hit that list a handful of times. With 20-20 hindsight, I'm pleased that I took the plunge and started writing.

That's enough of an intro, and I'm not a fan of talking about myself, so let me get back to where I was before I rudely interrupted myself.

The idea of *Multiverse* came about from a thought exercise. Without getting too much into the technical details, I love the idea of paradoxes. What is a paradox, well in this it's a situation where sensible things seemingly put together result in what comes out to be an absurd conclusion.

For instance, if you had the ability to go back in time and accidentally killed one of your ancestors, you couldn't possibly be born, and therefore you couldn't possibly have killed them. It's one of those difficult situations where the idea of traveling backward in time causes people lots of headaches, and mostly due to these kinds of paradoxes.

I wanted to play with that idea.

Let's not even go so far as to say you could travel in time, but what if you could send a message back in time. What could come of such an ability?

And thus this novel was born.

I did want to bring up something that is kind of amusing. I'm not the type of person to put myself in my own novels, or at least you're not going to find a Dr. Rothman in the novels I write because the whole idea of being IN a novel seems a bit weird to me. However, some of you may have noticed a conspicuous entry in the first chapter where the name Rothman is mentioned. Let me briefly explain:

Bizarre coincidences happen all the time, but this one is a doozy.

When I write a scene, especially when someone is in a car, I'll often get an address and destination and pull up the directions on Google Maps to understand how far, how long, what kind of traffic patterns to expect, etc.

I'll even get visuals so I can see what the surrounding area actually looks like.

This is all to add a feeling of reality to the scene.

When I was writing the first chapter, I randomly picked a starting point, had an established destination, picked a spot (randomly) on the map to zoom in on where I'd include the visual descriptions… and what do I see in the Google Maps in some random spot in New Jersey?

A sign that says Rothman... woah... coincidence? Yup!

I then realize it's for Rothman Orthopedics. WOAH! My father was an orthopedic surgeon... (no, he's long ago retired and never in New Jersey).

Of all the places to zoom into... I picked the exact spot where that building was on the side of the highway.

And that's how Rothman got mentioned IN the book.

As always, I will speak a bit in the addendum about some of the science in this novel, go over some of the concepts, and talk a bit more about those darned paradoxes.

For those of you who have read some of my other novels, especially the Levi Yoder series, you may have noticed that I crossed the streams a bit.

One of my ongoing book series is about a person named Levi Yoder. In the most recent book of that series, *The Swamp*, I introduced his eldest daughter, Alicia. She even had a few scenes of her own. Oddly enough, she was going to Princeton. I did enjoy exploring her role in this story and her interaction with the Outfit. I hope you did as well.

As always, I'd love to hear comments and feedback.

Please share your thoughts/reviews about the story on Amazon and with your friends. It's only through reviews and word of mouth that this story will find other readers, and I do hope this book (and the rest of my books) find as wide an audience as possible.

I should also note that for the fans of a particular book or series, I'm heavily influenced by my readership on what gets attention next. An example of that being my first book, Primordial Threat, a book that was not going to have a follow-on title. But when I released it, it became a hit in the US and abroad, so due to demand, I released a second in what is now known as the Exodus Series.

Also, for those who might have thoughts regarding Alicia, tell me what they are: Would you want to see more of her? If so, would you want her with her father or on her own?

I should note that if you're interested in getting updates about my latest work, join my mailing list at:

https://mailinglist.michaelarothman.com/new-reader

Mike Rothman
August 21, 2022

Update (January, 2024): Since the release of this book, I've gotten overwhelming requests for more on Alicia, and since I'm heavily influenced by reader feedback, I've since turned this into a series with ongoing books with Alicia as the primary character.

Given that, I have two previews of others works added to this novel, the first is a science-laden work of science fiction that those of you who may have liked this story would likely also enjoy called *Primordial Threat.*

The next preview is for a title that continues Alicia's story and her evolution known as *New Arcadia.*

PREVIEW – NEW ARCADIA

The mist hung low in the forest, and the agent's footsteps squished through the damp ground, kicking up the aroma of peat moss—an earthy, dark, rich scent that was reminiscent of wet wool, with a hint of rot. In the distance, he caught sight of a barbed wire fence, the first sign of the high-security camp that wasn't supposed to be there.

Crouching low, the agent continued to advance toward the camp, but froze suddenly upon hearing a crunching and snapping sound underfoot. Dread consumed him when he recognized the sound of children's bones breaking.

It was another shallow grave just outside the camp codenamed New Arcadia.

Despite the horror of the situation, the agent took another step forward.

He didn't hear the sniper round traveling at twice the speed of sound before it slammed into him.

The world turned black.

In a sound-isolated room fifty feet below Fort Meade, Doug Mason watched as two of his specialists worked on a patient lying on a hospital gurney.

One was a neuroscientist monitoring a flatscreen that had a bundle of wires attached to the patient's scalp. The other was a tiny bespectacled man who had been a practicing anesthesiologist before Mason recruited him into the Outfit.

The Outfit was a clandestine government agency that didn't officially exist, and its members were an exclusive bunch, hand-picked for their special skills. These two had come from the private sector, and now served a higher calling… one that involved any number of unusual tasks, in all of which national security was at stake. Today was no exception.

Mason shifted his gaze to the head of the gurney. "Jerry, he'll be able to respond to questions, right?"

"Oh, most definitely." The neuroscientist pointed to the monitor, which displayed a variety of squiggly patterns. "We've got a classic EEG signature of unconsciousness at the moment. Mohan's going to chemically immobilize Agent Chen, and the sedative he's on should give up the ghost. Then he'll wake."

"It's got to be strange waking up and not even being able to blink," Mason said. He'd never witnessed a programming session before, though that was mostly because it had only been done a handful of times, all when he wasn't on the premises.

"It's best that he can't move for a variety of reasons, but the most important have to do with the auditory and visual programming sequences." The neuroscientist adjusted a setting on what looked like a virtual reality headset the patient was wearing. "When we first began experimenting with neuro-programming, the subjects couldn't handle it. The results were miserable."

"What do you mean, couldn't handle it? Was it painful?"

The gray-haired man shrugged. "Hard to say. Before we started inducing paralysis in the subjects, they had an autonomic reaction to the process, flailed uncontrollably, and even when we strapped them to the hospital bed we couldn't get a complete lock on the programming. This is very fidgety, cutting-edge stuff. And the subjects usually don't even realize what's going on during the programming."

The anesthesiologist cut in. "Let's get things rolling." His Indian accent was quite strong. He cleaned the injection port on the IV with an alcohol swab, then injected a clear liquid into it. "This is Quelicin," he explained to Mason. "The good stuff. He'll be completely immobile. I'll attach an infusion pump to the IV so that he gets a constant four milligrams per minute throughout the procedure."

Mason watched the two men work together as a team. He felt uneasy about this whole thing. He knew it was necessary—the news out of China was grim, and Agent Chen was required for a very special mission—but that did nothing to calm his nerves.

"I pushed a counter to the sedative," said the anesthesiologist. "He should be awake now." He broke a capsule under the man's nose, and the smell of ammonia permeated the air. "Did he respond?"

"Yup. He's awake," said the neuroscientist, who was focusing on the monitor.

The anesthesiologist spoke. "Agent Chen, this is Doctor Patel. Can you hear me?"

Mason couldn't make heads or tails of what was on the monitor, but it clearly meant something to the neuroscientist, who said: "He hears you."

"Agent Chen, we're about to start the session. Just relax. You won't remember any of this when this is all over."

The neuroscientist pulled up a new screen on the monitor. This one flashed a series of patterns.

"Sending a baseline set of signals…"

A buzzing noise leaked from the agent's headset. A 3D representation of the brain appeared on screen, rotating, with portions of it highlighted.

"Do those highlights indicate where you're setting the memories?" Mason asked.

"Yes. This will be programming run one of three."

"Why do you have to do it three times?"

"We've found that repetition helps the memories stick. And it's not just pure repetition. On the third run we induce a slow-wave sleep to consolidate the memory—"

"I thought something like that would require REM sleep," Mason interjected.

"No. The slow-wave sleep that comes right after you fall

asleep is when memory consolidation occurs. So I induce that state with a slow-wave frequency generator and then trigger delta waves with about ten milliamps of current through the electrodes attached to the agent's forehead and the base of his skull.

"This isn't a great analogy, but conceptually it's similar to when your computer gets an update and you have to reboot before it can process the changes. And sometimes you have to reboot it yet again once things have been configured. The brain has a similar process."

The scientist tapped some things on the screen, and text scrolled rapidly past, along with images of places and people. All the things pertinent to an upcoming mission.

"Okay, Mohan, I've got the signals oriented. I'm about to hit go. Is he good?"

"Blood pressure is at a baseline of 115 over 78, oxygen is at 100%, and heart rate is 45. All good to go."

"Here goes."

A portion of the neuroscientist's screen blurred into streams of unrecognizable character patterns, not unlike the kind shown in the movie *The Matrix*. Mason looked over at the agent and saw that Chen's pale skin was now turning pink, almost as if he were having an allergic reaction or a hot flash.

The anesthesiologist adjusted the respirator, and its cyclic rate increased, giving the agent more breaths per minute. "BP is now 165 over 80, and heart rate has spiked to 115. We're still okay."

As the programming continued, the agent's skin went from

pink to red, and dots of perspiration appeared everywhere his skin was exposed.

"How much longer?" Mohan said, adjusting the respirator once again, his expression tense. "BP is now 205 over 84, and heart rate is at 185."

Mason clenched his jaw as his gaze panned back and forth between the physicians and Agent Chen.

"Almost done," Jerry said. "Five… four… three… two… one… done!"

The white noise that had permeated the room stopped, and the only sound came from the respirator trying to keep up with the demands of a patient who had been put through the wringer.

Letting out a breath he hadn't realized he'd been holding, Mason felt a wave of guilt wash over him. No wonder the subject had to be immobilized for this. What kind of hell was he putting these people through? And was it worth it?

"Patient's stats are dropping back into normal range. BP is 135 over 78 and heart rate is 70. Both are drifting lower."

Mason turned to the neuroscientist. "Can he hear me?"

Jerry nodded.

"Chris. Agent Chen, this is Director Mason. Are you okay to continue?"

The neuroscientist was watching his screen. "Can you ask your question again? I'm not sure the agent heard it. His brain is still processing the onslaught."

Mason leaned in closer. "Agent Chen, are you okay to continue?"

The neuroscientist nodded. "EEG waves match the affirmative responses we recorded before the testing began. He's good to go."

Mason took a step back and motioned for the doctors to continue. There weren't any laws against what they were all doing, but he felt like there probably should be.

All in the name of national security.

The fires of hell didn't seem that bad compared to how Alicia's face felt as it burned from the chemicals she'd been sprayed with. She jogged in place and heard the other trainees coughing and struggling against the effects of the pepper spray. Blinking away the chemicals didn't even help; her eyelids felt like flaming hot sandpaper. All she could do was grit her teeth and try to ignore the pain as she bounced up and down on the balls of her feet.

"Move it, move it, move it!"

One of the instructors shoved her toward the track, and it took everything Alicia had to *not* send a back fist to the guy's temple.

She and a dozen other FBI Academy trainees were on a remote portion of Marine Base Quantico. She'd been integrated into this training class only three days ago. Yet despite the dusty surroundings, the chemicals in her face, and her complete physical agony, she knew there was one thing she couldn't do.

Let these bastards get the best of her.

"The more you sweat and suffer here, the less you'll bleed

when on assignment. I want one and a half miles from all of you! That's six laps, for you people who aren't all that bright."

Blinking through the pain and tears, Alicia began running.

"Yoder, Sanchez, and Smith!"

Alicia and two other agents turned to the instructor.

He made a counterclockwise motion with his finger. "The other direction, numbskulls."

Alicia pressed a finger against the side of her nose, blew a seemingly impossible amount of snot in the instructor's general direction, and ran to catch up with the rest of the class.

Alicia felt much better after the run was over—though she still felt a burning sensation in the back of her throat. She hadn't been the first to complete the six laps, but she had finished in the front third of the trainees, which would have to be good enough. Halfway through the run, she had developed a pain in her lower abdomen. It didn't feel like a normal period cramp, but that was probably what it was. She sure as hell wasn't going to mention it; as the only woman in this class, she wasn't about to allow that to be an excuse.

She had never run with anything more than two-pound ankle weights in college, and she'd never have imagined just how exhausting it was to run in full tactical gear. All the trainees had been completely kitted out, from military-issue combat boots to an advanced battle vest with ballistic inserts, load distribution system, and what the instructor called SAPIs and ESBIs—small-arms protective inserts and enhanced side ballistic inserts. The whole thing probably only weighed fifteen or twenty pounds, but Alicia had felt every one of them.

The last two trainees came walking back from the track looking exhausted. Their eyes were bloodshot, and partially dried snot and Lord knows what else was streaked across their faces and into their hair. They looked like hell.

Alicia now knew the feeling—quite well.

When all of the would-be agents had completed the run and settled onto the benches, an instructor stepped in front of the group and spoke.

"Okay, trainees. We've got something special today."

He hitched his thumb toward the training site behind him—a dusty ghost town that had been constructed about a quarter mile away. It had been set up in a grid pattern, with a wide main street splitting it from north to south. Yesterday, when they'd used it to go through various close-quarters combat scenarios, corpses of burnt-out vehicles had lined the street, but today there was something else there, something metal. Alicia couldn't quite make it out from this distance.

The instructor smiled. "Some researchers out of DARPA have developed a new artificial intelligence unit, and we've plugged it into one of our EOD robots."

EOD was shorthand for explosive ordnance disposal—the bomb guys. And now Alicia realized what the metal object in the main street was. A couple weeks earlier she had worked with some folks from the Army's EOD group, and she'd gotten a chance to operate one of their remote bomb disposal units. It was kind of neat, reminding her of the robot from the cartoon

WALL-E. It even had arms that she could manipulate through a remote control.

"With this new AI enhancement, the robot is supposed to detect and identify combatants in the field. It's been through quite a bit of testing already, but before it can be put out into the field, it's going to need a lot more work. Today is your turn to see if you can fool the robot. All you need to do is go up to it and touch the thing without it raising its red flag, meaning it saw you. Any questions?"

One of the trainees raised his hand. "Sir? How far can it see?"

"Good question. The robot will analyze anything coming within a thousand-foot radius."

A voice broadcast from what looked like a walkie-talkie on the instructor's utility belt. *"We're ready."*

The instructor spoke into a shoulder-attached mic. "Roger that."

He pointed at the man who'd asked the question. "Smith, since you're the curious type, you can go first."

The trainee launched himself from the bench and jogged north, skirting the edge of the makeshift town, then vanished between the buildings. After a moment the robot turned eastward, sensing him.

Suddenly the trainee raced into view, and the robot's arm shot upward, with something red hanging from it.

"Subject detected," the walkie-talkie squawked. *"Send the next agent."*

The instructor pointed at another trainee. "Darby, you're up next."

Scott Darby, a tall blond giant of a man, stood and tapped the shoulder of the guy who'd been sitting next to him. Carl something. "Hey, want to try and tag team Robo-Grunt?"

"Sure."

The two men spoke in hushed whispers, then took off at a sprint. They split up, approaching their target from opposite directions.

Was one of them going to sacrifice himself so the other could tag the thing?

As they converged onto the town, the robot seemed skittish, scanning back and forth, clearly sensing movement. But the men were ducking behind buildings before the robot could zero in on them.

Then Carl launched a rock past his target.

But instead of following the movement of the rock, the robot turned, raised its arm, then spun, kicking up a cloud of dust.

Alicia wasn't quite sure what had just happened, but the voice on the walkie-talkie said, *"Both agents identified. Send your next."*

"Cortez, you're up."

The man sitting next to Alicia jumped up and raced forward. Like the others, he ducked behind the buildings and thus delayed his inevitable defeat. His tactic was to throw up a cloud of dirt to distract the robot. But the moment he leapt from cover, the robot flagged him.

Damn, that thing is fast.

"Yoder, you're up."

Alicia stood, then tilted her head to the supply shed. "Can I use the mosquito netting?" she asked.

The instructor shrugged. "Whatever's here, you can use."

Alicia unrolled nearly fifty feet of thick mosquito netting from the spool and wrapped herself with it. The instructor and trainees watched with confusion and interest as she created a puffy ghillie suit.

When she tied it off, she checked her shadow. She could barely see anything through the layers of mesh, but she'd created the desired effect: her shadow was round—not shaped like a human at all. Alicia hoped that the AI wouldn't know what to make of her.

Keeping her hands inside the suit, she pushed out the edges of the mesh, making herself look even rounder as she trudged northward.

She didn't bother skirting around buildings. She moved straight at the robot, her heart thudding in her ears as she wobbled forward.

It turned slightly as she got in range.

Alicia kept moving.

The robot shifted back and forth like it was suffering from a nervous tic. It clearly sensed her approach. But would it identify her as a combatant?

Alicia heard the whoosh of the robot's hydraulics. She saw the red cloth clutched in its robotic grip.

It's about to raise its arm.

But it was too late. Alicia bumped directly into it and yelled, "I tagged it!" She felt a wave of triumph.

Two men stepped from the nearest building. They were

dressed in street clothes and had picture badges clipped to their collars. One looked annoyed, but the other laughed.

"How did you know that your heat signature wouldn't be able to be detected through that mesh?"

Alicia shrugged. "I had no idea. I just figured if I didn't have a human outline, it might get fooled."

The other man grumbled, "Dumb luck."

"No, this was perfect," said the first man. He gave Alicia a thumbs-up. "I'd never have thought of this approach." He spoke into a handheld device. "It seems your trainee found a chink in our armor. We've got some work to do."

"Roger that. I'll dismiss the rest of the trainees for the day. Yoder, good job. We'll be back in the classroom at 0800."

As the scientists began unscrewing one of the panels on the robot, Alicia wriggled out of the layers of mosquito netting. Despite her little victory against WALL-E the Robo-Grunt, she couldn't help but feel anxiety over the training activities still to come. Unlike her classes in college, all of which provided a clear syllabus with what to expect, here she had been given absolutely no idea what the Outfit had in store for her.

She wasn't even completely sure what being an agent at the Outfit even entailed. The training seemed almost random. Last week it was working with some Marines on conditioning exercises. This week it was training at the FBI Academy. And next? Who knew?

She wished she at least had some grades to measure herself against. She had no idea if she was doing well or poorly. But that might change tomorrow. She had a mid-cycle evaluation with Mason at the Outfit's HQ, and she couldn't help but wonder what Mason would have to say about her performance.

It had been three months since Alicia had agreed to join the Outfit—a huge decision for her. It had not only meant moving to a new apartment in DC, it had meant leaving Princeton without having finished her master's degree in neuroscience. The unfinished degree didn't sit well with her, and now, as she drove past Lincoln Park, through the National Mall, past Foggy Bottom, and into old Georgetown, her mind was filled with doubt about her choices.

She placed a call on her phone and transferred it to the car's speakers.

"What's up, baby girl?"

The sound of her adoptive father's deep voice should have taken the edge off of her nerves, but it didn't.

"Dad, what the hell was I thinking? I feel like it was just yesterday that I was taking classes, an ordinary student, and now I'm training to be… hell, I don't even *know* what I'm training to be. Shooting drills, CQB training, and a few days ago they put me through an entire session on vehicle engagement tactics—learning how to drive and shoot at the same time, evasive maneuvers, anti-ambush drills… Dad, this is insane."

Her father chuckled. *"Alicia, take a deep breath. Where are you?"*

She took a deep breath and let it out. It did make her feel a little better. "I'm driving to HQ for my three-month review with Mason. And I'm really nervous about it."

"There's no reason for you to be nervous. You've got this. And besides, I've been keeping tabs, and everyone so far has had nothing but good things to say about your progress."

"Well sure, they wouldn't tell *you* if I'm doing poorly. You're Levi Yoder, Super Spy. I'm just… me." Alicia's throat tightened and her heart was racing. "Dad, I can't remember what made me say yes to this. And I mean that literally—it's like total blanks in my head. I think I might be losing it."

"I assure you, you're not losing it. And those gaps… honey, let's just say that they're there for a reason."

"What do you mean?"

"It's hard to explain. Sometimes when people go through trauma, things get blocked from your consciousness. It's totally normal."

A chill raced through her, and she began feeling light-headed. "You don't have to explain to me how the brain works —I'm the neuroscientist, remember? Or I was *going* to be. But —what trauma, Dad? Was I"—she swallowed—"was I… raped or something? What am I blocking out?"

"No, no, it was nothing like that. You just… you managed to get mixed up in something that involved the Outfit. You kicked ass, Alicia. But it was hard on you. Mason and I thought you might lose some of those memories of the incident, and honestly, I'm glad you did. You're better off, trust me. And if you're nervous about it, talk to Mason. He'll totally understand."

"Maybe."

"It's your call. But listen—I'm in DC today for a quick meeting. Maybe you could meet me upstairs for a bite to eat? How's noon sound?"

"It sounds great, Dad." Alicia wiped tears of frustration from her cheeks. "I'm sorry. I'm acting like a baby. I'm just nervous and… freaking out a bit."

"Alicia, you have nothing to worry about." She could hear the smile in his voice.

They ended the call as she pulled into an open spot on the side of the road in old Georgetown. Traffic had been unexpectedly light, and she was an hour early for her meeting, so she tuned the radio to an oldies station and tried to calm her nerves.

It wasn't helping. After thirty minutes, she gave up and got out of the car.

"Hey honey, you have any food I can have?"

She turned to see an old man in dirty threadbare clothing yelling at her from down the street. She grinned as she walked toward him. The "beggar" was a member of the Outfit, and the things he yelled were actually codes to notify anyone approaching headquarters if there was anything amiss. Asking for food was a sign that everything was clear. Had he asked for a drink… well, then Alicia was to leave the area immediately.

Ahead of her was a familiar sign. It featured a profile of a rooster on the left, and the head of a longhorn bull on the right. This area wasn't exactly upscale, but Alicia had gained some fondness for the dingy street front.

She walked into the Rooster and Bull, and the smells of stale beer and wood polish washed over her. The place was a dive bar… and also an entrance into one of the most secretive organizations in the world.

As always, the place was dimly lit, and the few tables and booths were all empty at this time of day. Behind the bar, a man toweled a glass dry. He nodded at her as she walked toward the back of the establishment.

Alicia entered the men's bathroom. A white-haired man sitting on a stool near the sink looked at her over his John Lennon-styled spectacles.

"Back again, little girl?"

She grinned. "Harold, how many pairs of tan slacks and plaid button-down shirts do you own? That's all I ever see you wear."

"Bah!" Harold held out a white towel. "My wife always harped about the same thing."

Alicia took the towel. It looked like an ordinary towel, but she knew it had a string of RFID tags sewn into it, and acted as a key of sorts.

"Sounds like your wife was a smart woman," she said, giving the old codger a wink.

For the blink of an eye, the old grump cracked a smile, then he muttered something unintelligible as he waved her away.

Alicia chuckled as she entered the third of the bathroom's three stalls—the one with an "Out of Order" sign taped to it. She shut the door behind her, then placed the special towel on the flushing lever and flushed the toilet.

Immediately the floor dropped—taking Alicia and the toilet with it. She put her hands on the tank to steady herself as she dropped with frightening speed down an incredibly deep shaft.

She'd taken this route dozens of times, yet her stomach still lurched.

After a few very long seconds, the walls fell away and the toilet-elevator slowed nearly to a stop. Alicia focused on regaining her balance as she descended into a featureless room deep underneath old Georgetown. The platform settled softly into a recess in the floor, and Alicia stepped off.

Just as quickly as it had dropped, the toilet-elevator launched back up again, disappearing into the shaft in the ceiling.

Alicia tossed the hand towel in a nearby basket, then walked to the room's only exit: a steel door with a security panel mounted to one side. She placed her splayed hand on the panel, and a blue line passed back and forth. Then a green LED flashed, and a click echoed from inside the wall.

"Stand clear," warned a digitized voice.

Three massive locking bolts slid out of their retaining blocks on the right side of the door, and the door slowly opened outward.

Alicia remembered the first time she'd been brought here, by her father and Director Mason. The place had reminded her of a 1950s bomb shelter, except that no bomb shelters she knew of had a four-foot thick, tungsten-steel alloy door weighing eighteen tons at its entrance.

She walked through the opening, around a corner, and down a hall that ended at another door, this one with a retinal scanner. She put her eye up to the box on the wall, and with a flash of green light, the door clicked.

Alicia pushed it open and stepped into the inner sanctum of the Outfit's US headquarters.

She was in a room larger than most warehouses. She stood on a metal walkway about twenty feet above the floor, giving her a clear view of the cubicles arranged in a grid below her, stretching as far as she could see. No matter what time of the day or night she arrived, she always found men and women working busily. Four huge display screens, each fifty feet across, hung from the ceiling at the center of the space, displaying information, maps, photographs, satellite feeds, and more, and the walkway she was on continued around the edges of the giant room, leading to offices whose windows also looked down on the central work area.

She was reminded, not for the first time, of the headquarters in the movie *Men in Black*, except there were no aliens—at least, not that she knew of.

She walked down a flight of metal stairs, stepped into the cubicle bullpen, and started the long walk to the far side of the cavern-like complex. When she finally reached conference room C1, where she was scheduled to meet with Mason, the butterflies in her stomach were threatening to come flying out of her mouth.

Despite her early arrival, she found the director already waiting, studying a photograph. She looked up at the wall clock and saw to her astonishment that she wasn't fifteen minutes early, she was forty-five minutes *late*.

"Oh my God, I don't—"

"Daylight savings?" Mason said. "Did you forget the time changed early this morning?"

He stared at her with his pale, silver-hued eyes. He was in his fifties, with light brown hair and a receding hairline, and there was something about how he held himself… his presence commanded attention. This man was the Outfit's most senior member in the US—at least, as far as she knew, and here she was showing up almost an hour late for her evaluation.

"I'm so sorry! Do we need to reschedule?"

Mason waved dismissively at her and slid the photo he'd been looking at across the conference room table. "Tell me what you see."

Alicia took a seat across from him and picked up the photo. It looked like some kind of business social. "Well, lots of Asian people, but I don't suppose you needed me to tell you that."

"Do you recognize anyone?"

She was about to shake her head when a woman caught her attention. She was only in profile, and she was a good distance from the camera, but…

"I'm not positive, but I think I do."

She felt a surge of apprehension. Her boss was expecting an answer—an *honest* answer—but Alicia didn't want to betray this woman's confidence. She was, after all, involved in the shady side of business.

"I… I think my father knows her."

"A very diplomatic way of putting it, young lady." Mason's stone-like expression softened, and he gave her a slight nod. "Very well, I'll talk to Levi in a bit."

He glanced at the wall clock and rose from his chair. "Unfortunately, I have another meeting at the top of the hour, so we'll have to postpone our review. I'll have my admin set something up." He walked to the door, put his hand on the knob, and looked back at Alicia. "And next time, don't be late."

She nodded.

As Mason opened the door, his phone rang, and he put it to his ear. "Hey, Levi. I'll be right up. My office." He looked back at Alicia once more. "This room is free for the next couple hours if you want to use it."

He closed the door silently behind him.

Alicia put her head in her hands. All her life she'd been an overachiever. She was always early for every engagement, meeting, class—everything. She couldn't believe she'd made such a dumb error. The training over the last weeks had been so intense, it had made her completely forget about the outside world… and ordinary things like *Daylight Saving Time*.

She'd been hoping that today's meeting would ease her anxiety. If she could just get some feedback on how she was doing—even if it was bad—she thought she'd feel more at ease. Instead she'd been almost an hour late to a meeting with one of the most important men in the entire Outfit.

She remembered her father's advice, and took a deep breath.

It didn't help.

— end of preview —

PREVIEW – PRIMORDIAL THREAT

"Dr. Radcliffe, I was wondering if you could take a look at the data I just got from my latest survey. Something's not right." Carl, one of the new hires for 2066, loomed over Burt's desk, sounding puzzled. Not unexpected, since he'd been on the job for less than a week.

"Did you talk to Jake Parish?" Burt didn't even look up. "He's maintaining the database for all the near-Earth objects."

"He's on sabbatical."

"Oh." Burt looked up from his own stack of astronomical survey data and took in Carl's six-and-a-half-foot form. He noticed the man's concerned expression and sighed. Even though Burt was only fifty, he'd found himself getting more and more cranky when people wasted his time. Trying to keep the annoyance from his voice, he carefully measured his words. "What exactly do you mean, something's not right? Can you be a bit more specific?"

Carl hesitated for a moment, then placed two printouts on Burt's desk. He pointed at an image from one of the observatories. "This is the survey image I took yesterday."

Burt leaned closer to scan the text describing a surveyed comet, its location, and its approximate size. Below the text was a dark image showing nothing but empty space.

"I was surveying the area where comet Kowalski C/2011 S2 was supposed to be," Carl continued, "but there's nothing in the imaging system's field of view." He tapped the other image. "Here you can see the same region, and this time I used the Hubble2 satellite. Still I got nothing there."

Burt suppressed an eye roll as he turned to the terminal on his right. There was no way an object multiple miles across had simply disappeared. He typed the name of the comet and yesterday's date. The data, projected at eye level, showed the space object's uneven shape, chemical composition, trajectory, and estimated location. He glanced at the printout and compared the coordinates. They matched. The comet should be there. Carl had obviously done something wrong.

With a huff of frustration, he handed the papers back to the confused researcher. "This doesn't make any sense. Take it to Dr. Patel and have her double-check your information."

Carl's eyes widened at the mention of Dr. Patel, and Burt had to hold back a smile. Neeta Patel, one of the other department heads at NASA's Jet Propulsion Labs, was known for having much less patience for wasting time than he did. But people learned the most by making mistakes, Burt had always believed, and Neeta would be a great teacher. She'd tell the newbie exactly what he'd done wrong—and she'd be entirely blunt about it. A lesson Carl wouldn't forget.

As the young researcher shuffled out of the office, Burt chuckled lightly, but his amusement faded as he turned to the large stack of papers on his desk.

He shook his head. "I hate sabbatical coverage."

"You agree with him?" Burt said, astonished.

Neeta sat on the far side of his desk, dressed in jeans and a black-and-orange CalTech hoodie. She was in her mid-thirties, with long black hair, and even in her casual wear she was an imposing figure. He'd worked with her for a few years, and she'd proven herself to be one of the most brilliant people he'd ever met.

Neeta leaned back in her chair and rubbed her eyes with the heels of her hands. "Yes, I agree with him," she said, her British accent apparent. "I was actually tracking an anomaly with another comet when Carl found me. Burt, I don't understand what's going on yet, but I expanded the survey areas for both of the near-Earth objects—the one I was looking into and the one Carl brought to me—and they were in totally different spots from where they should have been."

Burt frowned at the improbability of what Neeta was saying. "That doesn't make sense. The odds are almost infinitesimal that something could have hit one of the comets and knocked it from its trajectory. But two knocked from their trajectory? Could they have somehow collided?"

Neeta's hair swayed back and forth as she shook her head. "No chance. They haven't crossed orbital planes since the last time we verified their positions."

"I don't need to tell you that we've got to figure out what's going on. That's kind of our job."

"Of course." Neeta waved dismissively. "I already put a few people on surveying the areas in question to see if we have any more unexpected path deviations. Unfortunately, without twenty-four-hour telescope or satellite access, it might take a while. Those comets are way out near the Oort cloud."

Burt was about to respond when his phone rang. He tapped the wireless receiver in his ear.

"This is Burt Radcliffe."

"Dr. Radcliffe, this is Anita Wexler, Dr. Phillip Johnson's admin. He asked me to make arrangements for you to have a face-to-face meeting with him here in Washington, DC, at your earliest possible convenience. When can I send a car to pick you up?"

Burt tapped on his ear, muting the call, and said to Neeta, "Why would the new head of NASA want a one-on-one with me?"

Neeta shrugged. "Why the bloody hell are you asking me? Maybe you should ask him."

Burt tapped again on his ear. "Anita, is tomorrow morning early enough?"

"I'm sure that will work. I see a flight leaving LAX at eight. I'll arrange for a car to pick you up at your house no later than five. Is that okay?"

"That's fine."

"Thank you, Dr. Radcliffe. I'll book your flight, and you'll have a driver waiting for you upon your arrival."

As he clicked off, Burt looked over at Neeta once more. "Well, looks like I'm going to DC tomorrow."

She glanced down at his jeans and t-shirt. "Then I'd recommend you get home and make sure you have something decent to wear."

Jon Stryker slipped into his windbreaker, looked at himself in the bedroom mirror, and ran his fingers through his dark-brown hair.

Not bad for a thirty-four-year-old cop with two kids living with his sister.

He poked his head into his kids' room, from which came the gentle sound of Emma, the six-year-old, snoring in bed. It was only six a.m., too soon for even the little one to be awake yet.

He smiled at the sight. His youngest had once again lived up to her nickname: "Blanket Thief." Sometime during the night, she'd gotten up and taken the blankets off her eight-year-old brother's bed. She was now lying underneath both his blankets and her own, leaving him uncovered.

At least Isaac had on his flannel pajamas. His arms were wrapped tightly around his ragged teddy bear, and for now at least, the lack of blankets had left him unfazed. But he'd be howling about it as soon as he woke up and noticed his sister's burglary.

Blowing a kiss at them both, Stryker closed their bedroom door and followed the aroma of fresh-brewed coffee downstairs to the kitchen. He found both his sister and his ex-wife sitting at the small breakfast table, a pair of steaming mugs in front of them.

Seeing his ex was always a jolt. Every time he saw Lainie's pixie-like face, his mind flashed back to the moment when he'd received the divorce papers while deployed overseas. Though that had been four years ago, the hurt hadn't dulled. And it didn't help that she still looked as stunning as ever.

Stryker leaned over to give his sister a peck on the cheek, then did the same to Lainie. "I guess it's Saturday, eh?"

Lainie raised an eyebrow and gave him a grin. "Why else would I be here? I'm taking the kids to my parents for the weekend. Jessica was filling me in on how they're doing in school."

Stryker's sister taught at an elite prep school in Midtown, not far from his regular patrol of Times Square. The kids were lucky enough to attend the school tuition-free because of his sister's job—a fact that Stryker was ever-grateful for.

Jessica motioned toward the half-full coffee pot. "Today's batch is pretty strong, if you want some."

Stryker glanced at his watch and shook his head. "Thanks, but I can't. I have a rookie assigned to walk the beat with me today, so I need to get to the precinct early."

"You'll be back by four, right? You promised to help me hang stuff up in my classroom."

"I'll be there." Stryker grabbed his keys off the kitchen

counter and turned to Lainie. “Expect Isaac to start yelling when he wakes up. Emma stole his covers again.”

She smiled, and for a moment, Stryker saw the woman he’d married fourteen years ago. He steeled himself against her brilliant smile and reminded himself how much resentment they still held for each other. She hated that he risked his life to make a living, and he hated that she couldn’t respect his choice of career.

But they had kids together. And that meant they would always share a responsibility. Not to each other, not anymore, but to the kids.

With a wave, Stryker turned and headed for the door—and what was sure to be yet another uneventful day with the NYPD.

It was a crisp spring morning as Stryker walked the streets of Midtown Manhattan. He’d lived his entire life in the same neighborhood, but the vibe had changed a lot since he was a kid. The area had always been a tourist Mecca, especially with Times Square, the Empire State Building, and Grand Central all within walking distance, but Stryker missed the old gritty atmosphere, filled with the sounds of honking cars and revving engines. Those noises were long gone now that cars were almost all electric and every last vehicle had an Automated Vehicle Routing system built in. The city had required AVR for all cars within the city limits, and although the system saved untold lives by routing traffic flawlessly through the boroughs,

Stryker would never shake the feeling that it wasn't really New York without the snarled streets, sirens, and people yelling at each other about the traffic.

"Hey, Jonny," called a woman's husky voice from across the street. "You up for a good time?"

He looked across the street and saw Sheila, a stunning brunette in her late teens. She was wearing a skin-tight red dress that highlighted her substantial curves. Stryker had seen her hundreds of times on the street, but always near Times Square, not over here on Madison Avenue.

He crossed the street to speak to her, and caught a whiff of her jasmine perfume. "Sheila," he said, "it's not even seven in the morning. People are still asleep."

"You look awake to me," she countered with a sly smile.

Stryker shook his head. "Just do me a favor. If you're going to hawk your wares, please do it in your usual area of business. Or if you insist on hanging in this area, at least keep it quiet."

She put her hands on her hips and took a gliding step closer. "That wasn't a no," she purred.

He couldn't help but chuckle. "Sorry, honey. My shift starts in thirty minutes."

As he turned away, he shook his head. Even though prostitution was now legal in the city limits, the street cops tried to keep things civilized. After all, kids played here. In fact, not so long ago, Sheila used to be one of those kids. He'd watched her grow up in this very neighborhood.

He turned right on East 35th and strode purposefully past the Empire State Building, the edge of Koreatown, and into the Garment District, where the Midtown South Precinct was located. As he entered the precinct, he went straight to the locker room and began changing into his uniform.

A dozen other officers were already getting ready for the day. "Hey, Stryker," said one. "Did you hear about last night?"

Stryker looked over to the speaker, a younger officer named Brian Decker. The kid was checking himself in the mirror. "No, what'd I miss?"

"Jenkins and McCullough had to use OC on a bunch of whackos demonstrating in the lobby of the Grand Hyatt."

"OC" stood for oleoresin capsicum: pepper spray. Stryker had rarely had to use it in his four years on the street.

"Ouch," he said. "How many people were demonstrating?"

"Sharon told me they brought in almost a dozen."

Stryker shrugged a Kevlar vest around his trim six-foot frame and shook his head. "Any idea what they were belly-aching about?"

Still staring at himself in the mirror, Decker lightly slapped his cheeks and let out a yawn. "Who knows? You know how people are. They'll complain about anything."

That was true, but it didn't usually end up calling for pepper spray. Stryker was glad he hadn't been on duty.

He did a final check to ensure his firearm was securely holstered, then headed out of the locker room, grabbed a cup of coffee, and prepared himself for roll call.

Burt had never had a reason to meet the previous head of NASA, and why would he? The man was in charge of twenty thousand civilian employees; Burt was a nobody in comparison. And he couldn't fathom why he'd now been asked to talk face-to-face with his boss's boss… or maybe it was his boss's boss's boss. He couldn't quite be sure, especially with the way upper management played fifty-two-card pickup with the org charts.

But now he found himself standing in front of the desk of Phillip Johnson, the new NASA administrator. Johnson stood to greet him, revealing that he was nearly a half foot taller than Burt, and looked to be at least 250 pounds of solid muscle. Burt gave an involuntary start.

"Damn, Radcliffe, you look wound up tighter than a banjo string. Have a seat."

The administrator's southern accent caught Burt by surprise. He sat on one of the two padded leather chairs in front of the desk and focused on keeping the nervousness from his voice. "Dr. Johnson, it's an honor to meet you. I flew over as soon as your admin called, but she didn't tell me why you asked me here."

Johnson leaned forward over his desk and smiled, his brilliantly white teeth contrasting with his dark complexion. "I'll cut to the chase, Radcliffe. I just signed off on you becoming the new director of the Near-Earth Object program. You'll be reporting to the director of JPL. But I want all of your future status reports coming to me as well."

Burt felt the blood drain from his face. He blinked twice, uncertain if he'd heard the man correctly. "Sir? I probably shouldn't ask this, but… why me?"

Johnson laughed. "A while back, you worked on a

Bayesian learning computer system. You remember? It was being pitched by some generals as a new way of getting soldiers out of the business of war. Saving lives and all that."

Burt stared at the man. "Sir, that was over twenty years ago. I remember it well. I couldn't be a part of deploying a Turing-capable computer system, so I scrapped that part of my life and started over. What does any of that have to do with you wanting me to be the new director?"

Johnson drummed his fingers on his desk. "I was a colonel in the Army doing research at the US Army War College shortly thereafter, and I was charged with evaluating some of what you'd created. It was brilliant, if you don't mind my saying so. Frankly, it scared the bejeezus out of many of us. I still vividly remember a warning you gave in a paper you wrote about what might happen if computers were empowered to handle life-and-death choices: What if the machines figure out they're less expendable than we are? That stuck with me. As did all of your work."

Johnson leaned back in his chair and ran his hands over his clean-shaven scalp. "Anyway, when the head of JPL gave me a list of likely candidates for the directorship, and I saw your name on that list… that was good enough for me."

Burt suddenly realized his mouth was hanging open, and he was looking like an idiot in front of his boss. He quickly shut it. "Thank you, sir. I'll do my best."

"I know you will. I've got a special task for you." Johnson slid a storage card across the desk. "This is encrypted, so you'll only be able to read it in a secure location, but it has everything there is to know about DefenseNet. The president asked NASA to pick up that ball, and we've received extra funding to deploy the project. It's now your baby, Radcliffe. You got me?"

"DefenseNet? Wasn't that supposed to be a bunch of geosynchronous satellites to help detect and destroy incoming asteroids?"

Johnson stood and walked around the desk, and Burt also got to his feet. The man placed his thick arm over Burt's shoulders and escorted him toward the door. "That's exactly why I agreed to take it on—because I knew it was a project that NEO should be all over. And as head of NEO, that means I need you to be all over it."

The door slid open automatically as they approached, and Johnson pointed across the hall at a set of double doors. "That area is a SCIF. You have at least five hours before your flight, so you might want to take advantage of that place."

"Skiff?"

"Sensitive Compartmented Information Facility." The administrator pointed at the storage card in Burt's hand. "You'll find a secure reader in there so you can start noodling on what I've just gotten you into. There's also a SCIF at the JPL facility, though you've probably never needed to use it."

He gave Burt a final pat on the shoulder and then turned back to his office, the door sliding closed behind him.

Burt stared at the palm-sized plastic card in his hand, embossed with the words "Top Secret" in red.

What the hell just happened?

Burt poked his head into Neeta's office. "Have you looked over the DefenseNet plans I shared with you?" It had been a few hours since he'd returned home, and he'd given her the info right away.

Neeta swiped the air with her right hand, and her desktop computer projected the Earth's image, with two dozen interconnected satellites slowly orbiting around it. "Nah, I figured I'd get around to it when I had nothing better to do." Rolling her eyes, she motioned at the projection before her. "Of course I've been poring over the plans. What else would I be doing?"

"Sorry. I see you've begun modeling the network. That's great. Have you figured out why the satellites are interconnected? I still can't see the point of linking them like that."

"Unfortunately, no. Then again, I didn't have much to do with this when I was at the International Science Foundation, so I'm going only by the data you gave me. If we really want to know why, we'd have to ask Dave Holmes, the former head of the ISF, and as far as I know, he's dead—or hiding in some hole so deep that nobody's going to find him."

Burt sighed. "These plans aren't complete, or at least parts of them make no sense. I was reading through some of the notes that talked about space elevator anchors, but nowhere do I see any mention of tethers or what they'd be needed for. And there's no need for a hard connection to the satellites anyway. Hell, all we need is to equip each of the satellites with a bank of solar panels, and that'll charge the onboard batteries for the lasers. Any other communications can happen wirelessly."

Neeta frowned. "Dave was no fool. He wouldn't have designed something without a purpose."

"Yeah. And that's what makes me nervous about this whole project. I think we can build it and make it work, but are we even building the right thing? What did he really have in mind?"

At that moment the lights in the room flickered red, and the Potentially Hazardous Asteroid warning came up on the computer's monitor.

"Bloody hell," Neeta groaned. "I don't have time for a PHA alert."

Burt read the alert text. "A point-zero-zero minimum orbit intersection distance? That's going to ruin someone's day."

"I'll say." Neeta swiped the text from the monitor so that it projected in the air, then began typing. "Whatever it is, it's two hundred meters across, and the computers are giving it a ten percent chance of hitting us."

Burt ran the figures in his head as Neeta continued typing. "If we're talking about a dense rock, traveling at about fifteen kilometers per second, with an insertion angle of roughly forty-five degrees… we'll have a 400-megaton disaster if it hits. Definitely a city killer, if not a small state."

"I've got it at 430 megatons, but don't forget, seventy-one percent of the Earth's surface is water. It'll probably hit in the middle of the ocean.

"Causing a devastating tsunami."

"Yeah, well... less devastating than if it lands in downtown Chicago. Besides, the computers say it's going to take nearly a year for it to cross our orbit, well ahead of our current schedule for DefenseNet's power-on."

Burt looked up at the clock as he suppressed a yawn. "Before you leave, can you—"

"I know what I need to do."

"I know you do. I just don't like to assume anything."

Neeta harrumphed. "As soon as you leave, I'll round up the team and have them track this PHA down and figure out why it isn't on our list. Hopefully it'll be a false alarm."

"Thanks, Neeta." Burt finally allowed the yawn to escape. "Call me if there's anything that needs my attention."

As he turned away, Neeta spoke into the intercom system. "Jenkins, Hsiu, Smith, and Pederson, come to my office. We've got an unidentified PHA that needs our attention."

Burt felt a chill race through him as he hung up his bedside phone. "I can't believe I just finished talking with the Secretary of Defense," he muttered.

The tablet PC that he had accidentally knocked to the floor flashed red with another alert from the Jet Propulsion Lab. He picked it up and scrolled through a long list of incoming alerts.

When the phone rang again, he nearly jumped out of his skin. The answering machine picked up, and the frantic sound of Neeta's voice came over the speakerphone. "Damn it Burt, pick up! You're the bloody head of NEO and this place has gone bonkers. Hanford just sent—"

He hit the button to answer the call. "Neeta, get ready. I'm picking you up in ten minutes."

As Burt and Neeta took their seats in the airplane, they continued the debate they'd been having all the way from Pasadena to Edwards Air Force Base.

"The thing that bothers me the most isn't the number of alerts we've received; it's why we're suddenly getting them," Burt said. "I'll be frank, when I got that first report coming out of Hanford, it seemed ridiculous. But now—did all of our systems somehow get some kind of virus? That seems unlikely. So what does it all mean?"

Neeta tugged nervously at her long, black hair, which she'd gathered into a thick braid. "It seems like the universe has gone mental, hasn't it?"

Burt didn't like seeing her nervous like this. It was so unlike her. "Didn't you Brits invent the concept of keeping a stiff upper lip? You and I need to not get ahead of ourselves, and if we stay calm, the others won't make mistakes, nor will we. We can't afford mistakes. Agreed?"

Neeta took a deep breath and nodded.

The lights dimmed in the cabin as the small passenger jet began taxiing. Soon they were taking off, and Burt looked out the window at the unending line of headlights below. "It's 2066," he grumbled. "We have colonies on the moon, we've cured Multiple Sclerosis, and yet the LA city planners can't solve the five a.m. traffic snarls."

A 3D image of their flight plan appeared at eye level, and the pilot's voice broadcast through the cabin. *"Doctors Radcliffe and Patel, the Hanford site does not have a runway, so we'll be landing at Joint Base Lewis-McChord. It's currently oh-five-thirty hours and we should be touching down in approximately two hours. From there, you will be transported by helicopter to the Hanford site. The weather is clear along the West Coast and we should have a smooth flight."*

The glowing animation of their anticipated route to Washington State vanished.

"It's hard to believe what the Hanford people are reporting," Neeta said. "It all seems dodgy. But with all the data they've transmitted to us, it can't be a mistake, can it? The whole situation is…" Her voice trailed off.

Burt's ears popped as the plane banked slightly, and he swallowed hard as he felt the plane begin to level off. "Let's think this through," he said. "How is it possible that we suddenly have not one, not two, but *hundreds* of space rocks hurtling toward us from the edge of the solar system? Do you have any idea how we didn't see this coming?"

"I should have seen it." Neeta shook her head. "Most of those objects are traveling at tremendous speeds, and we could easily have missed some of the smaller ones, but bloody hell, one of those alerts is for something nearly a hundred miles across."

"Neeta, we're both only as good as the data we're given. I'm not blaming you, nor should you take any blame on yourself. I just can't fathom how something like this could happen all of a sudden."

With a deep, shuddering sigh, Neeta rested her head against the back of her seat. "At the pace some of that stuff is traveling, we've only got about ten months before some of that rubbish reaches us. I hate to say it, but it's probably even worse than we think, because at the current distance, we can't yet know how many smaller objects we'll be facing. Even if we get DefenseNet up six months ahead of schedule, it might not be enough."

Burt saw the worry in Neeta's brown eyes. "We've already gotten funding approval from the Secretary of Defense to accelerate DefenseNet's deployment. You talked to our crew at JPL already, right?"

"I've got them sorted out," Neeta agreed. "They'll start testing the DefenseNet lasers right away. But I'm worried about what we'll find out at Hanford. It can't be a coincidence that just as we detected all of these incoming objects, the fellows at Hanford start bleating about a gravitational wave disturbance originating in the same area of space. There's something out there. I'm worried that I somehow—"

"Neeta, stop blaming yourself." Burt shook his head. "There's no use second-guessing, we just have to deal with the facts at hand. That's why we're heading to this place in the middle of nowhere. There's got to be a logical reason why we've got a cloud of debris heading our way." He leaned back in his seat and closed his eyes. "Get some rest. We're going to have a very long day."

It was almost noon when Burt stepped off the helicopter and took in the empty, brown surroundings. As the downdraft of the chopper kicked up clouds of the loose bronze-colored dirt that dominated the landscape, he glanced in Neeta's direction and jutted his chin toward the low building in the distance. The electric whir of the helicopter's engine quieted as Neeta hopped out. She nodded at him, ducked and began jogging toward the main building of the Laser Interferometry Gravitational wave Observatory, otherwise known as LIGO.

While Neeta went inside to get things ready, Burt puffed on a cigarette and stared across the thirty square miles of brown emptiness surrounding the Hanford, Washington location, wishing he didn't have what felt like the weight of the world on his shoulders. In the distance, Jeeps carrying Military Police patrolled the edges of the newly-sealed site, while MPs guarded each of the building's entrances. As of four hours ago, by order of the Secretary of Defense, the site had been closed and troops from Joint Base Lewis-McChord had converged onto the observatory grounds, putting it into lockdown.

Burt took one last drag, dropped his cigarette, and ground it into the gravel with the heel of his cowboy boot. "Damn you," he said to the smoking butt, cursing his nicotine demon for breaking loose amid this tension.

With a dissatisfied grunt, Burt strode to the cinder-block building and displayed his badge to the heavily-armed soldier wearing the camouflage fatigues that were the standard issue Army Combat Uniform.

The steely-eyed MP held Burt's ID up at arm's length, comparing the picture with his haggard face. Then he unclipped a portable retinal scanner from his belt and placed it in front of Burt's right eye. "Doctor Radcliffe, please stand still."

A moment later, a green LED lit on the scanner and the soldier nodded. He returned Burt's ID, then stepped aside. Burt walked past, into the silent halls of the building that housed the LIGO control room. After his conversation with the Secretary of Defense, only a dozen people were authorized to enter the building, all of them senior scientists with Top Secret clearances. No other countries had broken their silence yet, though Burt knew that observatories in Germany and Australia had detected the same event. They all would come to the same conclusions once they'd analyzed the data. If the public found out, there would be chaos in the streets.

He walked through the musty, beige-colored halls of the Hanford facility and turned into the control room. Burt felt like a bear jarred from hibernation, and his mood soured further when he inhaled the control room's acrid odor of burnt popcorn. He shook his head as he spied a half-opened bag lying next to an ancient microwave on the back counter, blackened kernels spilling from it.

The forty-by-twenty-foot room seemed eerily like the one in which he'd spent the last ten years in at the Jet Propulsion Labs in Pasadena. However, instead of the quiet nervous energy he'd expected to encounter, he found Neeta and another engineer arguing loudly about the observatory's readings.

"What the hell do you mean you saw a blip in that sector three months ago and didn't notify anyone?" Neeta looked like a thunderhead ready to explode as she confronted the LIGO engineer who was easily a foot taller and well over twice her weight.

"Doctor Patel, I don't think you understand." The red-cheeked scientist turned from Neeta's ominous stare and pressed his lips together as he tapped heavily on the terminal in front of him. After a few seconds, he pointed at the main screen on the wall, which showed a signal graph dated nearly three months earlier. "We detected a gravitational anomaly in the same general direction eighty-nine days ago, but per our protocol, we didn't alert anyone because we couldn't get a solid confirmation in the readings from the other sites—"

"Well, your protocol is shit, Steve. I should have been told. You *do* realize what we're facing, right?"

Glancing at the badge clipped on Steve's broad chest, Burt recognized his name and knew that he was the lead engineer at the Hanford site. Clearing his throat, Burt turned to the harried scientist. "Neeta's right, we should have been notified. Why weren't you able to confirm the readings?"

Steve turned in his seat and stared at Burt as he settled into one of the swivel chairs, regarding him with a worried expression. "Director Radcliffe, we couldn't confirm the location with only our readings. It was a weak signal blip, so we didn't have high confidence. The LIGO site in Australia was offline for repair at the time, and our location in Livingstone only got a flicker whose strength was insufficient to confirm a hit. We didn't get any solid new readings from that sector until about 3:00 a.m. this morning."

Neeta's eyebrows knit together as her scowl deepened. Just as she opened her mouth, Burt held up his hand to forestall what he feared would end up being an unproductive fight with the local staff. Neeta snapped her mouth shut and continued fuming as Burt grabbed a rubber band that happened to be lying on the nearby tabletop. He gathered his shoulder-length hair into a ponytail, fully aware of how atypical it was for a man in his position to wear a ponytail, button-down shirt, cowboy boots, and blue jeans. But even though he was fifty, he still thought of himself as one of the engineers.

"Listen, Steve, what's done is done." Even though Burt felt frustrated with the LIGO staff, he needed to keep the peace. "I received your e-mail notification this morning and that's why Neeta and I are here. What do you have for us?"

The engineer anxiously tapped a few keys on the terminal and one of the monitors on the wall displayed a series of recent "hits" that the observatory had detected. "Director Radcliffe—"

"Call me Burt."

"Burt, LIGO has registered thousands of sources for gravity waves over the years. We only see these unusual gravitational waves when large masses accelerate rapidly, causing a disturbance in space-time. Almost like a pebble dropped into a calm lakc, wc'rc ablc to dctcct thc slightcst ripplcs of the event—"

"Steve, I've been doing this kind of crap long before you'd ever taken your first math class. Just give me the technical details."

The engineer blinked. "Sorry, sir. Uh, as you probably know, the gravitational waves we receive are usually produced by the merging of binary systems, such as two neutron stars colliding. Or if there's outflow from a star rotating around a black hole, we might see hints of that as well. However, we don't often receive bursts of gravitational waves. In fact, we've only encountered a dozen or so in the last decade, and we've never determined what caused them. Yet as of 2:53 a.m. this morning, we've registered over a dozen bursts of gravitational waves—"

"And you've checked with the other LIGO sites and confirmed the origin of these bursts?" Burt leaned forward, studying the pale face of the scientist.

"Yes, sir. We've triangulated with the other two sites, zeroing in on the same quadrant in space, and...." He tilted his head toward Neeta. "Per Doctor Patel's suggestion, I contacted NASA. They've routed a secure channel to us for the use of the IXO 2 satellites. We have full access to the satellite web. Only five minutes ago, I had the satellites aim their x-ray detectors at the source of the gravitational waves."

Steve punched a few keys on the terminal. The main screen on the wall displayed a running time counter, but was otherwise black, like a perfectly clean old-style chalkboard.

Burt leaned back and stared at the empty image on the one-hundred-inch screen, as Neeta asked in a much calmer tone than she'd used before, "Steve, when's the last gravity burst you detected?"

"About fift—" Steve glanced at a wall monitor and pointed at the flickering light coming from a live video feed monitoring one of the detectors within the site. "Wait, the laser has gone out of phase!" He looked around the room as the burst of activity registered on all of the control room's screens. "We're getting a new set of signals!"

Burt stood, walked past the engineers gathered around the computer terminal, and stared at the main screen. He glanced at the video feed showing the laser interferometer image on the leftmost wall monitor. He knew that the flickering light in the video feed was a sign that the facility had been hit by a gravitational disturbance, temporarily knocking one of the arms of the laser interferometer out of phase.

Everyone breathlessly watched the various screens flicker and update. Some monitors showed the intensity of the gravity waves, while others displayed the received data from the other LIGO sites.

Burt focused on the main screen; the empty blackness of the monitor drew all his attention, while all else faded into the background.

Suddenly, a white dot appeared.

Amid what had been blackness, a small, bright spot came to life, sending Burt's heart racing.

He pointed up at the monitor and turned toward the scientists huddled around terminals fifteen-feet away. "There! Is that a hit from the x-ray detectors?"

Steve dove at his keyboard and pounded a series of commands into the terminal. "Sir, I'm verifying..."

Burt strode to the gathered scientists, as raw data scrolled on the screen and Neeta pointed at one column. "There it is," she yelled. "We got a positive hit from the x-ray satellite."

Burt stared at the lone dot on the black monitor and knew what he was seeing. But they needed more data. More time.

An engineer raced to a garbage can and the sound of painful heaving echoed through the control room as he emptied his stomach. Everyone in the room was a highly qualified scientist, an expert in their field. They all knew what they'd just detected within the boundaries of their own solar system.

Wiping nervous sweat from his forehead, Burt announced,

"All we can do is wait for more signals. We need to know how big it is—its trajectory. How much time we have."

"Sir?" A trembling engineer looked up at him. "What can we do?"

The chill that Burt felt wasn't from the air-conditioned room. It felt as if the grim hand of the Reaper were reaching for a victim. He knew what the consequence of their discovery was. X-rays were typically only produced by very high-temperature events. Material being heated by unimaginably strong gravitational fields was the primary cause of such emissions.

"Let's focus on getting more data. We don't even know which direction it's going yet." Burt sighed, plopped himself on the nearest chair, and waited. It was the only thing any of them could do.

Burt prayed that the cause of the x-rays wasn't heading their way. It was one thing for DefenseNet to deal with asteroids. There were ways to handle them, given enough time. Even with Moon-sized objects, something could conceivably be done. He looked up at that glaring spot, contrasted against the blackness of the screen, and his chest tightened with worry.

As Burt waited, his gut told him that what he was staring at would be the end of them all. They'd be consumed by the insatiable hunger coming from an interstellar whirlpool of death.

A black hole.

A handful of hours had passed, and Burt paced along one of the musty hallways in the LIGO facility, trying to clear his head.

Having verified the existence of a black hole within the boundaries of the solar system explained many things. Black holes typically spun at a ferocious rate, and even though people thought of them as voracious space-based vacuum cleaners that ate everything in sight, most didn't understand that black holes were very messy eaters.

Sometimes, the twisting of gravity around the black hole would fling things away, like an infant with his or her undesired pea soup.

Burt's stomach churned as he considered the options.

"Let's just pray this thing is just skirting past," he muttered to himself. "Then maybe we have a chance."

Then he froze, as he heard Neeta's voice coming from one of the nearby offices. "Mum, I'm okay. I just wanted to hear your voice. Give Daddy a hug for me."

"Princess?" A man's voice came across the office's speakerphone. *"It's been ages since we've seen you. Are you okay? Has some boy broken your heart?"* The man chuckled lightly.

"Dad, I'm thirty-seven. Nobody's gotten my heart to break it. I'm kind of married to my work, and you know that."

Burt felt a surge of guilt as he found himself listening to Neeta's private conversation. She never spoke about anything but work, so it seemed strange for him to think of her actually having a family.

"Pumpkin, then maybe it's about time you let me help find you a proper husband—"

"Rajesh Patel!" A woman's voice yelled in the background. "*You stop harassing our daughter. She'll find someone and give us grandkids when she's good and ready."*

"Daddy, I love you, but I have to go. Hug each other, and if you don't hear from me for a while, just know I'm pretty busy at work. I love you both."

"We love you too, Poppet." Her mom's voice echoed warmly from thousands of miles away.

The buzz from the connection became silent, and almost immediately Neeta walked out of the office and gasped with surprise as she saw Burt standing in the hallway.

She quickly wiped the tears from her face. Burt stared at her, not sure he'd ever seen this side to the woman.

Ignoring the tears, he asked, "Do you want to grab some coffee with me?"

Neeta nodded as Burt turned and headed toward the break room.

Burt stared at the large center screen of the control room and sighed. Nearly one-hundred dots were lit, all of them appearing along the edge of a dark circle. Each spot represented an object's last gasp as the massive forces of the black hole heated and ripped it into subatomic particles before swallowing it.

He aimed a red laser pointer at the edges of the circle and glanced at the pale-faced engineer, who'd taken over at the terminal. "Give me a width. What are we dealing with?"

Closing his eyes, Burt listened to the tapping of keys and the engineer's trembling voice as he announced, "Sir, the diameter of the event horizon seems to be approximately three kilometers."

Burt was surprised by the reported size. Over one-hundred years ago, three famous physicists had established the Tolman-Oppenheimer-Volkoff limit, which dictated the upper limit for the mass of a neutron star. Doing the math in his head, he knew exactly what they were dealing with. "Well, isn't that interesting. We're dealing with a two-mile-wide rip in the fabric of space."

One scientist, a middle-aged man with a brilliant shock of red hair, asked, "But, sir, how's that possible? That's below the TOV limit, isn't it?"

Burt nodded. "About one-half of a solar mass, if my mental calculations are right."

He glanced at Neeta, and she nodded grimly. "Confirmed."

Suddenly, his old-style phone vibrated in his pocket. He retrieved it and glanced at the name: his brother. "Now is definitely not the time," he muttered, as he shoved the phone back in his pocket.

Then he looked up and addressed the room. "Half a solar mass, eh? Folks, that would explain why nobody had detected it until now. Its minimal gravitational lensing wouldn't have given us a visual clue, allowing it to sort of 'sneak up' on us. We're clearly dealing with a primordial black hole. Something birthed while the universe was in its infancy and during a time when temperatures and pressures still allowed for such things to be created. It's no different, nor any less dangerous, than the black holes we've all learned about in school. I suppose that's something ... we've detected the first of its kind. Or more to the point, it's discovered us."

Glancing at the dots on the screen, Burt knew that as each

dot appeared, the satellites would register its location. "Have the computers plotted a confirmed trajectory yet? Do we have a speed?"

The engineer at the terminal stared open-mouthed as data scrolled across the screen. He seemed frozen in place, so Neeta shoved him aside and took over.

"We have a confirmed trajectory," she said. "It's heading toward the center of the galaxy." Neeta rapidly typed a new set of commands and her frown deepened. "I'm afraid that we're directly in its path."

With that statement, Burt knew that the world's fate was sealed.

A deathly calm settled over him. It was as if a shroud had dampened any emotion he should be feeling. Quietly, he asked, "How long do we have?"

"Director Radcliffe, we have 345 days at the current speed and trajectory before the black hole crosses our orbit."

"Start a countdown. E-minus 345 days." His pronouncement was effectively a countdown to the end of humanity. With a grim sense of obligation, Burt rose to his feet and motioned to Neeta. "I'll need you. This is something we'll have to tell the current administration in DC, face-to-face. They'll be asking about contingencies." He pointed at the other engineers and snapped his fingers. "Nobody is allowed to say a word about this outside of this room. The rest of you, keep monitoring, and let me know if anything changes."

Neeta walked toward him, a confused expression on her face. "Contingencies?" She whispered, "I don't understand, what contingencies?"

The concept was almost laughable. Even if life on Earth managed to survive the onslaught from dozens of killer asteroids, nothing could survive when the black hole raced across Earth's orbit.

"Don't worry," said Burt, "I'll be doing most of the talking." Opening the control room's door, he glanced over his shoulder at Neeta. "We're about to inform the President of the United States that we all have less than a year to live."

— end of preview —

ADDENDUM

If you've read my books in the past, you've come to expect this scientist to weave in some science regardless of what genre the book is. I don't like to be predictable, but here we are, once again, at the addendum, and as with most novels, I've introduced some things that might warrant some explanations.

Inevitably this is a work of science fiction, but strewn throughout is a lot of science fact. What I try to do in this addendum is point out the various elements and talk about them at a fairly high level.

In *Multiverse* we talk about many science-based topics that could each warrant a series of books to give them any level of justice, but for purposes of distilling things down to their essence, I'll do my best to explain what a particular topic or buzzword actually means and cover what's mostly real versus where I've taken some liberties.

I also want you to realize that the topics I'm going to cover are extremely complex, and it gets much more complex as you peel through the layers of that onion. The best I'm going to be able to do is give you a handy idea of what it's about and sufficient keywords that you can go ahead and dig further if you're so inclined.

Again, I've always been a believer in learning through research, and folks who are truly interested in the science behind some of these things will learn best by having to look some of these things up. I'll give you a head start and help with *what* you need to look up, the rest will be up to you.

Tachyons – are they real?

This novel started very quickly with the idea that there's such a thing as a tachyon. But do they really exist?

First, let's talk about the idea of something going faster than the speed of light.

You might say, "But I thought nothing could go faster than the speed of light."

That is something that is a common misconception of what Einstein's theories state, and I did correctly state in the novel some of the rules.

The first one being that nothing that is initially moving slower than the speed of light can be accelerated to exceed the speed of light.

This is true.

However, that does not state that nothing can travel faster than light. It leaves open the concept for particles to exist that move faster than light from the moment they are created. If such particles did exist, however, Special Relativity implies that they could never be slowed down to velocities below the speed of light.

The equations associated with mass and speed are weirdly symmetric when it comes to the barrier associated with the speed of light. It would take infinite energy to push a normal (baryonic) particle with mass to the speed of light. As it would take infinite energy to *slow* a tachyonic (superluminal) particle to the speed of light.

It's weird, I know.

That's some of the details you saw in the novel where the scientists were monkeying around with accelerating particles and decelerating them using massive amounts of energy to accomplish some of what Professor Salomon was trying to do.

Here's another weird way to look at it: Tachyonic particles moving infinitely fast have zero energy, just like baryonic particles with no velocity on our side of the barrier. Infinity is a mirror of zero in this case.

This whole concept of faster-than-light particles (tachyons) has been fodder for science fiction for ages. I'm lucky enough to have had discussions with Greg Benford, a theoretical physicist and one of the great authors of what's often considered "hard" science fiction, meaning science fiction greatly based on science versus handwavery.

He pointed me to a lot of the current research, and after a lot of reading I came to some of the same conclusions many other scientists had come to… I just don't know if tachyons exist.

But let's talk about what we *think* might be true, after all that's what theoretical research is all about. We don't know until we know.

There was a report from two Australian experimenters in 1972 titled "Possible observation of tachyons associated with extensive air showers" by Roger Clay and Philip Crouch.

Their experiment was dealing with a weather balloon high up in the atmosphere (20 km) with a particle detector attempting to catch an expected cosmic ray bombardment. To summarize, they measured the arrival of a tachyon traveling at 2.5 times the speed of light.

Interesting.

The science and measurement methodology they used was deemed sound. However, those results are now fifty years old and have not since been duplicated. Statistically, they should have been.

The premise of a tachyon existing is reasonable, and the existence of tachyons is certainly the kind of thing which is allowed by Einstein's Special Relativity.

For this novel, we have to simply presume via a leap of faith.

Tachyons – if real, then time travel?

With the theory of relativity in hand, we already know that time dilation exists as associated with increasing our speed. For example, time passes a bit slower when you travel on a jet than on the ground. See the Hafele and Keating experiments I refer to in the Time Travel section of this addendum.

Obviously the warping/dilation of time is very small when

doing such a thing, but the dilation increases as you approach the speed of light. For instance, if you were traveling very close to the speed of light, you could in a blink of an eye have millions of years pass by in the real world where for you, only a fraction of a second had elapsed.

Using the same equations, we predict that if a particle could exceed the speed of light, the warping of time would become negative, and the particle would then travel backwards in time.

Detecting a tachyon:

We haven't yet reliably found tachyons such that we could definitively state how we'd detect them, but one of the simplest methods would be what I described in the novel, which has to do with Cherenkov radiation.

What is Cherenkov radiation?

Simply put, Cherenkov radiation is seen when a charged particle travels through some substance (medium) with a speed greater than the speed of light.

Today, we often see Cherenkov radiation in water-cooled nuclear power plants. What's interesting is that the speed of light varies depending on what substance light is going through. For instance, water slows light down to about 75% of its normal speed. Yet when a nuclear core is powered up, if you were to watch it happen, you'd see a sudden blue glow appear.

What's happening is that when a nuclear core is put online, trillions of nuclear fissions per second are occurring, and from each of those events, tremendous energy is radiating outward. Some of the particles emitted are beta particles with very high levels of kinetic energy. So much so that they're pushed outward at a speed that exceeds the speed of light in water.

Think of each of those particles bursting through a barrier akin to a sonic boom. But that boom is yielding that blue glow that you see.

The idea for detecting a tachyon would be no different, but you'd want to detect it in a vacuum where the speed of light isn't being slowed. And that's in effect what we've described in the novel.

Now, let's be honest, we don't know if tachyons are charged particles. If they aren't, then things become harder to detect.

And thus as an author's prerogative, I chose to make the tachyons a charged particle. Otherwise, we get into a lot more difficulties than I felt was necessary for the story.

Paradoxes – the headache of the science world:

Whenever time travel is brought up, especially traveling backwards in time, the topic of paradoxes inevitably come into play. It's the naysayer in the celebration, the veritable turd in the punch bowl of science. Ugh… paradoxes.

But, what are they?

The simplest paradox to describe related to time travel is called the grandfather paradox.

The grandfather paradox is a situation that arises when a person travels back in time only to kill their grandfather. Having killed him, then the killer's parent could no longer be born, and thus leaving us with the conundrum of how did the killer even exist to have killed the grandfather?

The grandfather paradox is taken as an argument against the logical possibility of traveling backward in time.

And now you know why scientists always have headaches.

Well, there is something called the Novikov self-consistency principle. Its entire premise is to address the paradoxes associated with time travel, which is a hidden “feature” of general relativity.

The implication is that there is a single timeline for the universe you’re in, the time traveler would not be permitted to affect the past so that it perturbs the future.

That does sort of plays into the idea of free will and such, but the idea being you’d physically be unable to affect the past.

But if that’s the case, then if you go back in time and kill your grandfather, how does that not change anything?

This is where quantum physics states that an event may have several possible outcomes with different likelihoods occurring.

We saw hints of that in the novel where Mason recalled various instances of things happening throughout the timeline.

But is that science or made up?

Well, we are certainly in the realm of real science, but it’s theoretical with many PhDs and big-brained folks behind it.

But what does that in practicality even mean?

Okay, let’s get ready to dive into the deep end of science. Ready? Here goes…

In the "many worlds" interpretation of quantum theory, things like the killing of one's grandfather are seen as various possible outcomes occurring in different, "parallel" timelines. With this interpretation, the grandfather paradox could be addressed if the killer starts off in a timeline where the grandfather lived long enough to have his children, and thus the killer was born, and then—moving along a parallel time track where they were never born. In essence they're a new element to a new universe.

And thus we have coined the term multiverse.

Multiverse – it's a thing?

The existence of a multiverse is a topic that has been debated in the physics community for years. A hypothesis that there are many (possibly infinite) copies of our universe that all exist in parallel to each other. Take the sum total of all the matter, energy, time, and space in all of these universes, and you have the "multiverse."

Although the idea has long been popular in science fiction and fantasy novels, many well-regarded figures in the scientific community (e.g. Stephen Hawking and Michio Kaku) are supporters of the concept. A related theory, known as counterpart theory, hypothesizes that in multiple copies of a given world, each item or event is not necessarily identical, but a copy in which variability may exist. Taking it one step further, there is something known as "many-worlds interpretation." This is a mechanism by which one can conceive that the actual world we live in is but one of many possible worlds. And more to the point, for each different way the world could have evolved, there is a distinct and separate world that represents that outcome.

If that seems confusing, welcome to the multiverse.

Time Travel:

When Einstein first described general relatively in 1915, he described our universe in terms of the three dimensions of space that we're very well aware of and the fourth dimension being time itself. This is where the term space-time comes about, it's the term scientists use to describe all four dimensions of our universe.

General relativity is describing spacetime itself. Spacetime is actually a model in which space and time are woven together to simplify talking about the four dimensions that would normally involve space and time. Here, Einstein determined that large objects cause a distortion in spacetime, and that distortion is known as gravity.

The idea of traveling forward in time isn't at all controversial. In fact, it's been proven to be true.

In science the effect is generally called time dilation, and it has been experimentally verified. I'll refer you to the U.S. Naval Observatory experiments by Hafele and Keating, which documented what happened when four incredibly accurate atomic clocks were synchronized and two of them were flown around the world while the other two remained stationary. When the clocks were brought back together, the time had shifted ever-so-slightly for the clocks which had been traveling at jet-like speeds. For them, they'd traveled forward in time by a fraction of a second. Admittedly nothing too exciting, but it proved a principle of time travel in a forward direction was possible.

However, going back in time poses interesting issues.

I already covered the concept of tachyons and their ability to go backwards in time from our frame of reference. Here I describe yet another method, which wasn't practical in a modern-era novel. This would be reserved for a far-future type adventure.

In 1974, Frank Tipler took Einstein's equations for relativity and realized that it was at least logical that a time-traveling device could be constructed.

Of course, the equations described on paper don't translate well to practical solutions with the level of science and know-how we have today. But as a thought experiment, Tipler posed what such a thing might look like if we ever had such technology.

Let's start with a huge amount of mass: the equivalent of ten sun's worth of mass. I know, I know, you're already thinking, we've gone off the deep end and are in crazy town. Bear with me.

If we packed that much mass in the equivalent space that a black hole would occupy, we would be talking about something less than twenty miles across.

All things considered, that's not *that* big, at least in size.

Tipler proposed that this amount of mass, instead of a ball, let's create a cylinder. Sort of like the cardboard center of a roll of paper towels—just bigger.

Imagine that the cylinder was rotating very very fast.

When you combine the immense gravitational pull of the mass, coupled with the very fast rotation, you get something called a frame-dragging effect.

What is that?

The cylinder would in fact be dragging space-time along with it, and if you followed the rotation in one direction, you'd find yourself in a CTC (closed timelike curve) that rockets you into the past.

A CTC is essentially where time loops back on itself so that when you believe you're moving forward, ultimately you come back to where you started and realize that along the way you were actually going back in time. Expand that out to eternity and you can imagine yourself going back an arbitrary amount of time.

If you moved in the other direction, you'd be going into the future.

I know, I know – these are very advanced concepts in theoretical physics, but these are all things you can look up if you so desire.

There are of course a variety of huge difficulties in constructing such a thing. Variables such as having exotic matter that contained negative energy, or an infinite-length construction.

ABOUT THE AUTHOR

I am an Army brat, a polyglot, and the first person in my family born in the United States. This heavily influenced my youth by instilling in me a love of reading and a burning curiosity about the world and all of the things within it. As an adult, my love of travel and adventure has driven me to explore many exotic locations, and these places sometimes creep into the stories I write.

I hope you've found this story entertaining.

- Mike Rothman

For occasional news on my latest work, join my mailing list at:
https://mailinglist.michaelarothman.com/new-reader

You can find my blog at: www.michaelarothman.com
Facebook at: www.facebook.com/MichaelARothman
And on Twitter: @MichaelARothman